SMONK

WILLIAM MORROW

An Imprint of HarperCollins*Publishers*

SMONK

or

WIDOW TOWN

BEING THE SCABROUS ADVENTURES

OF **E. O. Smonk**

&

OF THE **Whore Evavangeline**

IN CLARKE COUNTY, ALABAMA,

EARLY IN THE LAST CENTURY . . .

Tom Franklin

SMONK. Copyright © 2006 by Tom Franklin. All rights reserved. Printed in the United States of America. No part of this book may be used or re-produced in any manner whatsoever without written permission except in the case of brief quotations embodied in critical articles and reviews. For information address HarperCollins Publishers, 10 East 53rd Street, New York, NY 10022.

HarperCollins books may be purchased for educational, business, or sales promotional use. For information please write: Special Markets Depart-ment, HarperCollins Publishers, 10 East 53rd Street, New York, NY 10022.

FIRST EDITION

Designed by Susan Yang

Library of Congress Cataloging-in-Publication Data

Franklin, Tom.
    Smonk, or, Widow town : being the scabrous adventures of E.O. Smonk & of the whore Evavangeline in Clarke County, Alabama, early in the last century . . . / Tom Franklin.— 1st ed.
        p. cm.
    ISBN-13: 978-0-06-084681-7
    ISBN-10: 0-06-084681-X
    1. Cowboys—Fiction. 2. Prostitutes—Fiction. 3. Clarke County (Ala.)—Fiction. I. Title: Smonk. II. Title: Widow town. III. Title.

PS3556.R343S66 2006
813'.54—dc22

                                                                2006043835

---

06 07 08 09 10 WBC/RRD 10 9 8 7 6 5 4 3 2 1

For Barry Hannah

CONTENTS

1. The Trial · 1

Arrival—Apparel & accouterments—Boy with balloon— Photographers—A wiseacre bailiff—The judge—Trapped—An unusual projectile—A machine gun—The mule absconded

2. The Tombigbee · 11

Shreveport Louisiana—Christian Deputies—A purported act of sodomy—A whipping—Deputy Gabriel Washington Ambrose— A boardinghouse in Mobile—Titties—A dive—The excision of a growth of mole—Upriver—A suspicious medical examination— A bay-side discussion—A fatal stabbing—Uniforms— An interrogation—An act of Christian charity—Murder & a stolen molar—Denizens of the river—Escape—The captain's grief

How doth the city sit solitary, that was full of people!
How is she become as a widow! She weepeth sore in
the night.

—LAMENTATIONS 1:1–2

"Magnifique!" ejaculated the Countess de Coude,
beneath her breath.

—EDGAR RICE BURROUGHS,
The Return of Tarzan

1

THE TRIAL

IT WAS THE EVE OF THE EVE OF HIS DEATH BY MURDER AND THERE
was harmonica music on the air when E. O. Smonk rode the dis-
puted mule over the railroad tracks and up the hill to the hotel
where his trial would be. It was October the first of that year. It had
been dry and dusty for six weeks and five days. The crops were
dead. It was Saturday. Ten after three o'clock in the afternoon according to the shadows of the bottles on the bottle tree.

Amid the row of long nickering horsefaces at the rail Smonk
slid off the mule into the sand and spat away his cigar stub and
stood glaring among the animal shoulders at his full height of five
and a quarter foot. He told a filthy blond boy holding a balloon to
watch the mule, which had an English saddle on its back and an
embroidered blanket from Bruges Belgium underneath. In a sheath
stitched to the saddle stood the polished butt of the Winchester rifle with which, not half an hour earlier, Smonk had dispatched four

of an Irishman's goats in their pen because the only thing he abhorred more than an Irish was an Irish goat. By way of brand the mule had a fresh .22 bullet hole through its left ear, same as Smonk's cows and pigs and hound dog did, even his cat.

That mule gits away, he told the boy, I'll brand ye balloon.

He struck a match with his thumbnail and lit another cigar. He noted there were no men on the porches, downstair or up, and slid the rifle from its sock and snicked the safety off. He backhanded dust from a mare's flank to get her the hell out of his way (they say he wouldn't walk behind a horse) and clumped up the steps into the balcony's shade and limped across the hotel porch, the planks groaning under his boots. The boy watched him: his immense dwarf shape, shoulders of a grizzly bear, that bushel basket of a head low and cocked, as if he was trying to determine the sex of something. His hands were wide as shovels and his fingers so long he could palm a man's skull but his lower half was smaller, thin horseshoe legs and little feet in their brand-new calf opera boots the color of chocolate, loose denim britches tucked in the tops. He wore a clean pressed white shirt and ruffled collar, suspenders, a black string tie with a pair of dice on the end and a tan duck coat. He was uncovered as usual—hats made his head sweat—and he wore the blue-lensed eyeglasses prescribed for sufferers of syphilis, which accounted him in its numbers. On a lanyard around his neck hung a whiskey gourd stoppered with a syrup cork.

He coughed.

Along with the Winchester he carried an ivory-handled walking cane with a sword concealed in the shaft and a derringer in the handle. He had four or five revolvers in various places within his clothing and cartridges clicking in his coat pockets and a knife in his boot. There were several bullet scars in his right shoulder and one in each forearm and another in his left foot. There were a dozen buckshot pocks peppered over the hairy knoll of his back and the trail of a knife scored across his belly. His left eye was gone a few years now, replaced by a white glass ball two sizes small. He had a goiter under his beard. He had gout, he had the clap, blood-sugar, neuralgia and ague. Malaria. The silk handkerchief balled in his pants pocket was blooded from the advanced consumption the doctor had just informed him he had.

You'll die from it, the doctor had said.

When? asked Smonk.

One of these days.

At the hotel door, he paused to collect his wind and glanced down behind him. Except for the boy slouching against a post with his balloon, an aired-up sheep stomach, there were no children to be seen, a more childless place you'd never find. Throughout town the whorish old biddies were pulling in shutters and closing doors, others hurrying across the street shadowed beneath their parasols, but every one of them peeping back over their shoulders to catch a gander at Smonk.

He pretended to tip a hat.

Then he noticed them—the two slickers standing across the road beside a buckboard wagon covered in a tarp. They were setting up the tripod legs of their camera and wore dandy-looking suits and shiny derbies.

Smonk, who could read lips, saw one say, There he is.

Inside the hotel the bailiff, who'd been blowing the harmonica, put it away and straightened his posture when he saw who it was coming and cleared his throat and announced it was no guns allowed in a courtroom.

This ain't a courtroom, Smonk said.

It is today by God, said the bailiff.

Smonk glanced out behind him as if he might leave, the hell with the farce of justice once and for all. But instead he handed the rifle over, barrels first, and as he laid one heavy revolver and then another on the whiskey keg the bailiff had for a desk, he looked down at the gaunt barefaced Scot in his overalls and bicycle cap pulled low, sitting on a wooden crate, the sideboard behind him jumbled with firearms deposited by those already inside.

Smonk studied the bailiff. I seen ye before.

Maybe ye did, the man said. Maybe I used to work as ye agent till ye sacked me from service and my wife run off after ye and cast me in such doldrums me and my boy Willie come up losing ever thing we had—land, house, barn, corn crib, still, crick. Ever blessed thing. Open up ye coat and show me inside there.

Smonk did. You lucky I didn't kill ye.

The bailiff pointed the rifle. That 'n too.

The one-eye licked his long red tongue over his lips and put his cigar in his teeth and unworked from his waistband a forty-one caliber Colt Navy pistol and laid it on the wood between them.

Keep these instruments safe, fellow. Maybe I'll tip ye a penny for looking after em good.

I wouldn't accept no tip penny from you, Mister Smonk, if it was the last penny minted in this land.

Smonk had coughed. Do what.

I said if it was to happen a copper blight over this whole county and a penny was selling for a dollar and a half and I hadn't eat a bite of food in a month and my boy was starving, I wouldn't take no penny from you. Not even if ye paid me a whole nother penny to take it.

But Smonk had turned away.

Angry harmonica notes preceded him as he twisted his shoulders to fit the door and stepped into the hot, smoky diningroom, cigar ash dusted down his tie like beard dander. The eating tables had been shoved against the walls and stacked surface to surface, the legs of the ones on top in the air like dead livestock. Justice of the Peace Elmer Tate and the lawyer and the banker and two or three farmers and the liveryman and that doctor from before checking his watch and Hobbs the undertaker, all deacons, looked at him. The talking had hushed, the men quiet as chairs. The nine ball flashing its number across the billiard table in the corner didn't make its hole and ticked off the seven and stopped dead on the felt.

Smonk leaned against the wall, it gave a little. He coughed into his handkerchief and dabbed his lips and stuffed the cloth into his pocket, the conversation and game of billiards picking back up.

For a moment nothing happened except the quip of a mockingbird from outside and Smonk unstoppering his gourd. Then the door opened at the opposite end of the room and into the light walked the circuit judge, a Democrat, Mason and former army officer equally renowned for his drinking and his muttonchops. He acknowledged no other man as he excused his way through them and stepped onto the wooden dais erected for this occasion and seated himself behind the table set up for him, a glass of water there and a notepad, quill and ink bottle. He wore a black suit and hat like a preacher and for a gavel used the butt end of a new Smith & Wesson Schofield .45.

Order now, order, he called, removing his hat. Be seated, gentlemen. He screwed his monocle in.

Ever body set down, called the bailiff. And git ye got-dern cover off.

The men snatched off their hats and scuffed into chairs. In the rear of the room, Smonk kept standing. He ashed his cigar. For once he wished he wore a hat so he could leave it on. A sombrero, say.

Let's see. The judge cleared his throat. First on the docket here is the people of Old Texas Alabama versus Eugene Oregon Smonk.

Not first, the defendant growled. The whole docket. Today I'm yer whole fucking docket.

Anger charged the diningroom: the state flag in the corner seemed to quiver though the air between the men was as still as the inside of a rock. From somewhere out beyond the dusty desiccated sugarcane came the high parched yap of a mad-dog.

Afternoon, gentlemen. Smonk grinned. Judge.

He pulled his shoulders off the wall and hung his cane on his arm and puffed his cigar and stopped up his gourd. But he'd only made two steps toward his table when he paused and raised his head.

Something was different.

Somehow, the red-headed farmer glaring at him was not the same farmer Smonk had beaten with a coiled whip. The town clerk was not the same town clerk he had slapped down in the street, whose face he'd ground in the mud and money purse taken. Somehow that one there wasn't the banker he'd swindled out of seventy-five acres of bottomland including a creek. That one was not the liveryman whose daughter he'd won at rook and taken in the feed room in the back. Hobbs the undertaker was another undertaker entirely and Tate yonder wasn't the same spineless justice of the peace Smonk had been blackmailing near a year. They were all other faces, all other men.

He didn't know them. He didn't know them.

The bailiff wasn't a bailiff now but another man altogether. They were scuffling to their feet in a mob as the judge banged his pistol so hard the ink bottle jumped off.

Order! he called. God damn it, I said order!

But there was no order left.

Instead there were fire pokers and riding crops. An ash shovel. There were bricks and unlooped belts and letter openers and knots of kindling. An iron pump handle. A broken window's flashing knives. One soaked noose, cue sticks, table legs with nails crooked as fangs, the picks and pikes of splintered chairs.

The men advanced on Smonk with leery sidesteps. He ducked the hurled eight ball which smashed a window. He dropped his cigar to the floor and didn't bother to toe it out and it lay smoking between his boots. He took off his glasses and folded them away into his breast pocket, in no hurry despite the men closing in behind their weapons, so close the ones in front could see his red teeth.

Get him, said somebody in the corner.

But Smonk raised the prongs of his fingers and his assailants froze. He leaned back, haled a long tug of air and held it, as if he might say some truth they needed to hear.

They waited for him to speak.

Instead he coughed, blood smattering those faces closest. And in the same moment each fellow in the room tall enough to see witnessed Eugene Oregon Smonk's eye uncork from his head into the air.

For an instant it glinted in a ray of light through the window, then McKissick the bailiff caught it like a marble.

He opened his palm and grinned.

When he looked up Smonk had a derringer in one hand and sword in the other and he was backing toward the sideboard where all those lined-up rifles and pistols lay gleaming.

Well have at it, he yelled, you hongry bitches.

Meanwhile, the sun had shied behind a cloud. The horses along the rail outside were bland and peaceful, many with their eyes shut. Even the flies had landed. Across the street, the two photographers stood on either side of their wagon cracking their knuckles and glancing up the deserted street and down it.

The blond boy had tied his balloon in the raw hole in the mule's ear and was climbing into the saddle. He wiggled his behind. The stirrups, adjusted for Smonk, hung too far down so he didn't use them, even as the mule backed up on its own and faced east.

When the first shot came from inside, the photographers let fall their tripod and leapt into the wagon and flung away a green tarp to reveal a 1908 Model Hiram Maxim water-cooled machine gun bolted to its metal jackstand. One man checked the lock while the other twirled vises and tightened the petcock valve.

I heard he killed his own momma, he said.

For starters, said the other.

The blond boy slapped the mule across its withers and gigged it with his bare heels. Let's git to that orphanage, he said, saluting the machine gunners as they waited, one slowly returning the salute. The mule began to walk, and then trot, the bailiff's son not looking back despite the storm of gunfire, the balloon bobbing above them like a thought the mule was having, empty of history.

2

THE TOMBIGBEE

TWO WEEKS EARLIER, IN THE STATE OF LOUISIANA, THERE HAP-
pened a scrawny fifteen year old girl burnt brown by the sun and
whoring town to town unaware there were other options for a girl.
Evavangeline was her name, the only one she knew. There was
about ninety pounds' worth of her, and say five feet, plain, petite
and slightly buck-toothed. She had jags of red hair cut short by her
own hand because it was cooler that way and she bore a large red
scar on the side of her neck. More often than not she'd be mistaken
for a boy and recently had been chased out of Shreveport for
sodomy and romanticisms with a member of "his" own gender.

A group of well-uniformed Christian Deputies had burst in
upon the hot upstairs hotel room where the two were transacting
their business in the fashion of dogs, and Evavangeline had sprung
from the bed as if ejaculated. She'd crashed unpaid out the window, clutching an armload of men's clothing before her privates.

The deputies fell upon her co-fornicator and dragged him naked and hollering down rough pine steps and through the muddy street and strung him up by his wrists and administered him a whipping. He bellowed at each lick and cried for them to run fetch her—

It warn't no her you pervert, said the Christian Deputy horse-whipping him.

I swar it was, cried the man. She were a gal! A gal I say!

They were behind the jail, a crowd gathering to watch. People pointing that the man being whipped still bore his member in the strategic position.

I sucked on her titties! the beaten man cried. The whip snapped mud off his shoulders. Wee tomboys I'll grant ye, but teats sure as the world! I swar!

If that had been a woman, chided the tall, long-chinned head Christian Deputy, blushing aback his white stallion, then we'd have no reason to chase "her," now, would we? Perhaps a dress violation. Or you could file a charge of robbery, if you want us to interrupt your "whooping" so you can fill out the paperwork and list each stolen garment.

I do! the recipient of the beating cried. A sock! he cried. A real old union suit! A hank of rope!

He continued to bawl out the names of garments, his flagpole ever faithful.

Is they even such a thang as a *dress* violation in this jurisprudence, boss? asked Ambrose, the deputies' second-in-command, a short, stocky Negro who could read. His shirt sleeves and pants cuffs were rolled to accommodate his shorter limbs and his ascot had bunched at his chin. Look, he said and gestured at the scene around them. Dirty, diseased creatures of indiscriminate gender slogging through the mud wore rags, newspapers, sack cloths, loin cloths, croaker sacks, animal skins and corn shucks. Some were naked and hairy as apes.

Go, find out, said Walton, for that was the head Christian Deputy's Christian name. "Seek and ye shall find. Ask and it shall be given unto you."

Ah. Re-search, said Ambrose.

A bodice damn ye, cried the man being beaten. A red lacy garter!

You have to *search* for it first, before you can prefix it with "re," haven't you? asked Walton.

You'd thank so, said his ebony-skinned lieutenant. But what I heard now's they demarcating it *re*-search. They do that once in a while. Ever few years. Change a word or come up with a new one altogether. It don't make a shit normally—

Deputy Ambrose, warned his leader. You "cuss" again, I'll have your badge.

◦◦◦

A week later the gal Evavangeline stood in a boardinghouse bedroom in Mobile Alabama stark naked, frowning at her cactus of a body. Her titties barely qualified for the word. Old checker-playing geezers along the waterfront had better humps. And that goddamn scar Ned had give her! Big as a damn half-dollar piece! She spat into her palm, thinking to try and scrub it off. But she didn't. It wouldn't come off no matter how much she scratched at it and the truth was she liked it for a reminder of him. When it itched she thought Ned might be trying to tell her something. Or just saying hello. I'm out here somewhere.

In the mirror she thumped her nipples, which made them rise. She wondered about getting knocked up because she knew it made your titties grow. What she didn't know was if they shrank back after you had the kid. Seemed like maybe they'd stay full as long as the kid sucked on them. The stickler was that she didn't want a damn youngun to tote along, just some bigger titties. Maybe after she got the kid she could ditch it and find her a customer who'd suck the milk. There had to be men would go for that. Main thing she knew after all these years of being alive was that men existed with every possible appetite.

She gazed at her belly and wondered how a girl got knocked up. She was as skinny as a skeleton and no matter how much she ate she couldn't put on no fat. But you got fat when you got knocked up. Maybe it was a pill you bought or something you shot. She bet a doctor could tell her.

The morning suffered on and she snuck down the drainpipe of the boardinghouse without paying the lady and found a window table at a dive overlooking the bay and sipped dark rum and slowly ate the cork and listened to the hurdy-gurdy and smoked hash mixed with tobacco as endless boats bobbed past and crows and seagulls dipped in the breeze. She ordered another rum. She saw a man get mugged on the wharf. She dozed for a while and woke thinking how much she loved money. She saw a shark attack a small dinghy. She visited the privy and on her return saw a pair of rats fornicating under the piano stool. The mugged man still lying where he'd fallen on the boards.

Inside, the smoke was so thick it was like sitting in a low cave. No one who entered displayed the stylings of a doctor, though what that might have been she had no clue. She hoped it would be self-telling. A black bag maybe. One of those contraptions on the head. If somebody were to get shot, she mused, a doc would likely appear.

She ordered another rum.

The place stank of fish and privy. Flies and gnats so thick the wind from their wings was nearly a comfort. Because of Evavangeline's clothing and scrubby hair, a wispy red-eyed whore floated up and said, You wanna buy a girl a drank, handsome?

No, thank ye.

You lean the other way?

My leaning's my own business.

The whore's husband, the famously hot-headed owner of the dive, heard her. Whoa, Nellie, he said. Hold it right there.

He had a growth of mole the size of a man's thumb dangling from his chin. Blackly purple with a marbling of red, veiny, sparsely haired and peeling a tad, it was hard not to stare at, jiggling as it did when he talked.

Hell Mary, she said. Do it grow?

Buster boy— The owner pointed a bottle of bourbon at her. If you (A) keep looking at my birthmark, and (B) ever talk to my wife like that again, I'll (C) bust this here whiskey over ye head and make ye (E) pay the two bits the drank cost and (R) mop up the mess.

Is that right.

Yeah that's right, dandy boy.

Don't call me no dandy boy.

Why not? *Dandy boy?*

Cause I'm dranking. It don't do to mess with me in such times.

That's it. He slammed his hand on the countertop. I'm furious now.

He tugged at a revolver in his waistband but the gal jumped up with a sawed-down singleshot sixteen from under the table. Several glasses exploded behind him and he flew backward without even flapping his arms and his bowler hat landed spinning on the bar.

She flattened it with her open palm. I told ye.

You damn shore did, said his widow, pouring herself a whiskey heading for the cashbox.

Evavangeline hopped over the bar, her ears ringing. She knelt beside the man and tugged the long revolver from his waistband and checked its loads and stood up and cocked it with her thumb and closed her left eye for better aim and bit her bottom lip as was her habit when shooting and shot the growth of mole from the owner's chin without blinking at the noise. She inhaled smoke from the barrel then grabbed the mole which was burning on one end and swaddled it in the owner's dishrag for later study. Nobody in the place seemed to mind, not his wife, not the other patrons, not even the rats who'd dogged each other halfway across the floor, and no doctor had arisen from his chair. The hurdy-gurdy was playing "I'm a Good Ole Rebel." Evavangeline vaulted through an open window and darted along the wharf carrying her guns, ducking ships' moorings and upsetting a Hasidic Jew with an armload of beaver pelts.

∞

Still thinking about doctors, she stowed away aboard the next steamboat upriver. She had no idea where she was going but she had always been a creature of strong instinct, and north felt right. She slept on deck and stayed sober, shooting dice in the afternoons with a group of niggers. It was hot. Her head especially. The niggers were full of stories of a character they called Snert or something. She barely listened it was so hot. When the boat docked and took on passengers she would ask the gentlemen embarking and disembarking if he was a doctor.

No one owned up.

Then, at the muggy river town of McIntosh, one stubby Irish dribbling piss off the side of the boat admitted to Evavangeline that yes he was indeedy the ship's sawbones and further earned her credibility when he asked, You a gal under them duds and that dirt?

In his tiny room he lit a stick of incense and a candle which gave hardly any light. He smoked some skunkweed without offering to share and cranked his Gramophone and after a few loud pops some scratchy fiddles played slow and sad. She was naked, elbows and knees on his bunk, blindfolded by the silk cloth he said the Hypocritic Code called for. He popped his knuckles and spat on his finger and wormed it up her chute and wiggled it.

It's a dollar, she repeated. I done told ye.

How's that feel, aye? he asked. He inched in another finger.

How's what feel?

He withdrew and sniffed the fingers.

What the hell can ye tell from that, *doc?*

Ye mineral content, for one thing, he said. Ye 've got a strong sulfur ardor. Odd. How bout this, aye?

There was a rustle of clothing. Behind the blindfold her eyes rolled. Here it came. He grasped her hipbones and grunted and worked a slightly bigger thing in.

This is the old Druidic way of examining patients, he explained. From the Bible or Montgomery Ward catalogue one. I'm an avid reader. We train our fleshly tools here to be especially sensitive, like a thermometer only in all modesty somewhat bigger, and for a fee of two dollars we can dispense a kind of miracle salve into the anal rectum and *uuuuuh—*

She'd contracted her nethers as Ned had taught her—done correctly, as effective as grabbing a man by the throat.

He was gasping, pounding her back.

Is that ye pinky? she asked, her teeth gritted.

Inside her it shriveled. She loosed her clench and let him pull it out. She got up and sat with her legs hanging off the bunk and removed the blindfold. I said it was a dollar.

You bitch. He fisted the wall and the record skipped. I know jest what yer eaten up with. What disease, I mean. You reek of it. And there ain't no cure.

Are you really a doctor?

He laughed.

Will it land me dead?

You'll be curious about that fer a spell, aye? He laughed more. Now get out of my room you lice-ridden heathen and jump off this boat, before I tell em what you really are.

Simmering mad, she climbed back atop the deck to seek another opinion. She determined this time to request proof of medical accomplishment. A note you got from finishing one of them doctor schools. She couldn't read but expected she could judge it from the quality of the paper. Hell, even a tooth-puller would do. What did he mean what she *really* was? What was she?

She looked about the deck. Perhaps she could show the famously hot-headed dead dive-owner's growth of mole. If someone could identify it, it would indicate medical knowledge.

She waited in the sun with the niggers from the dice game.

Telling their crazy stories. She bit her fist. That Irish doctor. Fake doctor. Whatever he was. She smashed a horsefly on her neck and threw it in the water where a shellcracker was waiting to suck it under the waves. One of the niggers told her the way a girl got knocked up was by laying with a man and she disbelieved him. She dug the mole from her pocket and unspooled it from its rag. She sniffed it, she held it up by a long hair and watched it point north. She drew a knife from her boot and poked it. The black parts were softer. She touched it with her tongue.

No other man crossing the gangplank in McIntosh admitted to the medical arts, though, and presently the boat shrilled its steam whistle and sucked its paddlewheel to life and they lurched off. A couple of jokers fired pistols in the air, and as the scorched landscape wrenched itself past like a beaten army, Evavangeline realized that for the rest of her life she would wonder if she was dying.

Meanwhile, a number of whores and several sots had witnessed the murder and mutilation of the famously hot-headed owner of the dive.

The well-dressed troop of Christian Deputies who'd whipped (and then released) the gal's sexual co-conspirator in Shreveport had tracked her to Mobile, and within two days Walton had bribed most involved and found where she'd resided during her week in the bay city: a boardinghouse on Dauphin Street. Of some repute. A blind man running for state representative had dined there once. And on a separate occasion a dysenterious matador from Atlanta had used its privy for the better part of half an hour. And then, the *coup de gras,* that long extemporaneous political debate on Populism between Professor *Emeritus* R. M. Brutus Theodore "Patch" McCorquodale IV, Ph.D., and Bud Rope. Right on these here boards, the "half-breed" proprietor-lady was known to say, tapping her walking cane. Her two halves were Caucasian and Indian, if Walton's re-search was as accurate as he believed it to be.

Why in the world would the perverted sodomite they were pursuing choose such a high-profile locale?

With the bay tapping the sand and forever astonishing the crabs beyond the rim of their campfirelight, Walton led a discussion among his Christian Deputies where they sat in good posture after a meal of liver and kidney beans, earnestly dissecting their quarry's character. Aside from the men being a bit gassy it was pleasant. The leader had a small chalkboard and stand on which he drew diagrams, charts, maps, and stick figures. He wrote words and underlined them. "CLASS." Didn't their misguided prey feel out-of-his-element there in the famous boardinghouse? Among "GOOD" (Walton wrote furiously) "PEOPLE"? Why wasn't he sleeping in an alley, or in a seedy hotel, where "TRASH" traditionally stayed and where "SIN" took place? Did he feel safer there? Less conspicuous? Or was he trying to rise above his "STATION"? And if so, "WHY"?

What's *our* station, Mister Walton? inquired a tall one-eared deputy with his shirttail out. He'd raised his hand.

Walton had written, "A-R-I-S-T-O-C-R-A-" but paused. Why do you ask? Loon, is it? And please, call me Captain.

Well, the deputy said, it lines up like this here. I prefers me a cathouse to a boardinghouse. I'd ruther sleep on the ground than in some bed. Do that make me trash?

Why certainly not, Walton said. Deputy Ambrose, tell him.

Ambrose looked puzzled. He scratched his "Afro" which had a knife handle protruding from it. He came over to Walton and on tip-toes whispered, I thank that 'n is trash, Mister Walton.

What 'd that little nigger say? Loon asked his buddy.

Nonsense. All of it! Walton dusted chalk from his gloves. By virtue of my being a "Yankee," he announced, I hereby deem you all worthy.

He raised his hand sartorially.

There, he said. Anything else?

❧

Farther north, the steamship shouldered up the brown ribbon of the Tombigbee, shrunk by the drought to half its width and narrower for oncoming boats and lower for stobs. On board, Evavangeline had run out of money. Long about midnight she swiped a black gourd of tequila from the galley and drank it. She let a thin dapper Irish in a dirty white chef's hat lead her to a hidden spot on the deck behind some empty whiskey barrels with dead moss between the slats.

It's a dollar, she said, turning to give him access.

I like hair, he whispered. Under the armpits. I like to smell armpits.

Did I say—ouch!—it was a dollar?

He had his hands down her pants, groping about, lifting her feet off the deck.

Where's ye member? His tongue a hot leech in her ear.

My what? Where's my dollar?

Yer big ole cock-a-doodle-do. I want to suck on it, honey.

You pervert. She spun and shoved him darker into the barrels.

She hitched up her pants and patted her sleeves as if to dust herself of his deviance.

I'll have ye ass, the chef said. He came at her growling in his throat, a pug of a man now, glint of a paring knife in the moonlight. But even drunk she dodged and his blade slit no deeper than her shirt. He switched hands like a knifefighter and jabbed at her again but she was suddenly behind him with her arm around his neck and a hawkbill blade hooked in his gut.

Aye, he said. Killed me.

She looked around but the watchman had passed out on deck like a sack of manure.

Dragging the dead pervert toward the rail, she darted her fingers through his pockets. A silver dollar and a rabbit's foot, obviously defective. She shoved him over the side and threw the charm after and stumbled below deck toward the doctor or phony doctor's room. She fell over a naked man passed out drunk. It felt like the tequila was sloshing in her head. The worm tunneling through her brain. It ain't right, what he did, she told the narrow bucking hall. She stumbled over a sleeping child. When she found the doctor or fake doctor's door she kicked it apart and fell through the splinters.

He sat up in bed, wearing a woman's gown. Candles were burning. The Gramophone crackling.

Wait! he cried. He was wearing lipstick.

What in the world? She kicked his chamber pot aside and tugged at the revolver in her waistband. It was caught.

The man was begging, saying he was joshing her, she wasn't really going to die.

To shut him up she snaked her head in and bit a hunk out of his neck and spat it on his sheets like an oyster. He gaped at her then began to scream. She unsnagged the gun and grabbed him by the waddle under his chin and shot him in his right eye and then steadying his head shot him in his left and then straight through the nose, his lips still forming words. Turning his chin left, right, she put one in each earhole at certain angles so that there was little left above the lower jaw, the top half of his head back-hanging like a hood of hair. His bottom row of teeth was intact, she noticed, her face red from his splatter. She tipped out the blood and prized free a gold molar with her knife and let him go and when he fell his head bled across the bunk like a can of paint overturned. She stepped back reloading. The gunpowder at such range had burned the web of skin between her thumb and forefinger. The Gramophone's needle had been knocked ajar and she set it back and then, for a moment of her life, as smoke curled in the air, she listened to strings of Handel.

Anon. A lovely, leafy day. Sunlight and high cloudwork serrating the sky.

After breakfasting on cheese and "grits" and having a productive B.M. in the reeds, Walton clopped his eager stallion along Dauphin Street, making an entry in his logbook, majestic magnolias scenting the bay air with their hearty perfumes and massive live oaks columning the street, the humid shadows back from the road half-claiming mansions stately and proud, some burnt or in disrepair from the War lo these years hence but still displaying their once-splendor in the way only ruins can.

Behold Nature's Holy Cathedral, Walton proclaimed, cross-stitched with Man's finest architecture, and leavened by his will for destruction. Blessed be Thy name, Lord, that I am Thy servant proceeding on a Mission to spread Thy Gospel and dispense Thy Justice among these wretched heathens. He began to pump his fist in the air and hum "Onward Christian Soldiers." He saluted a drunk trying to urinate on a streetlamp and in return the man brandished his middle finger or "shot him a bird" in the vernacular and cursed in French.

Walton turned a cold profile and trod on. The previous night's fireside discussion had yielded nothing except cross words that ended with several deputies trying to "lynch" poor Ambrose. Confiscating their noose, the commander had dismissed the men for some "R & R"; he suspected that most of them had gone whoring and drinking as this morning he'd found several empty liquor bottles and more than a few feminine undergarments scattered among their soiled belongings. And even snoring they'd been scratching at their privates; which, of course, meant another infestation of "crabs." Ah, the yoke of command weighed heavy.

Since he'd been unable to roust them from their slumber, and since the sight of the frilly, indeed *diaphanous* pantaloons, girdles, slips, garters, corsets, bras, et cetera, was distracting him from his mission, and because Ambrose was nowhere to be found, Walton had decided to visit the boardinghouse alone. Indeed, it might be less intimidating for his subject that way. He was brilliant, quick-witted and a charmer, Phail Walton, who prided himself on having no sexual impulse whatsoever. *Nil. Nada.* He used his male member to void through, and that was it. A purely functional length of hose. Voiding, he wouldn't even touch it, would merely let it protrude and perform its task; and if it ever betrayed him and became

engorged in his pants, he would pinch the purple turtle's-head end,
like Mother used to, and it would recede. When he had a night
emission he would slam his fingers in the door come dawn and
drink a pint of his own urine.

The twelve or so deputies (the number varied, sometimes day
to day) who accompanied him on his adventures were required to
believe similarly, though not as strongly as Walton did; they never
had to purposefully injure themselves, for instance. He led prayer
meetings at night where the men held hands around the fire. He
made them find one thing each day for which to thank God. He
frowned on whiskey drinking and encouraged washing and dental
hygiene. He gave his testimony frequently. He urged the deputies
to commit good deeds, such as taking an old woman's elbow as she
crossed a street or thwarting a bank robbery. He taught the troops
hymns and patriotic songs and had them memorize the poetry of
Lord Byron and that of a startling new voice, a certain Mister
Whitman:

The young men float on their backs, their white bellies bulge
   to the sun, they do not ask who seizes fast to them,
They do not know who puffs and declines with pendant and
   bending arch,
They do not think whom they souse with spray.

In general, the deputies were eager learners.
   What the hell—
   Language, said Walton at his chalkboard.
   Heck. What the *heck* do it mean, "puffed and declined"?
   Ah, said their leader. Excellent question! Anybody? Anybody?

Nobody.

Well, said Walton, writing, it's a "<u>M-E-T-A-P-H-O-R</u>."

The deputies nodded.

That's what I knowed it was, said Loon.

On occasion, Walton would discover one of the men drunk, "stoned," or rubbing himself against some whore's bottom. Or concealing a sackful of stolen money. About this subject their commander was a forgiving sort and would simply and sadly give the backslider a dressing-down, confiscate any contraband, and dock the deputy's pay. Cursing, however, was another matter entirely. It was not tolerated. Walton could recite a list of names dozens long of men unable to retain his status as a Christian Deputy; and in nine of ten cases it wasn't excessive robbery, murder, arson, treason or even unusual or deviant sexual proclivities but *profanity* that saw these men's careers wilt.

Walton and his deputies wore matching uniforms—duster coats, crimson shirts and khaki pants with extra thigh-pockets filled with snake-bite kits, cartridges, harmonicas, jew's harps, spoons, flasks (medicinal only), chewing gum, telescopes, pencils, Bibles, thimbles, compasses, pocketknives, jelly beans, wire brushes, magnifying glasses and whistles, among other items. Walton supplied each man and paid a monthly wage from his mother's dwindling bank account in Philadelphia. The deputies wore across their eyes an expensive new instrument called Dark-Lensed Goggles ($1.11 per pair). The goggles made them look like the outer-space monsters they'd been hearing about of late but cut down on headaches from the sun and theoretically gave one certain advantages in a gun battle on a bright day. The men wore identical tall black polished Creedmoor riding boots tucked crisply in their pants. They wore golden ascots. They wore stiff-brimmed hats and leather gloves with fringes. Each bore a Colt revolver on his gunbelt and a Winchester thirty-thirty strapped across his back. An imitation United States cavalry sword (half the price of the original) on his hip.

Now, in full uniform, armed and "goggled," Walton on his mission of reconnaissance marched across the Dauphin Street boardinghouse's famous porch with his left hand resting on his sword handle and with his right rapped thrice on the door. The homely, bonneted woman who answered refused to cooperate unless bribed, and after having been "jewed" down from her original asking price of eleven dollars to ten and four bits, the woman spat a glob of snuff juice between two fingers and stated the name, which Walton repeated to himself in a whisper and had her spell again as he penciled it in his Christian Deputy logbook. He noticed she spelled it differently this time.

Evavangeline, is what he wrote. Then he underlined it.

It's an odd name, he observed. Perhaps an alias.

It ain't that odd. My given name's Yulena. Yulena Carp. What's yern, Mister Walton?

Phail. And it's *Captain* Walton. Please.

Fail? My word. They never give you much of a chance, did they?

Oh! Ha, ha! he said. No, dear woman, it's with a "P-H," as in the scientific way to measure acidity. Now, he said, smiling, when did you last see this Evavangeline creature?

She held up five fingers, he four, she five, he paid.

Left two days ago, the boardinghouse proprietor-lady said.

Skipped out on her bill, she did. If you wanted to make good on it, I'd appreciate it.

Of course. Though I'm surprised you didn't have her pay in advance.

I would of. That's our usual policy. But she wanted to whore and cut me in for half, ye see. And sure enough, she whored a whole day, it was a line clear out the door, then the little tart vacated without giving me my cut.

I'm flabbergasted, Mrs. Carp, that you would allow such behavior on your premises.

What ye got in mind?

The woman parted her lips in what the head deputy took as an overture. Before he could stop himself and despite her advanced age, he had imagined her naked and suddenly his "bad job" (as Mother called it) sprang to life in his tight pants. Yulena Carp raised her eyebrows. Unable to pinch himself in her presence, he turned his back and bent forward and closed his eyes, imagined sawing off the hand of an innocent child. He felt himself calm.

Excuse me. He faced her and cleared his throat. However, I'm not so sure our quarry is a "she" after all.

Do what?

She's a man! We caught her. Him. In, er, congress. With another gentleman. The other gentleman swore it was a woman with whom he was in congress with, but I and my subordinates have good reason to believe that he is prevaricating.

The Lord's Name in vain! she hissed. How ye know?

Walton tapped his goggle lense. From witness of these very eyes. He was—forgive me!—committing a perversion in the method of species *caninus* with the other gentleman we caught.

Sodomy, good woman, sodomy! Ungodly, it was. The depth of wickedness. Fornicating like heinous canines. And before we could apprehend him, off she flew like a demon out the window. We provided the sinner we did catch with a good thrashing, but that other "ornery" S.O.B.—sorry old boy—has thus far escaped his come-uppance.

Wait. You followed him all the way from Louisiana? Jest to give him a whooping?

Walton paused. We did. We Christian Deputies are very committed to our quest. The fact of the tavern owner's murder and mutilation is just good fortune. Our instincts feel, shall we say, vindicated. Also, we believe she "mugged" a man outside the tavern as well.

So you seen this Evavangeline's . . . ? The boardinghouse woman did the Indian finger-sign for "white man's pecker" (a hand at the crotch with the pinky hanging down).

Oh, we "seen" it all right.

And now you fixing to track him?

To the end. I swear it. He tapped one of his extra pockets. On this Bible printed in Miniature.

Say, now. She seemed distracted by his garb. Them's nice pants.

If you covet these "britches," all you need do is tell me and I'll give them to you.

How come?

It's in my Christian Deputy Code. I despise things of the flesh. Objects, I mean. I'm eager to divest myself of worldly belongings. The Good Book teaches, "Fling aside such *accouterment* like dust in the wind." I'm paraphrasing.

The boardinghouse woman pointed out the parlor window.

Would ye be willing to divest ye self of that horsey and saddle rig yonder? You do that you can keep them pants. And that queer tie around ye neck too.

It's an ascot, Walton said, gazing out to where his tall white stallion stood. Ron. The very definition of "steed." Straight-legged, straight-backed, straight-tempered. Gun-broken. Tireless in a hunt. Eyes like amber. Terrified of chickens, but since few fowl intervened in their peripatetic lives, this was manageable. The Christian Deputy leader's hazel eyes misted at the gorgeous gray-tipped mane he had a deputy trim and comb each morning for an hour. And the rig! Across Ron's rippling spine sat the stock saddle that had cost his mother fifty dollars at Sears, Roebuck & Co. The finest genuine oiled California skirting leather. Sixteen inch tree. Steel fork. Beaded roll cantle.

Yet when Walton departed the boardinghouse he did so on barefoot, having retained only his uniform and goggles, which she didn't ask for. Perhaps she thought them his actual eyes; good country people had before. Meanwhile, the pockets in his pants hung like an octogenarian's dugs.

The boardinghouse woman sat on her famous porch wearing her new Creedmoor boots propped on the rail, spitting snuff juice and rolling a cigarette. She struck a match and lit the smoke and gestured to Walton's departing back. Sign of a polecat. A dandy boy. A large anus. The word———, for which English has no synonym.

❦

Upriver, dawn's dry herald brought to the hungover steamship crew news of the pervert Evavangeline had gutted the midnight before. It went bunk to bunk in whispers and giggles. Instead of falling into the water like decent folk, the pervert had gotten tangled in a fishnet hung along the ship's port side. Throughout the night a pulsing contingent of catfish, carp, grinnel, gar, sucker, alligators and even a few river-lost sand sharks disoriented by fresh water had followed the boat, swirling in the ooze. In the morning light, enormous orange crawfish with their pinchers clicking rode the body, one arm of which trailing in the water was festooned with moccasins attached at the fang. When one became too blooded it fell loose and sank in the clouds in the sky in the river.

On board the steamboat came the further news of the doctor's head shot half off in his bed, his jimmied-out molar. Bad luck for Evavangeline in that he had been not only the ship's physician but the captain's younger brother. More bad luck yet in that the pervert she'd knifed behind the barrels had been the ship's cook as well as the captain's older brother.

She ought never drink tequila.

The captain went about howling and throwing things from the ship. He rent his clothing and pulled clumps from his beard and rammed his head into the galley wall.

Hungover, Evavangeline watched from beneath a tarp. When she yawned the dried blood on her chin cracked. She swiped it with the back of her hand. On the open deck somebody was telling the captain that his brother the cook had last been seen with a fellow who matched a certain description. Somebody else said that same character had been seen going below with the doc. Evavangeline, meanwhile, tiptoed to the edge of the boat and slunk over the rail like a vapor and slid down a rope. Behind the barrels, the captain's pet spider monkey found the growth of mole from the famously hot-headed dead dive-owner and raced across the deck and leapt to the captain's shoulder and began to earnestly screw the mole into his ear.

He grabbed the monkey and flung it overboard. He picked up the growth of mole from the deck and glared at it. Its hairs had grown longer since last it was seen.

It's a shriveled banana, the first mate said, salivating.

Naw, it's a pickled nigger thumb, said the second mate, also salivating.

The captain threw them both overboard.

From the river the two thrashing officers saw Evavangeline dog-paddling toward land and tried to point her out, but the crew at the boat's high rail was giving them the finger and mooning them and pissing on them and shooting at them. Somebody threw a pig.

Then one of the men was snatched underwater. He came up, flung back and fore spewing bile, bit in half by the largest alligator in Alabama. The crowd went *Ahhhhhh*. The officer bobbed for a moment, looking very surprised. He began to point at objects and call them Robert: a cypress knee, a beaver's mound, a dragonfly rising from the water. Then he went down again. The other officer was screaming as things began to tear at him and he went under as well and nothing remained save his woolen skull cap, tossed in waves the color of blood.

In the meantime, Evavangeline kicked quietly toward shore, circumventing the feeding frenzy which had the men along the boat rail cheering and trying to throw one another in.

Lord God! bellowed the captain to the sky. He began to punch himself in the face. The sailors noticed and elbowed each other. He fell to his knees. He thrust the mole heavenward and squeezed it so hard it squirted from his grip and went skittering over the deck.

It's a pecker! he yelled. What manner of man-eater, O Lord, have I brought upriver?

3

THE BALLOON

MEANWHILE, IN OLD TEXAS, IT SEEMED THE BAILIFF'S BOY WITH THE balloon had vamoosed with the mule, and for a moment, a revolver in his left hand and sword in his right, E. O. Smonk had given the line of horses shirking at the rail his savage consideration. But he detested the preening highnesses and now could be found hobbling east along a row of storefronts, ducking bullets and favoring his gouty foot and using his sword as a cane and firing the revolver over his shoulder. Thinking Next time jest take a fucking horse.

Across the street, the mercenaries covered Smonk's escape from their wagon, one firing the machine gun while the other readied a second lock and added water for coolant. The man at the trigger was screaming as he obliterated the hotel, shutters snapped off their hinges and posts sawed to dust and windows dissolving to silver mists and shingles flapping off and one short board twirling in the alley like a child.

The panicked horses kicked and rolled, a roan's head gone, a rumpshot bay burying its hind hooves in a sorrel's stomach, nails shrieking and wood splintering as the horses drew the rails away like a curtain, buckling the upstairs deck, the back of the building suddenly ablaze with fire, men spilling onto the porch dancing as if on stage, in their dying poses flinging out their arms or backflipping with their boots left upright on the floor. They cursed and cried to Jesus. They fingered their holes to dam the blood. They tried to remember how their legs worked. What their names were. They raised their palms but the bullets were true to the faces behind, a cheek gone, a lower jaw, grin of false teeth clacking to the floorboards and one shot-off finger pointing through the air still bearing its wedding band.

Fire leapfrogged over the floors, peeling up doorjambs and across the ceiling and walling the air with smoke. When the man at the trigger paused to let the other change locks, the citizens in the hotel began to clamber away from the fire by jumping through windows. They lurched from the ruined porch, some with their hats and coattails on fire, but froze when they saw a third man striding toward them in the smoke, stepping over bodies in the dirt, a German automatic rifle in one hand and a stick of dynamite fizzing in the other.

❦

At the bottom of the hill, lumbering along panting for air, Smonk felt the concussion of the explosion before he heard it. Windows shook and shook the widows' faces behind, faces already flinted into the masks they'd wear to the grave. Then he heard the Maxim resume its work. He tipped an imaginary hat to a widow on her steps trying to cock a rifle with both thumbs with a result of shooting herself in the foot. He was still chuckling when the undertaker's widow appeared from a doorway holding a revolver in both hands and shot him broad in the chest. His gourd exploded but otherwise unharmed he grabbed her with his sword hand and danced her around and pulled her face to his and kissed her flush on the mouth and when he let go he'd taken her pistol and she bore his blood on her lips like paint, her back braced against the wall behind her.

He popped off the gun's four rounds in three seconds and tossed it away and turned a second corner into an alley and shrugged out of his coat and left it crumpled in the dirt, his shoulders jerked by a fit of coughing and sneezes that mapped the oak trunk before him bright red.

He was edging down the alley when glass shattered by his head and a rifle barrel nosed out. Still coughing, he grabbed it from the widow's fingers and looked it up and down with his good eye. Marlin repeater, full magazine judging the weight. He caught the hand swiping from the window and crushed its fingers like a sack of twigs and began to limp, again firing over his shoulder, levering with a flick of his wrist, ducking as a shot apothecary's sign swung from its chain like a pendulum. A nail sparked by his foot and a post splintered by his cheek, but that was the closest they came to killing him as Smonk broke the empty rifle over his knee and burst into the livery barn. He saw no mule, donkey or pony and had little choice but the tall gray mare in the first stall, the only animal saddled and bridled. The livery attendant's widow charged screeching from the dark holding a pitchfork woven with hay but he parried it with his sword and knocked her aside. He'd wiggled his good foot into the stirrup when she attacked again with a snub-nosed pistol. He snatched it away and smashed the gun into her cheek and flung himself onto the horse and told it Git.

The gray kicked boards loose in the wall behind and swung its head and tried to bite him but he punched its muzzle away and evened the reins. The woman grabbed his saddle strap as Smonk dug his heels in the horse's flanks and they trundled her through the dust in the bay door and left her balled on the ground. A wave of cinders blistered past: Adios, Tate Hotel. Smonk fired the snub into the sky to get the horse's attention and soon had her majesty goaded to an awkward lope. He looped the reins around his fingers and whacked her rump with his sword until the ground drummed beneath them and they hurtled across the railroad tracks and east, clinking bottles on the bottle tree, gunfire fading behind like a cel-ebration of fireworks.

When it was safe he blew a mouthful of frothy blood and aimed the pistol and centered the last bullet through the gray's left ear. The horse leapt a crossfence and whinnied and twisted in the air in some fit of pain or ecstasy and landed with the squat rider bounc-ing and low, the pair blurring, elongating, barely a hoof to earth, inspired by God or bespooked by the devil who could tell.

Meanwhile Will McKissick, the bailiff, coughed himself awake. Pushing a body off his own, he sat up plastered in gore. I'm in Hell, he thought. Things around him were moving and hot. Vaguely he heard gunshots. Screams. He fought to his knees, half aware of the dead and dying on the floor. Place shot to pieces. Air boiling. Splinters of glass stuck in the walls.

He fanned his face. Remembered being eight years old, the first time he'd used a slingshot and pebble to pick a hummingbird out of the air. Under a mimosa tree not long before his daddy got shot. He remembered knowing from that moment onward that he was a bad boy who would grow into a bad man. Then he'd pegged another hummingbird, a hatchling just out of the nest, no larger than a bumblebee.

He steadied himself against the wall and coughed and pounded his chest. But those birds were in the past now. Them and everything else. Lately, despite the long, varied and original chart of sins awaiting him in the devil's ledger, he'd been fighting his evil inclinations and had broken his associations with the outlaw element and even settled down. An honest bailiff job. Several choices to marry. Redemption his target, no matter how long the shot. There was something round and blue in his brain. He could almost imagine it, but—

Smonk!

McKissick looked around. He wasn't in Hell. This was only its anteroom, Old Texas Alabama, where moments ago E. O. Smonk had grinned blood and drawn a sword from the air and conjured a pistol by brazen will and squirted out his eye.

McKissick opened his fingers. There it was. His breath whistled out. White glass marble with a few nicks. Blue dot in the middle. Warm. He smelled it. He rolled it in his palm and pecked it with his thumbnail. It seemed to be looking at him. He popped it in his mouth where it clicked against his teeth.

His head snapped. Gunshots! He skipped through the dead to the window and double-took when he saw two men in a wagon reloading—was it?—a got-dern *Gatling gun,* the design of which he'd never seen, a steam cloud hovering around them like a halo. Water-cooled. Fancy.

Expensive.

They ain't after no picture-graphs, he said to himself. Dern, I ought to knew it. Ye done got soft, Will, thoughts of revenge plus all these women at ye.

For he himself in his official capacity had questioned the strangers at their wagon before the trial. He himself the town bailiff had been convinced of their sincerity when they demonstrated the use of their camera, having him pose with his hair flattened by oil and a grimace on his face while they huddled together at the device under a blanket. Their intention was common practice, McKissick knew, to make a picture of a dead body, which would of been Smonk if things had gone according to plan. (Often the *New York Times* would pay a dollar for a picture of lynched niggers or shot-up outlaws. Those wily photographers would change the body—shave the fellow, say, or add an eyepatch—and send it back for another dollar.) As McKissick had stood getting his picture made, *not one hour before,* a number of the ladies had gathered to watch and he'd been buffaloed, proud to be the subject of artists.

Now something moved in the street. Justice of the Peace Tate, easily recognizable by his pompadour, was crawling through the dirt away from the murderers, blood strung from his chin.

McKissick saw a third killer by the hotel, a rifleman—probably the one who'd set the building afire—waving his arms so the men in the wagon wouldn't shoot him. He hurried through the street, sticks of dynamite in his back pockets. When he reached the justice, he shouldered his rifle and drew and pointed a revolver at the back of the man's head and fired. Dust puffed by his foot as a bullet missed him and the gunner turned the Maxim on its swivels and laid a hail of bullets across the windowfront of the apothecary's. Meanwhile, Mister Tate's hair had fallen but he kept crawling. The gunman shot once more then knelt and turned the man over and began going through his shirt.

There were more pockets of return fire now and the gunner swiveled the Maxim and dragged its anchor of bullets across the storefronts and ladies dove out of sight.

The rifleman in the street grabbed his chest and McKissick looked to the large house, second floor window, where Mrs. Tate, the justice's wife—*widow*—was levering her rifle to shoot again. The man she'd killed crumpled and lay on his side. The gunner tried to turn toward her house, catty-corner the hotel, but bumped the shoulder of the man filling the coolant.

McKissick was high-stepping through the logjam of arms and legs, dodging a fiery falling roof timber and grabbing Smonk's over & under which he'd squirreled away beneath the sideboard— he'd always admired the stout Winchester and knew it would be perfectly sighted. He hopped across the undertaker and clicked the rifle's safety with his thumb and knelt at the window and sighted the gunner no more than a second before he shot him in the temple and then shot the other man before the first landed.

McKissick stared down at the rifle, heavy in his hands, the line of upswept gray smoke from its barrels a shade lighter than the smoke in the air. You done good, he told the over & under.

Since coming to, he'd been conscious of an ache in his left side, and now that he had a quiet moment he reached inside his shirt. When he drew out his fingers bloody pellets of the rice he'd eaten for dinner were stuck there. Smonk's got-dern sword must of run right through him. He steadied himself against the pinewood wainscotting. Gritted his teeth.

Surrender? someone called.

Across the room through coils of smoke a revolver butt flagged with a white handkerchief raised itself above an overturned table. The judge's eyebrows inched up and then his face. He waved.

You that goddamn bailiff, he called. Ain't ye? I forget ye name. Mic-something.

How come ye ain't dead? McKissick asked.

How come you ain't?

I jest about am. Case ye ain't noticed.

God damn, said the judge, fanning at smoke. Might we finish this discussion elsewhere?

A woman screamed from outside. McKissick ducked through the window and stood blinking on the splintered porch. The wind changed the smoke's course and the street appeared before him. He lowered the rifle.

The dead were strewn and splashed along the porch, halves and quarters of horses and men splattered in puddles of tar in the street. A crater smoking where it looked like a bomb had gone off and arms and half-legs and other fragments here and there. The world seemed too bright. McKissick felt like somebody had boxed his ears. Women followed their own screams outside and whisking their skirts over the dirt sprang corpse to corpse calling out the names of the dead. At the corner of what used to be the hotel a woman held a severed hand by its pinky and screamed, Oliver! Over in the alley by the store McKissick saw the abandoned gun, still steaming, pointed at him. He tongued Smonk's eye around the horseshoe of his jaw.

Inside the hotel, the judge crashed over the table and fell off his dais. God damn, he cried. My arm's on fire!

The bailiff ignored him. He looked up the street and down. His memory was coming back. The mule . . .

The balloon!

Where's my boy? he yelled, so hard his wound farted. He unstuck his hand from his side and raised it to the sky, rice on his fingers. Willie! he yelled.

Still making their noise, the widows in silhouette looked up from the murdered while behind them the hotel roof collapsed, fire and smoke bursting out the top windows and a moment later those on the ground floor, the air fogged with smoke and the yowls so baleful and plaintive it seemed Hell had breeched its levee and poured forth its river of dead.

Eugene Oregon Smonk, McKissick yelled, *is done stold my gotdern boy!*

❧

Ike was waiting for Smonk at the three-way crossing, smoking his cob pipe and fanning his face with his hat. He'd shaved clean but for a bristly goatee, and under thick eyebrows white as a cottonmouth's yawn his pupil bores were pinheads, watching. Old as he was and weary, he leaned against the railing of his farm wagon holding the mule thief's hand high behind his head as the boy squirmed, kicked, spat and cursed. The mule was biting up sheaves of grass, the balloon still floating above. The mare shivered under Smonk so he dismounted and slapped her hard on the rump. Farewell yer highness, he said and watched her gone in a rattle of dust and grasshoppers.

Ike tossed him a jug which he caught onehanded. He thumbed off its thong and drank a long time with little care for what spilled into his whiskers.

The boy groaned.

Smonk gazed down. Almighty damn, he said and took another swig. Go on turn him loose, I.

Ike released the hand and the boy fell to the ground.

You run, Smonk said, I'll shoot ye in the ass.

Dad *gum* that hurt. From beside the wagon wheel, the boy glared up at Ike.

What would ye name be? Smonk asked.

I ain't got to tell you, the boy said. William R. McKissick Junior.

Well, Junior. I seen ye before. Ain't I? I mean before I told ye to watch my mule which you will not be paid for, case ye was wondering.

Yessir. *Our* mule. You seen me fore that.

I thought I recognized ye daddy. A fucking bailiff, no less. Smonk's knees clicked as he squatted then sat against the wheel spokes to catch his breath. He had both hips eaten up with the rheumatism, and every time he got down like this it felt like he might never rise.

Reckon ye old man's bit by the respectable bug agin, he said. Well, I wish him luck but don't allow none 'll smile down on him, life he's led.

The boy's eyes egged when he saw Smonk's speckled plank of a face up close, his bloody teeth and lips, the bright red string dripping into his beard, the hole an eyeball once held.

The boy pointed. Something got ye eye.

Smonk touched the hole. This? He put his fingertip in it.

The boy leaned in for a closer look. How deep can it go?

Smonk made a noise in his chest like rocks grumbling and spat under the wagon. Hear that, I? How deep do it go?

He did a trick where he pretended to put his whole trigger finger in but in truth he was just bending it back.

The boy laughed and clapped his hands.

Smonk lit a cigar. You ever seen a picture of a pirate?

Naw sir, what's that?

A robber that uses a ship and robs other ships. Out in the high seas. They carry curved swords called cutlasses and kill whales for fun and fly a goddamn skull for a flag. Wear eyepatches too and about half the time they got these birds riding on they shoulder. I never did put the two together till it was too late. See, I'd always wanted to be a pirate, way back a hundred years ago when I was a youngun like you, reading dime novels, and in them days I reckon it might of been possible. But then I growed up as ye will if somebody don't murder ye first and anyway one month of June not too long back I spent playing blackjack in a gutted-out church in Biloxi Mississippi. Remember, Ike? This coon-ass dealer used to wear him one of them pirate birds on his shoulder and I got to coveting that goddamn bird. It would say *ante* and *bust*, and it was the funniest thing. It never got old. Not one time. *Ante. Bust!* The whores loved it. If a man had owned that bird the whores would of fucked him for free.

The boy listened beatifically. The word *whore* had risen the devil's tool in his britches.

Smonk didn't notice or if he did didn't say. It was one of them perfect nights, he talked on, smoking. I got on a hot streak and couldn't of lost if I'd wanted to. Done won all they money and then won they pistols and a week of free whoring and a knife and a beefsteak ever day for the rest of my life and the steeple off they church. But it was near four in the morning fore finally I won the bird. And on threes! When I left that parrot was setting right cheer. He tapped his shoulder.

They was waiting for me in the alley, them coon-asses. I shot them I could and stobbed one or two and was about to kick the last one to death fore Ike pulled me off. And the whole time the bird never flew off my shoulder. When I finished it said *Bust.*

Overhead, Ike made a sound with his lips. A whistle of air.

I know, I know. Smonk winked and ashed his cigar. Brother Isaac here, he whispered to the boy, never did cater to that bird. Used to say don't trust it. Say *Let's eat it* ever time we got hongry. But I'd always concealed me a weakness for things of the air. I cherish a damn hoot owl. The ravens out west. Even yer common finches and spares. Bats, too. Always contained me a soft feeling towards a bat.

The boy wished he had a pet bat. It could fly and fetch things. Nothing big, just bat-size things. Ladies' earrings. A pocketwatch. Flitter of wings and the tiny shiny objects of the world at your command.

Smonk waited till he was paying attention again.

So I come to enjoy this particular bird's company and let him ride my shoulder ever minute of the day. I remember it could say *fart* and sang *Clementine* and it could do any birdcall it ever heard. Squirrels barking. A bobcat. Opera. It was jest a treasure. Then one night I was drunk on some vile potato splo a goddamn Irish foisted on me and without a speck of warning that cunning bird reaches over and takes out my goddamn eye with his beak, jest like that. Smonk snapped his fingers. Swallered it like a pill.

The boy slapped his own forehead. Dad gum! What ye do?

First thing I done I sobered up right quick, case he meant to go for the other one. Then I plucked him of his feathers and twisted off his little yaller legs and his beak and et him alive.

Dang, said the boy. How'd he taste? Had ye give him a name?

I had. Stan. Such was the name I give him. He jest looked like a Stan to me. And good. He tasted real good to be such a traitor. Somehow he was still tender.

Ike's eyes shrank in their wrinkles, which was how you knew he was smiling, as he studied the horizon for pursuers, and Smonk rubbed his goiter thoughtfully. During all this excitement the mule had wandered up and was pushing its snout against his shoulder, the saddle off center from its run and sweat tracks down its gray sides. Burrs in its tail. Smonk ignored the mule for the whore it was, off with the first little shit to put ass to it, and studied the boy.

Didn't I use to hold congress with ye momma?

Sir?

Fuck her, ye twit.

Yessir. I were six year old and a half that last time ye got some. I'm near bout twelve now and this much taller. He held his hand to his throat as a measure. But I remember it real good.

She like it when I nailed her?

Seemed to, yessir. The boy paused and peered into Smonk's

eye. Daddy says you a coldblooded killer. He says you ain't like normal folks. Says you of the devil. You gone kill me, too, Mister Smonk?

Smonk glanced at Ike.

Well, he said. I reckon ye daddy would know plenty about the devil. But I done met my quota today, so naw, I ain't gone kill ye. But get the hell out of here lest I change my mind.

The boy disappeared into the sugarcane.

Smonk let Ike haul him to his feet where he drank more whiskey, easing the pressure of his goiter with a series of crisp belches. He tossed the jug back and chewed his cigar.

You called it, I, he said. Trap, sure as sin. I'll concede ye that one.

Ike puffed his pipe and his gaze swept the horizon.

Smonk followed where he looked and saw the road he'd just blistered with speed. The red dust still settling. The sugarcane had been baked by the unremitting sun and the stalks if you touched one would crumble in your hand. The sky beyond glaring white while every leaf of every tree or bush had been coated red, the far-reaching sugarcane itself crimson in the distance.

Ike said nothing. He looked behind him where a hawk dropped from the sky into the cane and rose back up, the fieldmouse in its grip still clutching sprigs of straw in its tiny fingers. The lessons the world taught were everywhere.

Mister Smonk?

The boy. Tapping his elbow.

Junior, Smonk said not looking down, if I want any more shit outta you, I'll squeeze ye head.

I wondered might I get my balloon back's all. You can keep that dern mule. It kicked me one time.

Smonk looked at the balloon over his shoulder, gray-blue and traced with veins and linked by a string to the mule's ear. He looked at the boy's dirty face, its skewed grin and missing front teeth and dimples and glittering blue eyes.

He reached in his bootleg with a grimace and withdrew a gleam of light that when turned in the air became a pearl-handled Mississippi Gambler stiletto with a groove in the blade for bloodletting.

Eugene, Ike said.

Smonk winked and flipped the knife in his palm and presented the handle. Here.

The boy snatched it away.

Now git.

But—

Smonk took his cigar out of his mouth and touched its fire to the balloon.

Dad gum, the boy said when it popped. How bout the string, then?

⚬⚬⚬

Running west into the dying sun, the boy knew better than to go back to Old Texas. All the men were dead there, including William R. McKissick Junior's daddy, the bailiff. First William R. McKissick Junior's momma taking off after Mister E. O. Smonk and now his daddy the bailiff shot dead by Mister E. O. Smonk.

The boy ran, holding the knife Mister E. O. Smonk had given him. He pretended it was a birthday present from his momma.

His daddy—before he was a bailiff and before Mister E. O. Smonk had shot him dead in Old Texas—had been a paid employee for Mister E. O. Smonk. In Oklahoma or someplace.

Whenever Mister E. O. Smonk used to come to see Daddy once or twice a year, it meant him and Daddy would get drunk on Mister E. O. Smonk's licker. Mister E. O. Smonk's giant head would loll and he would slide gold coins over the table at Daddy bribing Daddy to let him go on have a piece of Momma. Sometimes it took a hundred dollars or more but Smonk seemed to think everything had its price. Momma would of been acting peculiar all night anyway, how she bent over pretending to look for dustballs under the table where the dustballs had been growing like a beloved crop the entirety of William R. McKissick Junior's life. And her with no drawers on. William R. McKissick Junior used to hide under the table trying to see her nethers, taking out his devil's tool and disobeying the Bible. Then, as coins rasped across the table, Daddy would say Ah hell, go ahead to Mister E. O. Smonk and Mister E. O. Smonk would grunt up off the chair unbuttoning his britches with coins falling out of his pockets thumping like hail on the floor and his suspenders falling down one then the other. Momma always chose that moment to pretend not to want none and make a fuss of being dragged in, getting her dress all tore, thigh-leg for all to see and her bottom too. Daddy would grab up the coins and stalk outside in a fury and start kicking the dog across the yard, or William R. McKissick Junior if he caught him under the table. From behind the sheet hung to divide the shack in half, the only thing louder than the bed creaking was Momma squealing.

And ever dern time, after Mister E. O. Smonk come out from behind the sheet, pulling on his suspenders and smelling his fingers, Momma would follow him, all slinky like. Wearing nothing but a shred of undergarment. In a good mood. Tired-looking. All smiley, a certain sweat about her.

Not noticing the menfolk at the table talking about murder, she'd scoop William R. McKissick Junior in her lap and hug and kiss him and smell behind his ear. Her cheeks flushed. Her bosom too. You could see most of em. Just not the nipple parts. William R. McKissick Junior would try to peek down her collar to see the nipple parts and he'd get him a devil's tool in his britches and Momma would feel it on her leg and pop the imprint of her hand into his bottom and say, *You stop that. You bad boy! You stop that right this second!*

He ran fast, now, the devil stirring in his pants at the memory. He waved his new knife, accelerating to a gallop, more of the air than earth, whooping and wheeling his arms.

For he was going at last to the woman who took in orphans! There were no other children in Old Texas and the boy wanted somebody to play with. Rumor claimed there were no rules in the orphanage ner chores neither and that you ate whatever you wanted whenever you wanted and went to bed when you chose and you could even screw the girls if you had a mind to. William R. McKissick Junior very much wanted to screw a girl. It was all he thought about. Screwing girls. Now here was his chance for some real cooter. He ran faster than he ever had before saying Cooter, cooter, cooter, cooter, cooter. Then he ran even faster than that, his new knife slicing the air like a curse on its course. If only he had the balloon.

4

THE CROW
HUNTERS

EARLY THAT SAME SATURDAY, SOMEWHERE BETWEEN THE RIVER town of McIntosh and wild loamy climes north, Evavangeline happened upon a quartet of ancient horsemen in their tattered battle grays all these decades later and bearing long untidy beards the color of war. She'd lost her boots and guns to the Tombigbee's currents and, because of her clothing and short hair, the foursome took her for a barefooted young whippersnapper as folk were wont to do in those simpler times and invited her along on a crow hunt up north ways. It was great fun, they promised, and they had whiskey.

You thank he's too old? she heard one ask another under his breath.

Naw, he replied, then shushed his companion.

What the dickens yall shushing about? Evavangeline called.

Don't be so testy, lad, said the man from his horse. You want a ride?

I'd ruther not. I can't abide me a damn horse.

You a fool to run.

Best not say nothing like that to me when we tap into that whiskey.

Preciate the warning.

Within half a day the crow hunters and their new young compatriot had arrived at a blind made of corn shucks and cane stalks and positioned in the northwest corner of a dried-out cornfield. The men dismounted as Evavangeline leaned against a tree to catch her wind. One of the crow hunters led the horses out of sight and returned later and they all knelt together and entered the blind and lay waiting, their breath meaty and rank. They told jokes on one another and passed the bottle and belched and farted so densely her eyes stung.

You got a extry gun? Evavangeline asked the man nearest her. Faded chevron of a sergeant on his shoulder.

Naw, he said. I jest got my three ones here.

Well, if another one appears by holy miracle in ye waistband or coat pocket or asshole, will ye lend me it a spell?

I will, said the man. He popped her on the rump.

The bottle came her way again. She drank a snort. She could feel it travel the length of her body like a herd of iddy biddy horses. With little naked men mounted upon them. With every swig there were more little horses and more little men.

A hunter told one about his army buddy getting his legs chopped off by mistake and they all laughed and one man spewed whiskey out his nose.

Don't be wastin that, the first hunter said.

It's yer turn, they said to Evavangeline. To tell one.

I ain't got nare.

Got a big ole red scar, one of the men said. On ye neck yonder.

Well, she said, there's a story.

She told about the time she got in a fight with two Irish. She and the Irish were hiding in an alley together. Evavangeline twelve or thereabouts. The potato-eaters, grown men, made fun of her red spot and she told them to go screw they selves. They came at her and she kicked the front one in the balls and got a fist in the jaw from the other. But his follow-through took him off balance and she uppercut him with her knee and split his lip.

Then I slit both they thoats and rolled em, she said. Did ye like that story?

Damnation, the hunter cried. I'm a veteran. Ever white man of my generation's been shot. If they ain't ye can't trust em. I meant no offense.

We all got scars, another man said.

In a huff, she climbed out the back to make water.

She was squatted there, her head cottony from the whiskey, when the veteran hooted. He'd stumbled out for a piss himself.

Hey fellers! he called. This here high-strung one's a split-tail!

She tried to rise but he grabbed her ankles. He dragged her hollering and bare-assed and clawing at the turf around to the front of the blind and the others climbed out with the bottle.

This here's a genuine piece of tail, boys, the veteran said. He unfastened his fly and leapt forward. He prized her knees apart and began to hum "On Christ the Solid Rock I Stand" and poke his dong about her thighs.

Boy hidy, said one of the men watching. I call next.

She tried to clamp her knees but he was in there. Then her hand happened upon the pistol he wore backward on his belt. She squeaked the gun from its holster and flipped it in the air like a circus shooter. In quick succession she shot the three men witnessing— gut, chest, neck—who hit the ground dead still holding their peckers before the fellow atop her realized she had the barrel under his chin.

Wait, he grunted, I'm fixing to get a nut—

But he didn't.

She shoved him away dead, his member still engorged and purple like an obscene mushroom. She swapt it off with his own bootknife and watched the stump blurt a rope of blood and spume like that fountain they had down in Mobile where men went to meet other men.

Sitting in the dirt, she held her head for a while, then pulled on her pants. Insects were gathering at the edge of the pooling blood like souls needing baptism. She wrenched the boots from the veteran and stabbed her feet into them. She reloaded his revolver and shot him a few more times in the gape where his jaw had been and collected their guns and then, despite her disinclination, she found the horses where they were tied and freed three and for herself chose the tall bay with spotted legs and leapt into the saddle.

In the afternoon the field began to fill up with crows gorging on corn. After a while they came through the stalks and gorged on the eyes of the men, and then their tongues.

∞

Meanwhile, time passes. The chase stretches. The men endure. Some forget who they're chasing or why.

But Walton never forgets. They've commandeered a steamship now, chugging upriver, the horses irritable, the men bored.

A river is no place for a man, the Christian Deputy leader thinks, pacing up the deck and back. On the bank he sees a wildcat lift its dripping muzzle from a slain "razorback" hog. Walton flings his hand in the air. There! That is the life for a man. Any moment that a man is not wearing a bloody beard he is less than he can be. The leader gave a two-fingered salute. You are manly, noble wild-cat! But not I, not with this, not with this, with this, this, this this this this *bull-crap*!

Lord forgive the profane word I just thought in my head. My flawed human brain! No excuse but my pent-up wrath at this sinner I'm chasing. I won't even say her name. She "galls" me, Lord. This Evavangeline. She tempts me, my Savior. They all think she's a man but I know the truth, O Lord Savior. Mine eyes are better than mine companions' eyes are and I was first in the door, Lord Jesus, and I know that while they are just mites, they are womanly breasts indeed, Lord Jesus Christ, and what else she had, O God in Heaven, I won't mention in Your Devine Presence, but You of course know Yourself, don't You, as Your Noble Lucky Hands formed it Themselves, didn't They, Lord? There it was, glistening, O Holy, just for the flick of a second, Lord Jesus Christ Above, and I saw it from behind! Her "cooter," Lord! Her delicious red vulva! Lord my Christ my Healer! And thus I am forever tempted by this woman. Evavangeline. Evavangeline. Hers is the first vulva I have seen other than Mother's, O Lamb of God O Perfect Prince. Please in the meantime forgive this hapless sinner, Lord. Amen.

Across the deck, on Walton's command, Ambrose was teaching the troops to read. There'd been grousing about having a Negro tutor the men, but Walton had delivered a stirring lecture about the necessity of the races getting along. It was why, he confessed, he'd chosen a Negro as his number two man. When no one seemed moved by their leader's oratory brilliance, however, he had threatened to dock the pay of any bigot. Meanwhile, Walton spotted the tip of a bow among the troops.

Red Man! he called, replacing his hat, securing the cinchcord underneath his chin.

A tall red-skinned man stepped up out of the crowd of students; the bow belonged to him.

You're Cherokee or something, aren't you? Walton said.

Something.

Don't get "riled." Why isn't your hair longer? In a braid? There's not really a C.D. rule about hair length. In fact, it might be fashionable if you were to let it grow—

Long hair is vanity.

Ah. Yes. We agree. I've been needing to "get my ears lowered" too. But listen. What's your opinion of, if we're tracking a certain convicted sodomite, and we're on a steamboat, say, forging upriver, and our quarry is probably, you know, on land by now, going really fast, train or horseback, whatever, and we're stuck here on this unholy lurching boat moving about a knot a day which is essentially not moving?

I'm not sure I understand, Mister Walton.

Captain Walton, please. Okay. I used to be a schoolmaster. He looked at his troop of eager readers. None of you all knew that, did you? Schoolmaster from Philadelphia. (Suddenly he ached for his chalkboard, but alas it was packed aback the mule.)

What I mean, he went on, is that I'm adroit at explaining things.

Especially with a blackboard. But let's try it this way, Red Man. Is it okay for us to get off this unholy raft and get the horses some exercise before they go crazy, and get the men some exercise before *they* go crazy? We'll gallop to the next dock and find out if she got off or stayed on. I mean he.

I see. The tall Indian leaned his bow aside and adjusted his quiver of arrows. He frowned and pursed his lips and squinted his eyes and gritted his gleaming teeth, as if for him thought manifested itself as a severe headache.

Walton's thoughts ran back to Evavangeline. To that day in Shreveport when she worked the door in the tavern across from the cheap hotel where he was living. (When they "bunked" in town on rare occasions, the other deputies usually shared a room, Ambrose out back in a barn or shed as most of these establishments harbored ill feelings for Negroes. But Walton always preserved his privacy for devotionals and prayer. It wasn't classist, he insisted to his mother in his long, florid letters, but was instead the necessary separation of leader from led.) On the day in question, he was ambling out of the barber's from having a shave and boot shine and saw her standing in the door under the saloon's awning. One in the afternoon. She was dressed like a schoolgirl. Pigtails. Her cheeks smattered with fake freckles. She fetchingly held a sign that said "Fuck $1" and was illustrated by a crude drawing of a man and woman copulating "doggie-style"; Walton assumed the latter was for Shreveport's copious illiterate. The leader of the Christian Deputies stood in the middle of the street watching the girl. Then she noticed him. He couldn't look away. A clatter of horse and buggy blocked them and then they saw one another again, his clothes flecked with mud and horseshit, a lump in his pants. She fingered the lapel of her shirt and flashed him a quick-tiny breast, startling and white in the sun and then gone, but not before he'd seen the bloodred nipple as big as a thirty-eight caliber cartridge.

Mother! Lord Jesus!

He'd covered his eyes with both hands and whirled, weeping. She went back inside.

The next day he'd spent in his room. He prayed and slammed his fingers in the drawer of the desk on which he ought to have been writing dialogue for the play he'd been outlining in his log-book. He would try that. He dipped his quill in the inkwell and swirled it around. He brought it up dripping and blotted it. It was hard to write with his fingers throbbing. He made a mental note to slam his other hand next time. Painfully, he began to make a letter. Capital "B." He followed it with a lowercase "r" and was well on his way to spelling "Breast" when he slammed down the pen. His fingernails were turning black, and he had a sudden restored memory of being dressed like a girl, his nails painted red. He covered his face with his hands and his eyes gazed out through the bars of his fingers.

O Lord Jesus Christ comfort me in my prison of pain!

He shut his eyes and prayed that he would be miraculously transported to another location, as when God had miraculously transported Lot and his family from the doomed sodomites in the cities of the plain. But opening his eyes he could still see the harlot out the window across the street wiggling her hips like an effigy of sin itself. Right there. In the doorway. Dressed as a squaw this time. A drunk sidled up to her and stared openly. He appraised a hand along her hip. She turned around at his behest and raised her leather skirt. O her bottom! Walton jerked his head hither and yon, discombobulating the things on his desk, but the man's own wide buttocks blocked the view of hers.

The Christian Deputy leader fell back onto his bed, sobbing and pinching himself.

In a flash he was at the window again.

Beneath the awning the drunk man was whispering in the girl's ear, braced on her shoulder to stay afoot. She nodded and they went inside. Walton watched, his breath fogging the glass, his heart an overheated toad frying in the cauldron of his ribs. Upstairs, across the street, the harlot appeared in a window to pull down the shades. Before she did, though, he saw her lick out her tongue at him.

Serpent!

He tried to fill a cup with urine so he might drink it, but his turgid member refused to cooperate, the down-bending so pleasurable in itself that it nearly betrayed him.

He had rushed downstairs right then, pants abulge, ascot atangle, and burst into the deputies' room, where the men were supposed to be engaged in an exercise about the sucking out of snake venom. There were several empty liquor bottles scattered about the floor that, without being asked, Loon testified had been left there by the room's previous tenants. He hiccupped.

Men, Walton cried. Sin! He pointed upstairs.

Thus rallied (Ambrose rounded up from witnessing to a group of degenerates playing "craps" in the alley), the entire troop lurched across the street in full uniform, several adjusting the things in their pockets, their leader seen by some to be pinching his male member through his tight pants. They entered the saloon, Red Man lowering his bow, an arrow notched, to fit inside. They bounded up the stairs, behind Walton. Red-faced, he had kicked down the door and burst in the room and away she'd flown out the window like a shade flapping up.

Meanwhile, on the boat, Red Man had recovered from his bout of thinking. No sir, he said. Regarding your question of abandoning ship for hot, dusty horse travel overland.

Why?

Because to track a man is to know him. To track a man is to honor him.

Pardon?

Knowing and honoring a man are aspects of tracking him. In my tribe before the Wars and dark years of reservation life, before I fled east to escape the Apache and Comanche and the Pawnee and the Rangers and revenuers and cavalry men and bounty hunters, I, like you, also was a teacher. Of young braves. Sometimes the other warriors called me coward for choosing to be with the little ones instead of out earning feathers and ribbons and pieces of clothing taken from massacred white men and women and children and kept and passed father to son in a family for as many generations as the piece of clothing lasted—sometimes just a scrap, the cuff from a shirt, or only a button—

What in the world are you talking about? Walton asked.

To track a man is to know him. To know him is to honor him. And to truly honor him (which is part of tracking him) you have to go exactly where he went, suffer his very path, riding when he rode, walking when he walked, as close as you can get, stepping when possible in his very footsteps. You finger every broken branch, touch each smudge of dirt with your eager tongue, you work at becoming him—

Wrong, said Walton. Why would I want to become a sodomite? Captain! he called.

A dour, scruffy man shuffled forward. Aye?

Steer us over to the bank, sir, hard aft. The leader clapped his hands. "Pronto!"

At this speed? We'll run aground.

Speed, sir? My gracious! You call this speed? Walton threw open his arms. Evolution is moving faster than we are!

Meanwhile, the deputies learning to write had been smudging "Walton" in asbestos on the side of the boat. While they worked, chewing their lips like giant, frightening children, Ambrose plucked a pencil from his Afro and saw how many littler words he could make from "Walton." He listed "wal," "ona," "alton" and "walto" (except for "w" and "l," he drew the line at single-letter words). He added "lto" to his list then looked up and noticed that Loon seemed to have a condition where he spelled all his words backward; so when he copied the Christian Deputy leader's name in his large, uneven characters, it caught Ambrose's attention.

Mister Walton, he said to his commander. You ever noticed what ye name is wrote backerds?

Great Scott. It's "not law."

The men, keen of ear, began to watch him murderously. They clattered to their feet in an asbestos cloud. Since the reading lesson, a plot of mutiny had circulated among their number. They'd decided that to earn any respect as a gang they had to kill somebody, Walton the logical choice. Ambrose next.

Not law, they chanted, coming forward drawing out their swords. Not law, not law, not law.

Deputy Ambrose! Walton whispered. Do something. That's an order.

Not law, not law, not law . . .

Red Man! the Negro called.

Everyone stopped saying "Not law" and looked at the tall Indian.

Ambrose jabbed his finger up in Red Man's face. Didn't you say ye Injun family and other ones like it 'd keep as keepsakes the clothes of—yer own words here—of "massacred white mens and womens and childrens"?

Yes, Red Man said. Why? Then his face sagged. Oh shit, he said.

Mister Walton done tole you bout cussing, Ambrose said, and without a moment's hesitation the stocky second-in-command drew his long-barreled revolver and shot the Indian in the forehead. Red Man stood for a moment, cross-eyed, then fell straight back, his bow toppling after. A plug of his head splashed in the water barrel.

Oh, Walton said. I may faint.

Yet the deflecting tactic worked, and as the blood pooled about the dead Indian's neck the remaining deputies forgot about Walton's backward-spelled name and the plot to murder him and, to a man, except Red Man, went back to their reading lesson, though visibly distracted.

That nigger better not kill me, a deputy said.

Nice work, Walton whispered to his second, once it was clear the danger had passed.

Ambrose eyed the men as they bent over their work. Can I shoot me a white 'n next?

Certainly not, said the leader. But you can "cover" yon captain so that he complies with my order.

Right, boss. Ambrose crossed to the steering platform and jammed his revolver in the man's ribs. Nigger with a gun, he whispered. Only thing missing is a reason.

There, called Walton, pointing to a small peninsula overhung with trees, jutting out into the river at a bend. Bank us there!

Kiss now, boys! the captain shouted. Here comes the end!

They exploded onto land. Ambrose flew overboard. Timbers splintered like gunshots. Bleating livestock flew past. The heavily packed mule crashed braying into the river, pulling a pair of horses with it. The men on the ship were too busy to watch, scrambling out of the way of sliding ponies and airborne barrels.

Walton used the forward momentum to his advantage, however, and, arms akimbo, pirouetted from the deck and grabbed a lowhanging limb. Those ballet lessons had done a bit of good, after all.

From the tree, he called out instructions. Deputies staggered about rubbing their heads, removing splinters. Two were swimming for the other side of the river. Deserters. If he could've spared the manpower, Walton would have sent after them. Meanwhile, a soggy Ambrose dragged ashore picking leeches off his arms and neck. The horses and pack mule at the bottom of the river were dead.

Look here, Ambrose said. Red Man lay in a heap where he'd been catapulted from the ship.

Walton watched his lieutenant kick him over. Underneath were small foot tracks.

Yep. It's him, said Ambrose. The pre-vert we're after. I'd know that sign anywheres. Reckon he come out the river barefoot, then took off.

They looked at Red Man's body, birdcalls piercing the human silence like bright arrows.

That, deputies, Walton said at length, is dedication. To discover "sign" even after death. Perhaps you oughtn't been so "trigger-happy," Deputy Ambrose.

But Mister Walton—

No excuses, please. Your pay is hereby docked.

Ambrose grumbled under his breath as Walton assembled the men for an inspirational talk on Red Man's service to his country. By now all the horses were ready save the ones dead in the river—for which the Christian Deputies observed a moment of silence—and leaving two eager volunteers to bury their fallen comrade, Walton and his men mounted up and were off.

∞

Within an hour they'd spotted dozens of buzzards circling in the sky. At the edge of a parched cornfield they gazed upon four dead men, a gory scene which Walton characterized in his logbook as a "carnage of Old Testament vicissitudes (sp?)."

The crows had given way to buzzards, slick reeking ungainly flesheaters, summoned by death like family members called home. The large sneering birds were everywhere, tubercular frowns pasted in the sky, leaning malignant growths of tumor in the limbs of trees.

The deputies dismounted in unison as they'd been instructed and drew their revolvers and aimed them all about, some men kneeling, one on his belly, as the drill called for. Walton came forward proudly, stepping over the prone man. Excuse me. He crossed the ground and knelt beside the jaw-shot veteran. The leader removed his glove then slid his goggles onto his forehead and pinched his nose shut at the horror, studying the body. Where was its member? Ill at the sight, he looked about and inspected the other three men, dispatched by precise shots. Their members, while all taken out of their pants, remained intact. Walton gagged. The buzzards had been having a "fiesta." The dead men's eyes had been picked out and were grotesque purple festers now.

The leader belched and turned away. What do you make of this, Deputy Ambrose? Anybody see the missing, er, part?

Naw, said the Negro, but I'm gone fuss less bout these here goggle-ma-jigs.

Walton belched again and replaced his own eyewear. Fan out, he said, his voice nasal.

The deputies unclenched their stances and pretended to look. Two began to vomit from the odor. Walton himself had begun gagging again. Another fellow was whistling, hands pocketed, walking backward toward the river.

Shew, said Ambrose. Stink don't it. He peered inside the blind. No pecker to report, Mister Walton, but they was here all right. Our pre-vert amongst em, look. Here's his tracks. They was waiting on something, looks like. Or somebody. You can see where they guns was laid. Here and here and here and here and here. And here and here. Here. Stink so bad from they farts you can smell the rabbit they'd eat for supper.

Walton clapped his hands. Guns, Deputy Ambrose. That's it! Guerilla warriors is what we have. Which explains the uniforms of these dead. Perhaps left over from the War, lo all these years later. "Sore" losers, these guerillas. Mis-perceived as heroes. Men unwilling to march out of the past. Praise God, we might just get a shot at testing our mettle in actual battle.

Battle? cried Loon.

Let me tell you what else I suspect, Deputy Ambrose. I suspect that somebody in their own party shot them. A traitor!

You mean didn't the pre-vert we after kill em, don't ye?

Listen. The reason I suspect a traitor, is that whoever killed these fellows could have never attacked head on. This place is a bunker.

A what?

Walton half-smiled. "Bunker." I'm circulating it as a new word here in the Southland. It's a secret club I and several of my old college chums originated. As social experiments, we coin new words and use them with authority. See if they catch on.

Ambrose pushed his goggles up on his forehead. You can't be doing that.

Oh, I can't, can't I?

You gots to be a lingrist or something. A senator. The word gots to be around a long time. Work its way into convocations. Official. Folks got to agree.

So why can't you and I agree? I'm practically an aristocrat, nearly a blueblood, and in addition to that a northerner. In other words *entitled*. You're a darky but one who can read. You're fairly well mannered, except for your propensity for profanity. I propose that you and I name the word and use it, Deputy Ambrose! "Bunker!" Such a stout word, I predict it catches on, especially if you'll employ it among your dusky pals when you return home on leave.

Ambrose thought about it. Why not. So that crow blind yonder's a bunker, and the pre-vert we're chasing killed them fellers?

Walton blinked. Exactly.

The men had begun howling with laughter; a deputy had been caught masturbating in the blind.

Walton called a meeting and informed the men that this deputy would now have the nickname "Onan." He described the Biblical masturbator, which caused a few sniggers among the troops.

Self-abuse, the Philadelphian admonished, is no laughing matter. Onan, your pay is hereby docked.

The men grew solemn.

Their leader clasped his hands behind his back and began to study the brown-stained grass for traces of further evidence. In the last few weeks, he had been trying to create descriptive nicknames for each deputy in hopes that it would bring them closer together and help him, Walton, tell the fellows apart. "Loon" and "Red Man" had caught on quickly and tipped him that these aliases must be psychologically and/or physically descriptive; if they were mildly insulting as well, the humorous aspect further aided the men's memories. The head deputy imagined that his subordinates bandied secret nicknames for him as well. "Sarge." "His Majesty." He wondered if they had conversations about him. They must. Aside from alcohol, tobacco, gambling, whores and a taste for mindless violence, what else did they have in common but Phail Walton? Often at night, as they bivouacked under the stars, he pretended to sleep, even committing counterfeit snores so that he might hear what they said about him. He'd recruited them from everywhere. Bums, mostly. Drunks. Criminals. Men "on the lam." While they suffered in steadfastness, loyalty, courage and obedience, they were cheap and easy to replace.

Look here, Ambrose called. Tracks go this a way. Peers like he made off with one of these fellers' horses. Stole the guns and this one's boots. Look how little his feet is. Like girl feet.

Add thievery to the list, Walton said. Mount up!

Shouldn't we bury these fellows here? Loon asked.

Shall I describe a certain pervert? Walton said. We're in pursuit? Besides, I think our last two grave-digging volunteers have joined their fellow deserters. I'm onto that "scam" and we're fast losing men.

But it ain't Christian, Loon persisted. I was brung up to bury folks. My daddy was a gravedigger and my granddaddy before him was too and my great-granddaddy and all my uncles and so forth was. My brothers was and one tomboy sister a bull-dyke. We all gravediggers is what I'm saying. We dig good ditches and privies, too. So I'm jest making a point. You got a man with a talent, me, it's a dang shame not to let him exercise his God-give gifts. What you think there, there, you, nigger—what's ye name agin?

Ooh, Mister Walton, Ambrose sneered, I agrees with the white fellers. He glared at them, one by one. Loon with his missing ear. Onan stepping from the bunker, smoking a cigarette. An as-yet-un-nicknamed deputy picking his teeth and on down the line.

Why don't we jest ignore the heat and spend a hour digging giant holes to stick these dead strangers in? the second-in-command snided. And then why don't we climb in this here smelly-ass bunker and sang a few hymns, too? Recite some Bible scriptures? Sang Christmas carols?

The deputies were shamed.

Walton gave his dark-skinned lieutenant a fond, thankful look, and the two men smiled at one another with unabashed collegiality.

Mount up, Walton called, but everybody had already.

5

THE MOB

Evening at last in old Texas. The parched oaks lining the
street. The dry throats of whippoorwills. The ladies of the town in
their mourning color numbly lugging pails of water uphill from
the well to fight fires arisen from cinders that combust upon landing like flies raised from hell. One elderly woman collapses in the
street and, spilling her water, begins to wail. A younger woman
takes up the buckets and totters back down to the bottom where
buzzards hop off and where, flat under a bristle of scrub brush
across the tracks, a wild cat ragged in its coat of dust waits, dying
of thirst, twitching with the ray bees.

The judge, meanwhile, was hiding in the cluttered back room
of the town clerk's office stuffing a valise with confidential records
in case he had to blackmail his way out of this brouhaha. The clerk,
and Justice of the Peace Elmer Tate, and Hobbs the undertaker and
a passel of business-owners, all killed, were to be memorialized in

a ceremony the following Monday, and the judge expected to be asked by their widows to say a few words about each man. He was in a slight panic because he didn't know any of them. He was always drunk on his stops here which had winnowed from bimonthly to once or twice a year. He usually passed sentence without remembering from one case to the next what he'd said. Most of the time he couldn't even find the tiny office they provided him.

He looked up to see the bailiff watching him from the door. A Winchester rifle in one hand.

Oh, said the judge. He shut the bag and buckled it.

I don't give a good got-dern what yer stealing, the bailiff said. Such cares is for the living, which I no longer count myself among. Did ye want to see me before I left?

I did, yes. Are ye shot?

Naw. The bailiff raised his shirt and revealed the purple anus of his wound. Stobbed a tad but it ain't the first time.

You might want to get that looked at, the judge said. Or the rest of us 'll stop counting ye among the living too.

The doc's dead. Shot thew his thoat, among other places. And I've had worse than this anyway. The pain 'll remind me of Smonk's treachery.

I could write ye a statement to similar effect. In the meantime, go on lower ye tunic. I get the picture. He opened a pocket of his valise and removed a flask. Cheers, he said and drank and dabbed his lips with a handkerchief and took a seat on one side of a small writing table and waited for the bailiff to roll a stool across and sit opposite him, laying his cap between them.

What's that in ye jaw? the judge asked. Hard candy?

Naw.

My ulcer's griping. A rock of candy 'll help sometimes. But that's neither here ner there because my ulcer ain't gone git no better until we do something about this Smonk dilemma. Cause now that you done shot them gun-killers instead of arresting em for questions, it's no way to link Smonk to em. Is it.

I reckon not.

You reckon right. *Legally,* anyhow. He cleared his throat. Now. I'm willing to take into account that you was protecting the town and won't file no charges of obstructing justice ner murder on ye.

Preciate it.

However. I'd like ye to listen real careful to a letter I got. He uncrinkled a piece of paper so oft-clutched in his sweaty palms it was thin as tissue. I'll skip the personal references and things I deem beyond ye and jest read the particulars. To save time. He cleared his throat again. To the attention of Judge et cetera et cetera, et cetera, et cetera. Ah. Here. "It is of Urgency that You come preside in the E. O. Smonk Trial. No Town has ever suffered more than Ours bedeviled and beset upon as We have been by this Devil or Homunculus or What Ever He claims to be He lives several Miles outside Town in a large Manson He comes to Town Saturday Nights and wrecks Havoc on our Citizens beating them with his Fist at Night when good People ought to be in Bed getting ready for their Day of Labor. In a bold Gesture We Citizens of Old Texas have brought criminal Charges against Mr. Smonk. Mr. Smonk claims He will attend the Trial only if a Judge of the State Circuit is brought to mediate the Matters. No One Man or Group of Men will go to his Land and arrest Him. He is armed with Weapons from the United States Army," et cetera, et cetera.

The part he didn't read further said: "Since We are on your Circuit, We find it curious that you have not visited our Village in more than one Year. What might the Governor think."

Signed, the judge finished, Justice of the Peace and Beat Supervisor and U.S. Postmaster M. Elmer Tate. Owner of the Tate Hotel.

He folded the letter away. After that alarming news, he said, I began to use my copious influence and asked around about our Mister Smonk, and listen what I found out. Jest listen. Apparently it's been years old E.O.'s done slipped around the law, hither and yon all over the goddamn country. Years I said. Rumors mostly. Accounts as far west as Nevada and as far south as Mexico north up to Dakota. Man that always gets what he wants. One way another. Threats of violence and actual violence. Lawyers when he can use em cheap, gunmen if he can't. Bribes, extortion, name it. Blackmail. No crime ner coercion small ner large enough, with no loyalty ner fealty to country ner king. But impossible to nab. What do ye think of that, bailiff?

What?

That he disappears at will and is gone for a year then turns up someplace else. That nobody knows where he come from ner what he is. He was likely born out west where the law's jest now setting its teeth. Such an abomination as Smonk is would of never been allowed to carry on so far here in the Confederacy. He paused and took a long drink and continued. The part I don't understand is that for some reason not given in this letter, he's chose my quadrant of the goddamn county for a base of operation in these his waning years.

The bailiff shifted in his chair.

You okay there? Please leave the room if ye need to pass gas.

I'm hunkydory. Can ye get to the point?

The goddamn point is we could of strang him up—fount him guilty, is what I'm saying—but instead this town of fools tries to lynch him unbeknownst to me and of course he escapes. Old Texas! What in the hell was yall thinking anyway? Leaving all ye guns on a sideboard? Not a single goddamn dead-eye sniper hid anywheres?

The women had guns. They was hid.

The women.

We figured he'd of smelt something if we done anything different like. Out of the ordinary.

Well, he might of at that. What I hear he's had his share of experiences walking into and out of courthouse doors and he's got an extry sense about him. How come nobody informed me of the plot?

The bailiff looked out a window.

Well?

Don't nobody trust ye.

There's a fine hidy-do, ain't it. God almighty damn. At least with Smonk a body knows where he stands.

The bailiff worked his jaw. Best take care not to sound like ye admire the bastard too much.

Who wouldn't admire the gall of a fellow brings a machine gun and a peck of hired killers to his own goddamn trial? Who wouldn't admire a fellow never leaves a trail of evidence? That's got this far in the world and galled so many folks and killed twice that number and cheated the rest, all without being blowed to itty bitty pieces or hanged by his goddamn neck or succumbing to one of the countless infirmities he seems to collect like a goddamn hobby, hell yeah I admire the son-of-a-bitch.

The judge took his monocle off and polished it with his hand-

kerchief. His eye looked small and weak without it, a puddle dry-
ing up. Well, he said, if you'll permit me, this next part's why I'm a
goddamn circuit judge and you only a bailiff. See, what none of
yall folks know out here in the wilderness between the rivers is that
I'm a man of principle like none you've met. When I learned of
this Smonk's existence, at great personal expense I sought him out
to discern and divine his motives. With only the good of my con-
stituents in mind and of course the interest of science and theology
as well.

The meeting had occurred a week before, the judge remembered, down south in Mobile, where he'd met Smonk for supper in
a dive overlooking the bay. Smonk had brought a big ball-headed
nigger and a chink whore in with him and several people got up
and left the room.

I don't usually eat with niggers, the judge had said, his black
coat folded over his arm. Chinks neither.

Smonk bumped the table sliding in. We don't usually eat with
judges.

They'd had shrimp, which the judge despised. Bugs were what
they looked like to him. He'd enjoyed the broiled potatoes, however, and speared them with his fork and added salt and chewed
slowly as Smonk gobbled his shrimp—legs and shell and back
veins in his beard—and rambled about the bridges he'd blown up
in the War with the Spanish. How crucial the placement of the
charge. How perfect the timing need be. How you always get your
pay in advance. The ball-headed nigger never said a word, just ate
quietly and with perfect manners which offended the judge. They
were in a corner booth overlooking the water and shaded by a shut-

ter propped open with a pool cue. Every door in the dive had a horseshoe nailed over it with the ends up.

His shoulders to the wall, Smonk smoked one cigar after another and ate a raw onion like an apple and had fits of coughing that shook the table. Once, he spilled a cup of salt then scooped a few grains and flicked them behind him. The judge had heard Smonk never left a building by any door except the one he'd entered. That he wouldn't touch a toadfrog. Wouldn't begin a trip on Sunday or bring anything black aboard a boat. Wouldn't carry a hoe, ax or shovel into a house. That he never stepped over a fishing pole or under a ladder. Never swept beneath a bed or sang before breakfast or watched the full moon through green leaves. He made a point of getting his hair wet in the first May rain shower and believed that to take the rings off your finger would bring heart trouble and that a mouse-hole gnawed in your floor had to be patched by someone other than yourself. He believed it was bad luck to take cats into a new house. He believed that whatever you dreamed while sleeping beneath a new quilt would shortly come true, and that a dream of muddy water meant death.

His hands were abnormally large, though whether that was normal for his own peculiar brand of physiology or a symptom of one of his many ailments, the judge could only postulate. Smonk's fingertops were hairy and his breath hot and acidic, hanging in the air like burnt skunk, occasioning the judge to chew with his hand-kerchief over his mouth. Smonk had positioned the whore under the table to rub his feet and once in a while he looked down and said something to her.

Oh, yah, she answered. Mista Smonk weal, weal hod. Weal, weal big. From under the table her hands appeared, a foot apart.

Trained her good, didn't I? Smonk said grinning to the nigger but the nigger didn't grin back or otherwise commit. Nor did he lower his eyes to the judge's satisfaction when the judge stared at him, but this seemed a prudent time to set one's sense of propriety aside for the greater good, so instead of having the impertinent fellow hanged, the judge had let it go for that day and turned to study Smonk's features. In profile E.O.'s nose and mouth extended farther than your normal white Christian's, an African feature which might locate some nigger in his past. And his eye, the one of use, was narrow, like a chink's. Hell, wondered the judge, am I even dealing with a white man at all? Smonk had parched skin the color and texture of an ancient saddle and matted red hair tied at his neck, a cascade of beard graying down his chest but red around the lips like a consumptive's. There's your coughing. It was impossible to say how old he was. Might be fifty, might be eighty. Could of been handsome too in his young days, but now with nicks and sores and carbuncles and liver spots, et cetera, and that purple scar the size of a goddamn dirtdobber nest going up his neck behind his ear, well hell, it looked like any day could end his journey of years.

Smonk had sensed this inspection and for a moment locked his eye—as clairvoyant and intent as a wolf's, gazing at snow with blood on it—with the judge's.

The judge looked away.

You want ye shrimps, fellow? Smonk asked.

Naw. The judge swallowed. I don't eat bugs.

Don't eat bugs.

Weal, weal, *weal* hod.

Little more was said. After Smonk waited for the judge to pay, they'd walked down a narrow flight of stairs and through a back alley past mounds of rotting shellfish and along the tracks to the rail station where three men were loading a buckboard wagon. Smonk shooed them away and offered the judge the sum of five hundred dollars in a cigar box for a verdict against the town of Old Texas. The judge removed his monocle and took the box and placed it under his arm. Smonk put his cigar in his teeth and rolled back a green tarp in the wagon and what the judge beheld caused him to drop the box.

Is that a goddamn Gatling gun?

Hell naw, Smonk said. I got dirt on a general up in Washington. This here is Mister Hiram Maxim's machine gun, the newest model. Makes a army Gat look like a goddamn flintlock.

Now, one week and one massacre later, the judge sat across from the bailiff and stuffed his handkerchief in the breast pocket of his coat and wished he had a rock of hard candy. From outside he heard a lady wailing.

Mic— Bailiff, he said, taking another swig, don't trouble to thank me for my legal or scientific pursuits regarding Smonk. He rose and shut the window. On the sill outside was a parched white splat of birdshit. A monarch butterfly flittered down and landed there, then fluttered on. Thought the shit was a goddamn flower. The judge smiled. It's been my pleasure and duty, he said, turning, to serve my fellow citizens, even unto the risk of my own life yea soul.

I ain't a bailiff no more. Didn't I say that?

The judge began to search his pockets ironically. Did ye file a letter of resignation in triplicate? If not yer still in the town's employ and I can't in good conscience accept a resignation now. In this current crisis. In other words, you the law.

What was they? asked the bailiff.

What was what.

Smonk's motives. Which ye set out to discern and divine.

Ah. The judge looked up and to the left and composed his thoughts. Wretched, he said. There's his motives, crystallized into one apt term. But what I'm trying to get at here is that with the justice of the peace et cetera et cetera murdered, the time's done arrived to circumvent the natural course of law.

You ain't got to go far to convince me, said the bailiff. Smonk kidnapped my youngun during his escape, if ye ain't heard. Or killed him one. If you'd of asked me first off, I'd of told ye Smonk's days is numbered fewer than the fingers on my hand and I'd of been gone.

Excellent. But ye gone need help. Man be a fool to take on E. O. Smonk without a goddamn army, jest about. I'm gone wire the governor post haste, but in the meantime is it anybody else left? Yall got to go after him now, this instant. Fore he disappears.

Holding the table for support, the bailiff stood to his feet. You dreaming if ye think he's gone disappear this time. If ye think this is done. You ain't the only one studied him, Yer Honor. I had my dark associations with ole Smonk too, matters not to speak of now. But in his mind, ye see, we attacked *him*. Now if we don't finish the job he's gone come back tomorrow or the next day with something bigger than that machine gun and burn Old Texas to the ground, or worse. This ain't over, is what I'm saying. It's jest begun.

God damn, said the judge. He sat looking perplexed. How in the hell do ye account for him?

I don't. They say when he come out his momma's wound he

caught his foot on something in her guts and snatched it loose. Say he weighed more than fourteen pounds. Say his eyes was open when the nigger midwife peeled back the caul and he sucked and gnawed on his momma's tit even after she'd bled to death and started to cool and he never would of stopped eating if the midwife hadn't prized her dern thumb in to break the seal. You know what else?

What?

They say he was born with teeth. Say the midwife died from the ray bees.

God damn, said the judge.

The bailiff put on his cap. It's some things in the world ye jest got to take for what they is. On they own terms. He took up his rifle. It's one other fellow wasn't numbered among the dead, I heard. Blacksmith down the way. I reckon me and him's the mob.

Well. If it's anything yall need, charge the town for it.

I might need a few more guns.

Fine.

And a hoss.

Whatever. The important thing is to catch him and kill him and mail me his goddamn glass eye, which I claim for a souvenir.

The bailiff moved his jaw. I best git on.

Do that. The judge raised his flask in a farewell toast. He had no intention of wiring the governor or anybody else. This backward secluded town had designed its own doom and could burn forgotten to the ground as far as he cared. And as for the bailiff, closing the door behind him, well, the judge expected never to see the poor idiot alive again.

Cheers, he told the room.

ಲೂ

Sucking Smonk's eye, McKissick limped out into the heat. For a moment he leaned against a column until a spell of nausea passed, then he walked faster, hand clamped to his wound. He went to the doctor's and the doctor's widow gave him some bandages and lamp oil and he made a poultice. Then he limped along the road to the opposite end of town to the blacksmith shed where he found Gates, a filthy man in his sixties, hammering coffin handles on an anvil. Four covered bodies laid out on various stacks of wood. He'd been staring into his fire and had difficulty seeing who it was.

Who's that? Will the bailiff?

I was once, said he. Who the hell are you? A blacksmith, or— he indicated the bodies—the damn undertaker?

Blacksmith. By God. My talent's about the only thing he ain't took from me. But since old Hobbs was shot, we all jest doing our own setting by. He nodded at the bailiff's side. Catch one?

Naw. Jobbed me with his sword.

The smith drank from a tin cup and then resumed his hammering. Don't touch them handles yonder. They still hot.

I'm going after him, McKissick said between hammerfalls. He took my boy. The judge is conscripted me.

Gates used a pair of tongs to turn the coffin handle which glowed orange and went back to whacking it on his anvil. Luck to ye.

McKissick limped to the corner of the shed and pulled back the sheet from a corpse and winced at the face stained in blood, much of the head mown away. Who's these fellows?

The hammering stopped. That one was Lurleen.

Dern, the bailiff said. Sorry. He cocked his head for a different angle.

Them others is my stepdaughters. Itina there and Clena and that one cut in half yonder's Revina. I still ain't found her legs though them toes on the salt lick there's probably hers. They long enough.

Dern. McKissick studied Gates's dead wife. How come she's wearing men's duds?

All of em is. So they could go see inside the courtroom when Smonk got ambushed. They hadn't ever saw such a show. We put they hair up under they hats and wrapped cloth around they knockers to flatten em. They was a family of big-bosomed girls, if ye remember.

McKissick did. The stepdaughters who'd lay with any man could muster a hard-on. Their mother who wasn't a whole hell of a lot older than her oldest daughter but a lot prettier. It was common knowledge around town that she'd had congress with Smonk.

Look close, the smith said, sipping from his cup. You can still see where we drawed mustaches on her lip with ash. We was laughing so hard. Them younguns started cutting up. Scratching they make-believe balls and pretending to hold giant peckers and take a piss. Itina went over to Revina and humped on her. We was all drunk.

My condolences. On the whole brood.

Thank ye. Mine on ye boy.

Hold off on condoling him, if ye don't mind.

Sorry. Didn't go to jinx ye.

McKissick picked up a coffin handle from where it lay cooling on a block and threw it down.

Hot, ain't it, Gates said. I told ye.

Naw. It jest don't take me long to look at a coffin handle. He blew on his palm. How much longer ye reckon ye gone be here laying em out?

Why?

I come see might ye go with me.

After Smonk? The blacksmith studied his black hands. Their black nails. It wouldn't be right, he said. I can't jest up and leave the girls.

What's worse, leaving em to set a spell here or letting go the scoundrel that killed em? Seems like you got a lot of reason to want Smonk dead. If it's true what they say about him and—not to speak ill of the dead—ye wife here. Seems you was spared. Like me. I ain't never thought much of God, but if this here ain't God saying get yer selves out on a mob I don't know what is.

The blacksmith didn't answer. Using his tongs, he raised a glowing bar from the fire and began to beat it.

Well? said McKissick.

Naw, said the blacksmith. I can't. I ain't shot a gun in I don't know when. Don't even own one. I'm a humble worker. If ye had twenty, thirty fellows, sure, I might go. But jest two of us? No thank ye.

They got a word for not going. It's called being a chickenshit.

That's five words.

Don't be counting my words, Gates. Judge says we can supply up, charged to the town. New firearms and such. Mounts.

Preciate it, naw. These handles won't forge they selves.

Suit ye self then, chickenshit. I'm taking off terectly, if ye grow some balls.

He raised his hand farewell, shape of a coffin handle burned into the skin, and limped out past the covered bodies. In the town proper he sidestepped a dead horse and turned the corner and limped past the wagon with the machine gun, two young women guarding it.

They were making eyes at him.

In the store the owner's widow had laid her husband's body on the shelf where the tins of potted meat were usually displayed. She'd dressed him in his church suit and boots.

I can't do business today, she told McKissick from behind her black veil. We closed for mourning.

Well, this re-supplying is on the judge, he said. He's sending me out after Smonk. I'm sure he'd be happy to pay double. The judge, I mean. Or triple.

What is it ye need?

He bought her entire supply of firearms: four pistols, three rifles and two shotguns. She tried to sell him a used twenty gauge single but he glanced at it and said, Junk.

Then he bought all her ammunition. After that he carried his packages to the livery where he bought a tall paint (on the judge) and had the liveryman's widow remove its shoes for a quieter ride. He noticed that the livery also sold fireworks, and he charged a box of Roman candles and several bundles of bottle rockets and fire-crackers, too. His boy Willie if he were still alive would love such noise and fire. And if not, the bailiff would shoot them off in his son's memory.

Then he was running back through the street, to the store, tromping up the steps, pounding on the glass.

Balloons, he told the lady, ye got any more sheep-guts?

Meanwhile, Gates the blacksmith had slipped off his apron and leather gloves and donned his hat and was walking toward the store when four women in black dresses and veils surrounded him with rifles. He raised his hands in surrender and they shoved him along at gunpoint to Mrs. Tate, widow of the justice of the peace and owner of most of the land around Old Texas and owner of the bank and the apothecary's. And the hotel, recently destroyed.

They found her in her dark house at the edge of town, in her parlor with the drapes drawn. She sat beside her dead husband, very upright in an upholstered chair, fanning herself primly with one hand and with the other holding his fingers. He lay on a sideboard, dressed in a brown suit. Using pins, she'd arranged his hair despite his deflated head and placed a towel under his neck for the drainage and spread a plaid cloth over where his face had been. A tiny woman with tiny hands, Mrs. Tate flipped down her veil when they entered.

The widows shoved Gates forward and he snatched off his cap and tried to smooth his wiry hair.

Are you drunk? she asked. Such your habit.

Nome. This all is sobered me up.

Mrs. Tate snapped closed her fan and rose to inspect Gates, circling him, her head level with his biceps, poking at his kidneys with the fan.

Why weren't you at the trial? she asked from behind him. Account for being alive. When so many better men have passed.

He stammered how he'd voted to lynch Smonk, how he'd

planned to attend the trial and celebration after, but the gun-killers had robbed him and knocked him in the head. Did she want to feel the whop? He knelt as she pressed the needles of her fingers on the soft lump at the base of his skull, her touch lingering to a caress as he stammered the tragedy of his own family, dead and tarped, one and all, back yonder in his shop.

What he didn't mention was that two of the three killers had visited his shed earlier that day, before the trial. Before the massacre. How the smith had not realized that *these two strangers with a packhorse full of guns on the day Smonk was going on trial meant something was up* was beyond him. He ought to of reported it. It wasn't like there was a pair of strangers through here every day. In fact, he couldn't remember the last new face he'd seen—other than Smonk's. The killers had asked about a whore and he'd pointed them to his house, but instead of paying him the three dollars, they'd knocked him in the head with a rifle butt and took the coins from his pocket and left him for dead and he'd lain half-conscious on the floor in his own head blood for over an hour. It was just like Lurleen and her girls not to come get him after laying with the killers, traipsing off to the trial in their men's duds. Lurleen would of done anything to see Smonk again, Gates knew—she still was in love with the one-eye. The blacksmith had just awakened on the floor and touched the throbbing lump at the top of his neck when he'd heard the machine gun going off.

I'm sorry for your loss, Mrs. Tate said. Though if those women had known their places they'd be alive yet. You need the church, Portis, you always have. Now more than ever.

Yessum.

Our Scripture is very clear on a woman's place. And the place of children.

Yessum.

A man's too, Portis.

Yessum.

She reclaimed her seat in front of him. I believe your story. She plucked a wet cloth from a washbowl and wiped her fingertips of his filth and waved the other widows out of the room and resumed fanning herself.

But when the time comes to pay the fiddler, she continued, we've all got to chip in. Ante up, as a sinner like *he* might say. So I must ask you, Portis, to delay your mourning and commit us two jobs. First, find that judge before he tries to flee. He's been unaccounted for since we put out the fire. And the more I've been considering it, the more I see he had to have been mixed up with Smonk. Else he'd be massacred too. Or at the very least knocked in the head like you or punctured like our new bailiff.

Yessum.

Second thing, she said, is that you must go with Bailiff McKissick. Make sure he kills Smonk. Help him. Come back and swear he's dead.

Yessum.

And there's only one way to prove that.

Yessum.

Do you know what that is, Portis?

Nome.

His eye. Bring me his eye.

Yessum. I will.

Good. Mrs. Tate gazed at her husband. She swatted a fly with her fan. She'd killed several already and formed a small pile at the justice's shoulder and Gates watched as she used her fan to herd the fresh smudge over with the others. Then she resumed fanning. Is it true that Smonk took McKissick's child? That boy William?

I heard it was.

Do I need to stress how your standing in our village will improve if you bring that little one back safely?

Nome.

You could be an important man in our town, Portis. Now that you're a widower. With so little competition.

Yessum.

I think you should wash, she said. So we can see what you look like, those of us in need of a man, you now in need of a wife.

Yessum.

In search of the judge, Gates ran building to building, zigzagging through alleys, and had not been looking a quarter-hour when he spotted a pair of legs jutting from the rear window of town hall. Gates recognized the judge's boots and seized him by the knees and wrestled him hard down into the dirt, papers from his bulging valise spilling into the sugarcane.

God damn, said the judge from the ground. He jabbed out his hand. Help me up and escort me to the gallows where I'll see ye hanged.

They sent for ye, Gates said, pulling him into a headlock.

God damn, the judge's muffled voice said. Let me go!

The blacksmith dragged the smaller man over the street as he flailed his arms and made a commotion of dust, still clinging to the valise. At the store across from the burnt-down hotel several women had congregated at the wagon in the alley as if the mounted gun had been scheduled to deliver a sermon or a serenade. When they saw the judge, they seized him from the smith and relieved him of his valise and raised him above their heads like a hero and he seemed to levitate down the street above them, his face the pallor of chalk.

Gates returned to his shack and sat alone at the table for the first time in ages—it was quiet without his wife's fussing and the step-daughters bickering at one another about whose turn it was to wash the clothes or who got to go and try to seduce McKissick. He left the table and rumbled in his dead wife's trunk and found a shard of pierglass, a fingernail of soap, a razor, a nub of brush and a cracked washbasin which he filled with water. He studied the reflection of his face and began to scrub and shave. Twenty minutes later a ruddy white man slightly cross-eyed and with one long eyebrow looked at him from the glass, the water in the basin black as ink and full of gray whiskers.

Not half bad, he said, for a fellow of sixty-some year.

There were no weapons in his shop, but wearing his church shirt under his overalls, he crossed the dirt hefting his iron tongs and assessed them workable. He moved Clena's legs and picked up a large pipe wrench and tested its screw. Lastly he put a fistful of nails in the bib pockets of his overalls.

I'll be back, he said to the room. I hope.

He put on his hat and took it off when he entered the store.

We closed, said the owner's widow. Unless it's billed to the judge.

Then tally em up.

With her following, Gates bought a new Stetson hat, a scarf, a denim shirt with silver star snaps, three pairs of corduroy pants, long johns, two pairs of socks, a telescope and a bugle and several coiled ropes and a horsehair whip and the most costly snakebite kit on the shelf and two machetes and a compass and a Bowie knife. He bought a sleeping bag and saddle and bridle and blanket and knapsack and five pounds of salt, a bag of jerked beef, sugar, coffee, flour, cans of sardines and oysters, crackers, apples, hard candy, cigars and lard.

He bought a root beer soda and, sucking on his straw, requested a matching pair of Colt revolvers with hair-triggers if she had them and a twelve gauge shotgun with a pump action, and several boxes of shells, sixes or lower. No slugs, please.

We out of guns, she said. Bullets too. McKissick bought em all.

Ever one?

Well. I kept Abner's birdshooter here. She drew the twenty gauge single from behind her counter.

How much?

What 'll the judge offer?

One hundred dollars.

Sold to the judge.

In the livery stable Gates bought a silver gelding fourteen hands high without even bartering or checking its legs or eyes and a pack mule which he instructed the liveryman's widow to lead to the store and load with his parcels, charged, including any special fees or taxes, to the judge.

You want these animals fed? the woman sobbed. She wore a sling around her arm and had a number of broken ribs. She also had two black eyes, a smashed nose and busted lips. Her dress was still torn and soiled with a hoofprint on her back. Either she was leaving it on as protest or it was her only one.

On the judge, Gates said. Was it you tried to stop Mister Smonk?

It was.

Look where it got ye.

Least I ain't the fools going after him now.

Gates had ridden less than a mile when the horse, which was blind, stepped in a hole and projected him in his new outfit into the dust. When he rose he saw the animal had broken its leg. He raised the twenty gauge to his shoulder but it clicked. He checked was it loaded, it was, and tried again. Click.

He was using his pipe wrench to finish the horse, which was taking quite a while, when a gun fired.

Gates leapt over the animal as it convulsed one last time. He lay panting on the turf, his hands and shirt sleeves bloodied.

It was McKissick, his revolver smoking. He rode up behind Gates and reined in his mount and looked down. Who the hell are you out in these suspicious times?

The other half ye mob. Portis. Who'd ye think?

Who?

Portis Gates. The blacksmith?

Oh. McKissick put the pistol away and fanned his face with his hat. I ain't never seen ye cleaned up's all. Didn't know you was so old. What the hell was you doing to that poor horse?

Putting it out of its misery. It got its leg broke and my shooter's gone south.

Here. McKissick tossed him a thirty-thirty.

Where we going?

The bailiff nodded east. Smonk's house first. Few more miles yonder-ways. He extended down a hand. We can ride double to save time.

And double they rode, east through fields of ruined cane, the blacksmith remarking how happy he was he hadn't put his whole lot in sugar, considering the spate of weather they'd had. Wasn't it something? How many weeks? Could McKissick remember the last drop of rain? Did McKissick think they could stop for some licker?

McKissick did not.

An odor had caught the wind and blew in their faces. What the hell is that? the blacksmith wanted to know and soon had his answer as they cupped their hands over their noses and McKissick tried to calm the horse, gazing down at a charred mess of burnt animal flesh beside the road, some dark satanic work of art, faces blended to other faces and eyes like strings of wax. Gates pointed out a few dog parts, a wildcat's padded foot, a coon's tailbone and a fox's skull. His partner spurred the antsy horse along. The blacksmith said he reckoned the ray bees plague that had haunted Old Texas these last years was spreading all over.

McKissick said nothing.

Meanwhile, Mrs. Tate pronounced the judge guilty despite his citing precedents and quoting the law in English and Latin and calling upon various prophets and heroes of the Old Testament as well as Homer, Sophocles, George Washington, Nathan Bedford Forrest and Buffalo Bill Cody who was a close personal friend. He reminded Mrs. Tate that she was a female, not a judge, as she bade the widows bind his hands. They scissored off his outer clothes and took his shoes and shoved him in undergarments wrung with sweat off the porch and past the gunwagon down the narrow alley to where his knees gave way as he beheld the town's rickety gallows.

Ye can't hang me! he cried. Ye can't!

You're right, said Mrs. Tate behind him.

At her command four widows seized his ankles and dragged him through the dust and upended his legs and two widows above from the gallows floor lowered a noose and hauled him into the air with a pulley through the trapdoor until he was hanging upside down. A dozen or so ladies began to pelt him with rocks and hit him with sticks of firewood like a piñata while two others over at the store backed a team of oxen toward the machine gun.

The judge swore and threatened and cajoled and shat hot mud down his back and stammered and tried to bribe them. His sour undershirt fell over his face as rocks bounced off him. At the creak of the gunwagon he cried, What's that noise I hear? Is it the sound of my own demise? Two ladies unhitched the oxen and led them to safety while several others mounted the buckboard and puzzled over the operation of the giant gun, handing its steam hose one to another with no idea of its function. Mrs. Tate was the one who discerned that the lock fit in the side slot. She stood on a peach box and used both hands to latch back the bolt and two fingers to squeeze the trigger which was easier than she'd thought.

The instant thunder brought screams from the ladies but removed the judge's right arm at the elbow and splintered one of the gallows-posts. The judge began to shriek and wriggle as the dirt stained beneath him and the widows nodded to one another and drew broom straws to establish a fair order and took turns at the trigger disintegrating the judge as a haze of steam rose from the water jacket and they fanned it with their hands and the gun hammered like a locomotive boring through the last tunnel to hell. The widows fired and fired and fired and fired until the final cartridge hull clattered to a stop on the wagon floor and what was left of the judge resembled a steaming mass of afterbirth, blue and dripping. The silence of the world shocked them all.

6

THE ORPHANAGE

IN THE MEANTIME, THE CROW HUNTER'S HORSE SHE'D TAKEN HAD bucked Evavangeline and fallen itself and then risen in a spray of gravel and legs and with dirt on its rump fled wobbling and whinnying like a sissy-horse, taking all those saddle-bagged guns with it.

She rose and dusted her pants and tied a bandanna around her head and walked several miles, pausing in a field to snap a section of sugarcane from a stalk. She shucked it but it was dry as kindling, like chewing sawdust. She walked on as the day's colors drained, coming upon a modest homestead, a mud cabin with a chimney composed of flat white stones and off to the side a rickety stick shelter with no pretensions of being a shed. In the pen alongside stood the same sissy-horse that had thrown her. She looked at it for a long time. It had that certain aloofness horses have. But beside it was a pony she noticed, black with a white star on its forehead.

Hey, she said to it.

Behind her there was a pump and a watering trough. An arbor with clusters of grapes which she stuffed in her mouth. All around was flat land here, with the woods miles behind her and sugarcane everywhere. The horizon east to west had grown murky with heat and overhead was the whitest sky she had ever seen. It was like the sun had exploded. The light running out.

She crossed the yard and half a dozen children surrounded her. They touched her clothes gently, as if she were an angel. They purred like kittens. They smelled like soap and blueberries. She felt her womb clench as if somebody had pulled shut the drawstrings of an empty sack. The children cooed at her. They seemed to float. Maybe this was how you got knocked up. She shut her eyes. They were rubbing her arms and legs and bottom though not lecherously, except perhaps for the oldest boy, who had a knife handle sticking out of his boot.

She woke in a dark room and sat up in bed wearing a clean nightshirt. She felt fresher than she could remember. Her hair wet. Her underarms burned, so she reached and felt them. Shaved. She felt her calves. Shaved too. She put her hand between her legs.

Least ye left me my thatch, she said.

Why was you dressed like a man?

The voice had come from the rocking chair beside the window. Now she could discern the woman's outline—weak chin, big overbite—as it rocked. She understood that she'd been hearing the creak of the chair for hours. The sound had been her sleep.

Go to bed, *William*, the woman hissed out the window. *Yer disobeying the Bible.*

Who you? Evavangeline asked.

An orphan keeper. Do you want to stay here? the woman asked. Our man's lost. Gone. For days now. His horse come home so we think he's dead.

I was escaping, Evavangeline said.

From who? Who from?

A evil man.

The woman stopped rocking. Can you tell me the particulars of him?

Evavangeline's instinct urged her to lie, so she described not the veteran but, instead, the strange man she'd heard about from the dice-playing niggers on the river. They say he killed his momma when he was born. Say he bombed bridges in the War. They say he never sleeps and knows the devil by first name. Say he likes to drank the pee of young girls. They say he has white blood, nigger blood, Indian blood, all three. That he can see in the dark.

The woman left her rocking chair and came to sit beside the girl on the bed. You mean ole Smonk, she said. Minute there I thought you was gone describe me my own husbandman. He wasn't a good man, not no more. Not since the weather got so contentious. Like the saying goes, if you seek him, check Hell first. But you can stay, we got room. She set her hands on the girl's thighs, her thumbs nearing Evavangeline's privates. She leaned in and feathered her lips against the hot skin of her throat.

You exhausted and wounded, the lady whispered. I done tended ye hurt places. I been feeding ye broth and tea. Come dawn you'll feel like a brand new girl. Things always look better in the light of day. You can stay with us if ye want to. But sleep now, the woman said, thumbing Evavangeline's magic pea better than any man, her voice like a fiddle bow pulled real slow over the gut. *Sleep.*

But she couldn't sleep, even after the dyke had left her in spasms and shut the door. She lay awake tingling, wondering if she was an orphan or not. The earliest thing she could remember in the days before Ned was the gypsy witch named Alice Hanover. Days she rarely let herself think of now. How she would watch the old witchwoman perform her black magic, pantomiming her spells into existence, into beings you could only see in the blackest pitch of night. Rising up out of the ground they would stamp whatever they had for feet and look about with their horrible innocence, their skin blacker than the night around them. When they moved it looked as if darkness were swallowing itself. The old woman would summon these things indiscriminately and for the highest bidder and let them loose on whom her employer told with money her only thought. Sometimes these summoned would execute their sentence upon the intended and then, instead of dishappening back underground, be taken by a wind and remain lost in the world. It happened more the older Alice Hanover got. They were glints now, the girl knew, half here, half someplace else, the shadow of a tree moving when the tree was not, the thing that bumps you in the dark.

Once, she'd gone with Alice Hanover to hex a whole family. Perhaps the witchwoman, who bragged she was a hundred-sixty years old, had sensed her own end drawing near and, despite her hatred of every other person, thought it necessary to bestow her knowledge on a student. Otherwise her spells would be gone forever, a language when its last speaker dies.

In the gal's memory she and Alice Hanover were shreds of shadow sliding under that night's halfmoon, figments creeping through the bright-blooming cotton to the edge of the homestead, the pair peering through a log fence so recently cut it still smelled green. The witch clucked her tongue and the dog fell dead on the porch. Evavangeline watched the old woman close her eyes and point her gnarled left trigger finger and begin to spin her right hand, palm cupped and suddenly full of water. In a clear quiet voice Alice Hanover spoke words Evavangeline had never heard uttered before nor since. They were ———, ———, — and ———.

For a moment the night hushed, as if it had noticed them.

Then blades of grass began to whisper, cotton bolls nodding on their stems.

Her skirt-tails ajostle, Evavangeline heard leaves rattle in the branches. She heard a horse nicker. A shutter bang open. The chickens started to cluck. Wind picked up and her hair stood on end and the breeze cooled her scalp. A light flickered on inside the shack and somebody screamed and the baby began to squall. Lightning cracked the starless dome of space and showed the powderhorn of black air weaving over the cotton destroying all in its wake, barbed wire whipping and rocking chairs and corn cribs and cows and large snakes raining down, the funnel's great endhole snorting the face of the land, the grass on the cabin's roof standing and then the roof still in its shape rose and folded like a letter. And one by one among floating chairs and washpots the flailing enemies of Alice Hanover's customers rose screaming, even the naked baby and its doll made of corn shucks. Shorn from the baby's hands, the doll turned a child's eternity in the air then landed at Evavangeline's feet like a gift.

For a moment she considered it. She picked it up.

———, said Alice Hanover and unscrolled her smoking fingers.

Thus Evavangeline handed over the only toy she had ever touched.

Alice Hanover held it aloft in her flat palm like someone freeing a dove and let the wind claim it and the girl watched the scrub of doll lift from the gypsy's fingers into the air and striptease apart a shuck at a time until the lightning stopped and the wind died and the doll lay scattered in places unseen.

Later she lay awake on the ground by the wheel of Alice Hanover's wagon where she slept each night. She knew the gypsy was above, in the covered buckboard asleep on her ticking with her eyes open, and that she must move quick else the old crone would kill her with a grunt before Evavangeline could draw the blade over that warty throat and unriver its blood. She would never be able to do it, to get in the wagon, sink the knife. The gypsy was too wily. Evavangeline lay like a bruise on the cold skin of the earth, her ear to its dirt, her teeth clenched so tightly she could hear the ocean a hundred miles south, while above her the wagon planks creaked as Alice Hanover endured her slumber.

Evavangeline raised her fingers to the underside of the wagon's floor but didn't touch it. She felt the old woman's heat through the boards. She moved her fingers to the left, to the right. She pointed to a spot and jibbed her knife between the boards and through the old woman's ticking and her skin. Her onion of a heart. There was a squawk and lightning struck nearby. The knife kicked itself from between the boards and fell to the grass steaming. The wagon pitched and yawed and the night spoke words Evavangeline tried her best not to hear. It rained then snowed. The ground shook. Trees broke in half and fell all around. Worms squirted out of the dirt.

Then everything grew quiet and still. Blood ran between the boards and covered the girl, afraid as she was to come out.

She waited. And waited.

She stayed there hardening in witchblood for three days until hunger like a father's foot drove her back into the world. And weeks, months, years, later, now and again, with a huffing man driving her across the mattress or the ground, she would whisper two or three of the words of Alice Hanover. —— she would say. —— ——. The man would pause, breath held as the air changed, and say, What in the hell.

Then, because she never recited all the words in their right order, the air would move again and the man would resume his thrusting and she would pinch bloody crescents in the skin of her arm to assure herself that this was real and she was alive and—

You killed him, didn't you? the dyke said.

She stood backlit in the door holding a pair of boots in one hand and a pistol in the other.

Killed who? Evavangeline asked. She sat up.

My husband, said the dyke. These is his boots.

Evavangeline folded her arms. Well hell Mary, she said. I might jest did. Killed him I meant. What did he look like?

The boots hit the floor. He was a veteran!

Evavangeline leaned forward, her eyes gleaming in the light from the door. Was he also a crow hunter and a raper?

Sometimes! the woman shrieked. When he drank the devil's whiskey he loved to kill things! And rape them! But if he's dead and you ain't gone stay, then I got to feed all these younguns myself!

What about all that cane?

It's dried out. It's dead. We lost ever thing. Tate 'll foreclose on us less we git some money, fast.

Whose children did I see earlier?

My husband rounded em up to sell. He's supposed to deliver em tomorrow. But that ain't none of ye business.

The dyke raised her pistol but Evavangeline was already behind her. She kneed her in the kidney and the dyke turned, tearing Evavangeline's shirt and clawing at her eyes but the girl bit a swatch out of the dyke's neck and shoved her against a wall and clubbed her with a chamber pot when she bounced back and watched her sink in the corner. She bound and gagged the dyke then put her own clothes and the crow hunter's boots back on and crept through the house holding the pistol in one hand and an oil lamp in the other. She found the children sleeping on the floor in a room and woke them one by one and waited for them to put on their shoes, the ones who had them, and led them outside past the dyke and through the yard into the root cellar, slapping the oldest boy's hand from her ass.

Yall stay here, she said to them, till jest fore morning. If ye have to take a piss, use that stew pot yonder. Come first light yall find ye way home.

You a whore? the oldest boy asked. He had the blondest hair.

None ye business, she said. What's ye name?

William R. McKissick Junior. My daddy was the bailiff over in Old Texas fore Mister E. O. Smonk killed him. I lit out cause I heard it was a woman who took in orphans and would let you screw the girls. The boy cast an evil eye on the children. But so far won't none of these here ones screw and they ain't fed us yet. I got me half a mind to git on.

Evavangeline knelt. She took his hard shoulders in her hands and looked in his eyes. She could see he had an erection by the way his pants stood.

If I goose ye one time, she said to him, will ye do something for me?

Ma'am?

If I take care of that there, she said, thumping his britches, will ye then repay me with a promise?

Oh, yessum! he cried.

She led him to a dim recess in the cellar. It smelled like potatoes. The other children followed and watched. She undid his pants and squirted him into the darkness. He made a croaking noise.

Now, ye promise, she said.

He seemed drunk, a sleepy smile, string of drool. Yessum.

From here on, you'll watch after these here other younguns. Help em get home and don't let nothing happen to any of em. And don't try to screw em neither.

But—

Just do like I told you. Get em out of here fore first light.

Yessum, the boy said. Can ye do me that way one more time?

My lord. She reached forward and it was waiting for her, still bouncing from its rapid rise.

THE TENANTS

ON SMONK'S TRAIL, MCKISSICK AND GATES HAPPENED UPON A small flat-topped log barn dobbed with straw mortar and cotton, a thin man centered in its door whacking a wagon axle with a hammer. He stopped and rose from his haunches still holding the hammer and stood in the shade watching them walk up on the horse.

This here's Smonk's tenant farm, McKissick said. Which would make that feller Smonk's tenant.

How ye know? asked the blacksmith from behind him on the horse.

Never mind. It's a few things I know.

You ain't gone shoot him, are ye?

Not if I don't have to. Pipe down.

The bailiff halted the horse a dozen paces out from the barn.

The tenant farmer took off his hat and his hair kept the shape of its crown. Evening, he said.

Never mind that, McKissick said. We inquiring about Smonk. Eugene Smonk they call him.

I know of him, sure do, the tenant farmer said. He nodded at the bloody shirt. You want that looked at? Sister yonder's got the healing gift.

They followed his eyes uphill to a dim shack with a skeletal woman in a slip smudged against the wood like a wraith, her eyes black as snakeholes. A clothesline hung with undergarments stitched down the hillside and several gray guinea hens ran screaming over the grit.

You only pay what ye think ye ought to, the farmer said. Plus the cost of her apothecary bottle, if ye know what I mean. He winked. She'll do ye, too. For half a dollar. I'm the one ye pay.

Naw, McKissick said. I met a fellow once in a field told me I could go in the house and lay with his two daughters, right in yonder, he said. I paid him and when I went in it was two fellers. I said where's the girls and they said what girls. I told em I'd paid the feller outside and they said what feller. We looked out the window and that feller was nowheres to be seen. I killed them two when they started laughing at me and then I tracked down that other feller and killed him in Bessemer.

Well, that's about the most I ever heard ye say, said Gates.

McKissick had lowered his eyes. He raised them now. I'm carrying this here gut wound back to the man give it to me. To the man took ever thing of mine. My farm. Land. Took my boy. A hunk of my flesh here. Wife. My very soul.

That sounds like Mister Smonk, all right, said the tenant. He lives two miles yonder ways. The big spread. You'll know it. He gestured around. He owns all this here land.

Does he own you too? asked the bailiff.

The farmer shrugged.

Say yer woman 'll do a bit of whoring? Gates asked.

Finest suck ye ever had. I ought to know. The farmer winked again.

Say she's got a snort too?

Genuine pure corn licker.

Naw, said McKissick. We best attend our chore.

Reckon I could inquire what that is? the tenant said. Ye chore, I mean. Jest curious is all. Lonesome as it gits out here in the woods. Yall sure ye don't want a suck?

I could use me a suck be honest, said the smith. Wouldn't mind a snort neither. Reckon that judge would pay?

McKissick peered at Smonk's tenant. Naw about the suck and naw about the licker and hell naw about asking after our business. One more such question 'll earn you a bullet or two where they can't be dug out.

I didn't mean no offense.

Fools never do. If ye see Smonk, don't tell him you encountered us. Bout the only thing we got in our favor here is the element of surprise. Without looking at his companion the bailiff said, Give nosy here a pay-off.

Gates balanced his rifle on the horse's back and reached in his bib pocket and tossed down a rusty nail.

Obliged, the tenant farmer said, picking it up to bite, watching the two men continue along their way, the overloaded mule struggling behind.

❧

How many? Smonk asked from the bed, opening his eye. He'd been resting but knew without being told about their visitors.

From the window, watching the men ride into the sugarcane, Ike flashed two fingers.

Two? Shit. Smonk threw a bloody rag across the room. Shamefulest posse I ever heard of is my own. Two. Of all numbers. One's my former employee, I speck. Missed his liver. The other one, couldn't tell ye. Not that judge I guarantee ye that. Maybe some laggard didn't show up at my event. Smonk drank from his jug and belched and moved his sore foot to a cool spot on the quilt. They coming?

Ike shook his head.

Good. We'll catch our breath, get em on the flipside. He patted the ticking and the woman came from the shadows and lay beside him like a pool of warm wax and started under the sheet with her hand.

Naw, he said. Rub my damn foot.

Ike picked up an eight gauge doublebarrel shotgun from the corner by the door without looking at what the girl was doing and went to the porch putting on his hat and whistled for the tenant.

The man trudged up the hill. Don't be whistling at me, he said, sticking out his arm. Last time I checked my skin was still white and yers was still nigger-colored.

Ike looked where the men had gone into the trees, watchful that they might sneak back and spy, which he would of done had he been them. Watch the place a day, day and a half.

They wouldn't bite, the tenant reported. I said jest what I's supposed to. But they claim they going after Mister Smonk over his place. Like they knew him. It was two of em. One was gigged.

Well, said Ike. I speck you best git on. He's evicting ye.

What's that mean?

Kicking ye out.

A nigger? A dern nigger's booting us out? He reached into his back pocket and unfolded a Case pocketknife.

One of Ike's eyebrows spiked and his hand struck the knife from the tenant's hand and his own razor flashed and slit the farmer's throat and Ike had wiped it twice on the man's shirt as if it were a strop and slipped it back into his pocket before the tenant could fathom that today death was the color of a Negro.

It ain't fair, he squeaked.

Ike stepped aside as he fell. Fair, he said, as if there was such a thing.

❦

Meanwhile, Gates had become addicted to sucking the rust off nails. He had ulcerous spaces between his teeth and he would work the nails softly into his gums, where the rust dissolved. It felt good. Also, he had the shits and every half-mile or so had to be let off to do his business in the trees and then run to catch up with his ride.

Ain't you a fellow renowned for his sense of humor? he asked. Didn't somebody tell me that?

McKissick didn't turn. I was. Once.

Can ye say a dirty joke?

Naw.

Little conversation be nice is all. I can never remember no jokes.

I got me jest one more joke to say in my life, said the bailiff. After I've cut Smonk's thoat or gutted him nuts to neck or shot him in the heart, jest fore he dies, I'm gone show him his selfsame glass eye.

Back up a step, pard, said the blacksmith. You got his eyeball?

McKissick frowned over his shoulder but dislodged it from his jaw and spat it into his palm and displayed it. Maybe it would make the blacksmith hush. The fellow reached forth a finger to touch it but McKissick popped it back in his mouth.

Careful, he said. I ain't so sure he can't still see thew it. He looked around them. These is strange times.

I seen stranger, said the blacksmith. Did I ever tell ye about the time I seen a cannonball go right thew a boy? In the War? It left a perfect hole in his gut for a second. We all started laughing, what was left of the regiment, even the man with the hole in his middle, laughing, laughing, laughing. Then he fell dead and we laughed harder. We was falling down laughing. Cannonballs rolling past. We pissed ourselves, one and all, and kept on laughing. Then after a time we got quiet and went hid over behind some burnt-up hay wagons. We was about fourteen year old, I reckon. We couldn't look one another in the eyes no more. We made a pack right after that to never talk about what had happened. But you know something? I talk about it all the time. I'm surprised I ain't mentioned it before.

I am too.

Presently they rounded a turn on the road and beheld the

Smonk homestead at the end of a long double row of cedars. A former sugarcane plantation, the house was as stately as a hotel and boasted among its oddities a cast iron dome with a spike that reached higher than the trees. Fastened to the spike was a bronze weathervane in the shape of a gamecock. The house had three stories and eleven bedrooms, a billiard parlor and hidden arsenal. In the back there was a statue garden which Smonk let go wild and so the naked people frozen in marble looked as if they were being strangled by vines and ivy. To the left were several outbuildings including a barn and beyond the barn lay an apple orchard and on the other side of the house there was a stone well with a shed covering it and boards over the mouth and stones over the boards. The men glanced at one another. The house seemed deserted, its shutters closed except for one, tapping open and shut in the wind, unkempt ivy lacing the front columns and weeds through the porch. The dome windows were dark and there were perhaps a dozen dead dogs on the porch and others strewn in the yard.

Bad luck had sent an angry red moon which flung the men's shadows before them on the ground. The bailiff and blacksmith dismounted and crept along the twin rows of cedars leading the horse and mule as insects screamed in the trees and fields. They eased off the cobblestone road with the animals in tow and skirted the house and came in downwind through a scraggle of bitterweed, pausing in the moon shadow of the barn.

You want to rest up inside here a spell? the blacksmith asked.

I speck so, said McKissick. I done got dizzy.

Yeah. Gut wound 'll do that.

You ever had one?

Naw.

They entered the barn and moved quietly through the darkness among the lumbrous animals, the bailiff tying their mount and beast of burden to a crossbeam near the door. The blacksmith was thirsty so he set aside his weaponry and slipped between boards into a stall and squatted next to the cow and rang milk into a bucket by squeezing her udder. When he had his all he offered the bucket to the bailiff.

Naw, said he. I'll not take nourishment till Smonk's head is separated from his shoulders.

The blacksmith reached up and grasped the cow's ear to help him to his feet. He had a milk mustache. It might make ye somewhat less lightheaded, he said.

Don't worry about the weight of my head. It works fine enough to come up with a plan. Listen, McKissick said, and told how he would sneak up to the manor and break in and try to assassinate Smonk and rescue the boy, if he were still alive. If anybody who wasn't the bailiff or his son came out of the house, the blacksmith was to use the Winchester rifle to ambush him from the barn.

Gates agreed. But *his* plan—his *secret* plan—was to wait until McKissick had killed Smonk and then ambush and kill McKissick. Or even if they didn't find Smonk, which would of been fine with the blacksmith, he could still prove he killed Smonk by possessing his eye. He imagined showing it to several young girls and how their titties touched his elbow.

Can I see that eyeball agin? he asked.

Hell naw. Jest kill anybody comes out the house. Anybody cept me. Or Willie.

Gates gave a thumbs-up.

McKissick trotted off and left the blacksmith to peer through a crack in the barn wall wondering who Willie was. The bailiff closed the distance to the giant house, such an expert he seemed at skullduggery that even watching him the blacksmith sometimes lost track of the assassin's position.

As McKissick neared the house one live dog rose from among the dead ones and began to growl and snap. It came tottering down the stairs. It's got the ray bees, the blacksmith whispered to himself as the dog charged. McKissick dropped to one knee and steadied his pistol arm with the other and shot the dog once in the head and stood to watch its final staggering steps. It fell not five yards from his boots and he replaced the spent cartridge with a fresh one from his new gunbelt and looked back toward the barn.

Gates waved behind the boards but McKissick was back on the go, melting shadow to shadow across the open yard and blending alongside the house. He holstered his pistol and scaled one of the trellises and pried open the shutters of an upstairs window and his legs disappeared inside.

Waiting, Gates screwed his pipe wrench all the way out and then all the way back in. He did this several times. He saw a rat creeping up on him and stomped on its head and the pest lay wiggling. Damn, he said. You a big one ain't ye. He jingled the nails in his pocket then lined them up on the ledge of the cow's stall and selected the rustiest and sucked it into his gums. He saw another rat and threw a clod of mule shit at it. He found a pail and shat a hot stew and told the horse, Dang, that sum-bitch stinks so bad I can't hardly squat over it. Holding his nose, he carried the pail out the back door and urinated in the straw and, inside again, began to name all the dead citizens of Old Texas and knew he was leaving somebody out.

He'd arrived in the town two years prior, had been on the run from the law for bigamy and arson and trying to sell a wagonload of stolen exotic snakes. A posse had chased him out of Jackson Alabama and he'd fled south through the woods, exhausting the horse he'd stolen and splashing on foot into a swamp. From there he found the river and followed it up the country, enmeshed in such a tangle of wilderness he'd of gladly submitted to a noose just to get out of the damn mosquitoes. It might of been days or weeks he was lost, eating bugs and frogs, finding a new leech on his balls ever morning. At some point he'd mistaken a creek for the river and followed it inland, half-mad from malaria and worms in his stool, his beard wild and flowing, his clothing long since shredded, skin covered in tears and gashes. It was pure chance that Lurleen had been out looking for berries. She'd carried him on her back to Old Texas and called the doctor who ministered to him for weeks and by the time he was sitting up in bed he was somehow engaged to be married. He reckoned it didn't matter he had two wives already and took the plunge a third time.

It ought to of been a dream, Lurleen decent enough to look at, plus her daughters—the three of them prancing about the house trying to show him their wares. Lurleen made it plain that he could lay with any one of them he wanted, said it was all in the family. Said the town needed younguns or it would dry up and die. For a number of months Gates had found himself in heaven, four women with large knockers and appetites, constantly vying for his knob. But anything could get old and within a year he dreaded each time they came to him, every night and morning, raising their skirts. He'd sneak down to his shop where he hid his whiskey and there would be Clena bent over his anvil with her bloomers down.

Thrown in the mix, too, was Old Texas—the entire town—

with its strangenesses and secrets. Where *were* the children? Why the shortage? Lurleen said it was because of the War. Said all the men and boys had gone off to fight and left the women alone. The other men who were there were men like Gates, fellows who'd found their way here and married a widow and were themselves as happily sexed as any men anywhere. But whenever a gal got knocked up, it was something happened to the baby. Better not to ask, Lurleen had said. It's church business. And Gates, always one to mind his own affairs, hadn't.

He'd accumulated about enough of the mysteries when Smonk had started coming to town, though. Year ago. To tell the truth, he'd kind of liked Old E.O. He was ugly but he always had licker to sell, and if you didn't get crossways of him, he wouldn't get crossways of you. He would beat you at cards, but as long as you paid he was pleasant enough. Good licker too. Plus he was another man for the stepdaughters to moon over. And Lurleen. He remembered the night of the barn dance when she was out on the hay with Smonk. Gates was adding licker to the punch bowl when McKissick elbowed him and said, Uh oh.

Smonk's hand was on Lurleen's caboose and ever body was looking to see what Gates would do. Had he had his druthers, the blacksmith would of told Smonk, Take her. Please.

Then McKissick pushed Gates out over the hay. Everybody had seen what was going on, so poor old Gates had little choice but to start his banty-rooster strut, raising his hand for the fiddler to stop and that knucklehead on the triangle too.

Smonk must of known Gates was coming though Gates was behind him. The one-eye twirled Lurleen out of the picture and stood with his back to the blacksmith, waiting.

Gates glared at him. Then he said, Reckon that's my woman, Smonk.

She is, Smonk said, is she?

He turned without looking at them and walked out of the barn. A strut of his own. Before he stepped outside he gave Gates's wife a wink. She squealed. She squealed and jumped up clapping her hands and ran out after him. She never looked back.

Poor old Gates. Standing there pulling on his thumb. No man wanted to go out after E. O. Smonk, in the dark. But Gates had no choice. Out he went.

They found him half an hour later in the livery barn with his head bashed in. Near about dead. The men had a town meeting about it and agreed to meet again, but finally it was their wives harping on them that made them round up a mob and ride out to Smonk's. Gates hadn't yet awakened from being conked and might never, for all they knew. That would be murder, the ladies had pointed out. And this town needed every man it could get.

Ten men went. All the other husbands. They flew a white flag approaching Smonk's plantation. The one-eye was sitting on the porch drinking a tumbler of bourbon and soaking his feet in brine. They all had guns. He held his dog back on a rope and listened to them say he was going to be taken in lawfully and detained lawfully and tried lawfully.

Smonk flicked a cigar into the yard. Then hanged lawfully?

The law will decide that, Justice Tate said.

You mean yer wife will.

Enough, Hobbs the undertaker said. You can't jest ride into a town and steal a fellow's wife and knock em in the head, Smonk.

Seems like you'd appreciate the business, undertaker.

Well I don't. Do ye see the position you've give us?

Smonk looked out at them. Their guns. They'd all donned neckties. If I can disprove the charge of rape, he asked, will yall drop the charge of knocking that jackass in the head?

The men grumbled among themselves. Fine, Justice Tate said. That could sure of been self-defense.

Smonk finished his bourbon and tossed the glass over his shoulder where it shattered against the door. Out slunk Gates's wife in a short slip. The men started coughing and clearing their throats. She had a brush and a dustpan. Without looking at them, she squatted down and started cleaning up the mess.

Hey, Smonk yelled back at her. Tell these ignoble bastards nobody didn't get nothing they didn't want.

She was sweeping pieces of glass in the pan. She wouldn't look up.

Well, demanded Justice of the Peace Tate. Speak up, Lurleen.

He ain't done nothing I didn't let him, she mumbled.

Good evening, bitches, Smonk said.

Gates had awakened a few days after that, perhaps not as sound as he'd once been but alive, and then, a week later, Lurleen Gates had come home claiming Smonk had kidnapped her. She said she'd only gone out in the dark because she didn't want the other ladies to hear the tongue-lashing she meant to put on old Smonk. Said she was sparing the town. Said Smonk did unmentionable things to her and made her lie. Said if the men of the town didn't go get him and put his life on trial they were a bunch of lily-livered sad sacks.

Now the blacksmith heard shots from Smonk's house and hurried to the bay door with the Winchester, stopping to untie the horse and mule for a quick escape. He was glad not to be involved in the actual killing of Smonk because everybody knew killing Smonk would be dern near impossible. He hoped McKissick was up to it. Hell, he'd rather buy Smonk a drink of licker than kill him. Smonk always had good licker. Or maybe Smonk and McKissick would kill one another and Gates could take them both back and be heralded a hero in Old Texas instead of a cuckolded fool. He hunkered down with the rifle and waited. Or dern. Maybe he wouldn't go back at all.

Smonk didn't like the stars. He didn't trust them. It felt like they were watching him from higher ground and cover of dark. In years past he'd insisted on rigging a tarp over Ike's wagon before he could sleep. The tarp made Ike tense and closed-in, and he finally put Smonk out and told him to sleep under the wagon. This had worked and now, as if they were brothers in bunk beds, they talked each night.

I had a dream, Smonk said tonight.

Don't tell ye dreams, said Ike.

They lay listening to bugs.

Tell me about that shark's tooth, Smonk said.

I fount it on the beach when I was a youngun, Ike said. On a giant pile of oyster shells. I couldn't even close my hand around it it was so big. I showed it to my daddy and he quit drinking long enough to be amazed. He was a drunk and a fisherman. He said it was a great white's tooth. Then he passed out.

In the morning I took the tooth and showed it around. My little buddies. One of em had this magnifying glass I'd always wanted. It would start fires. When he saw the shark tooth he offered a trade.

Then Daddy woke up and started looking for it. Looked ever where. He come fount me and said where the heck was it and I said traded and he went to whaling on me with a ax handle.

Smonk ashed his cigar. He turned his jug up. He had burlap bags nailed to the sides of the wagon to keep out the starlight and his rifle lay cleaned and oiled alongside him in its sock. He didn't use a bedroll, the ground better for his hips.

He'd just rolled over onto his back when, beneath him, as if such a phenomenon were natural and nightly, the ground shook, almost gently, whispering the grass and rocking the stones and squeaking the wagon hinges. Leaves in nearby trees shuddered though the wind had faded with dusk and the bugs went dead and for a moment the night held its breath. Then a great clack of thunder and several after-clacks rumbled the south, behind them.

Adios, plantation, Smonk muttered.

Reckon ye got him? Ike asked.

McKissick? Smonk blew a ray of smoke. Naw. That one's slick. His only failure is he bucks his own nature. He'll come at us tomorrow.

You want me—

Naw. Jest go on finish ye story.

Well, me and my daddy never had no easy time with the other. He was a mean drunk that was drunk all the time and I couldn't do nothing to please him. Nothing but leave. Which I done at the age of seven or eight. Went off and grew up to be a decent young church-going Negro. Didn't mind my lot which seemed like it was gone be picking cane. Anyway I had a aunt would write me letters and give me the family news. I never answered em but they'd find me here and there. One of em turned up in Alabama where I'd married a gal and we was fixing to start us a family. That was the letter that said Daddy was finally dying of the cancer.

Telegram, warn't it?

It was. I didn't know it was such a thing. The wagon creaked as Ike shifted his weight. The bugs were at it again.

I killed three horses and rurned another one getting up to St. Louis, Ike went on. And when I did I made a beeline to see Daddy straight away. Hadn't laid eyes on him in twenty-two years. I remember he was in the back room at the doctor's house. He didn't even know me at first. Had a hole eat out of his neck. Weighted about seventy pounds. I took off my hat and said who I was and he said come closer. When I leaned in to hear, he said, I still can't believe you traded that got-dern shark tooth.

Smonk began to cough and coughed for a long time.

When he finished, the bugs had gone quiet again.

It was the river, Smonk said. That I dreamed of. It was up in the tree branches it was so high.

Go to sleep, said Ike.

ᗡᕈᏇ

In Smonk's house McKissick was kicking through doors and belly-crawling down halls. Where the hell was E.O.? He'd fired dozens of times, at threatening lamps and figurines and at his own gaping reflection in windows and mirror-glasses. He'd found a room with twenty-five Model '94 thirty-thirty rifles racked on the walls, drawers of pistols and stacks of ammunition.

But no E.O.

He smelled something burning and, reloading, hurried through the hall peppered with his own bullets and down the curving staircase. In a low corner of the kitchen, smoke was leaking from a small door he hadn't yet seen, an aperture so squat it seemed designed for a child or dwarf. There was a string going under the door and he saw the string had been tight at one point, tripped no doubt by his own foot. He approached the door and tapped the planks with his pistol barrel, smoke seeping from the top of the door and through its knotholes and slits. He touched the hot wood with his knuckle and used his pistol barrel to unfasten the rawhide thong. When the door swung open a cloud of smoke belched out. He fanned his face and coughed, crying from heat, and bent to peer below the smoke, down the earthen steps, where in the hazy gloom lay piles of gunpowder bags and sticks of TNT in boxes and crates of nitroglycerine vials, some already on fire.

Shit, he said.

He fell backward over a chair and scrambled through the door. He crossed his forearms before his head and crashed through Smonk's picture window and shutters and rolled over the porch with wood dander and splinters of glass in his hair. Clinging to his pistol, he slid over broken panes and off the porch and landed running as the arsenal in Smonk's root cellar began its explosions, shaking the ground and the tops of trees and catapulting the porch columns over the weeds. The house disintegrating in all directions in blinding flame and glass and screaming nails and the iron dome rising in the air.

McKissick landed on his side near the cobblestone road and rolled as a sink buried itself in the grass by his head. Burning furniture splintered on the ground and a mattress bounced and the dome landed upside down on the corn crib and settled in the fire like an enormous iron helmet cast down by some firegod of old.

McKissick looked behind him where a cedar had burst into flames and then the next caught and the next and next like matchheads down the line.

He rolled in the grass, barely missed by a sideboard landing in splinters and the bottles of liquor inside casting currents of blue flame in every direction. He scrabbled away batting fire from his arms and legs. He looked mutely for the horse or his partner as stars landed around him. He was deaf. The back of his neck was blistered. He smelled burning hair. When he whistled for the horse smoke came out. The mule trotted past Smonk's well, and the bailiff saw a lovely burning shingle flapping down toward the animal's back, where the fireworks he'd bought in Old Texas sat in a bundle on top of their supplies.

No, he said.

Someone tugged his shirt. He looked but no one was there. Something clipped his ear and he understood the idiot blacksmith was shooting at him and he rolled behind the sink. When he peered over the iron, Gates was nowhere in sight.

McKissick's hearing was returning in one ear, the right. Maybe the left. He was black as a minstrel, tatters of smoking cloth dripping from his arms. Something hard in his gullet. His hair burnt off. Blisters already forming on his neck and the bald back of his head.

Where the hell was E.O.? He found his pistol smoking on the ground and fetched it and hit himself in the head with the heel of his hand to clear his thinking as he hurried toward the barn, his boots dissolving into tarry footprints as he ran. Metal eyelet marks burned into his skin.

The hayloft was on fire as he stood in the bay door looking. Animals screaming in their stalls. Burning chickens batting past. It might have occurred to him to set the larger animals loose but at that moment somebody jumped him from behind and hit him in the head. He rolled and put up his hands and caught the Winchester's forearm in one fist and barrel in the other as the blacksmith used his weight to force it toward his throat.

Wait, fool, he grunted. It's me. Ye partner.

Oh. Gates hesitated, then climbed off. Sorry, he said. I thought ye was a nigger.

Hell naw. I'm jest all burnt up.

I wondered why ye head was smoking.

McKissick squinted down at his side where fresh blood ran from his wound. Look here what ye done. I'm glad I only left ye a few cartridges. And gladder yet yer a terrible shot.

Sorry for the mistake. Gates extended his hand and helped McKissick to his feet and suddenly McKissick was pounding his own chest.

Dern, he said. He made gagging noises.

What is it? Ye heart muscle?

Naw. It's Smonk's got-dern eye. I reckon I swallered it.

The hay was burning high, fire licking along their legs, and they walked to the edge to watch from a safe distance the barn consumed. The not entirely unpleasant odor of burning cow.

Did ye kill him? Gates asked.

Not that I know of.

Did ye see him?

Yeah. We played a hand of rook and drunk a root beer sody.

Oh. Gates put his hands in his pockets and took them out again. Where to next, then?

McKissick turned. Try to find the horse first. That mule too. See what we can save. Then back to town. Meet him there.

They began to walk away from the fire, the bailiff stepping gingerly in his bare feet. What 'll ye take for ye shoes? he asked.

You can war em all the way home if ye agree to stop and visit that whore up the way. Git a taste.

Fine. We ought to go back by there anyways.

They shook on it, and Gates sat in the dirt and removed his shoes, well-worn suedes with yarn for lacing. He handed them up and watched McKissick pull them on using the side flaps.

Another, smaller explosion boomed behind them, the fire raging through the trees and the fields of sugarcane popping as they incinerated. Gates hung his rifle in the crook of his arm and they walked. He decided that if he killed McKissick now he'd have to sop around in his innards to find the eye, which didn't seem too pleasant, judging from the smell leaking out. Maybe let him move his bowels before murdering him. He cleared his throat.

Can I git a ration of bullets?

Hell naw.

A mile away they found the singed, shaken horse in a copse of ashen trees and McKissick spoke gentle words into its ear and within minutes he'd mounted up and helped his partner on and they rode west, behind them the crackle of fire and pop of wood. If the wind shifted it might overtake them but it looked as if a fire had burned through here already. Land so desolate, the old song went, that people used to have babies just for the food. McKissick's skin was scorched and blistered and tatters of clothing still clung to raw patches on his arms and legs. Except for the blacksmith's shoes and a crude loin cloth fashioned from a bandanna, he was naked. Gates was barefoot with his pants rolled halfway up his calves.

Presently they came upon the pack mule which had leapt in a dry pond bed and rolled in the dust to douse its fiery burden. While the fireworks had exploded and the other goods were smashed or scattered hither and yon, the animal itself was usable and the blacksmith accepted the reins and hoisted himself on without a saddle. The mule seemed eager to get the hell away which improved their pace. Stuck to the mule's mottled hair Gates found a small package wrapped in brown paper which he tossed to McKissick.

Willie, he said.

As all the balloon needed now was the boy's sweet breath to fill it, it could have been the bailiff's heart.

8

THE REDEEMER

Before dawn, on the Lord's day, Mrs. Tate crimped dead Elmer's pants cuffs the way she preferred them worn and smoothed the pants at the knobs of his knees and folded his hands which slid back as before. She returned with twine and tied the buttonholes together.

She shooed a fly. She puffed the shoulders of his Sunday coat and wondered should she have dressed him in his postmaster outfit instead. She returned from upstairs with his lucky handkerchief (which he'd forgotten the day of the trial) and tucked it into his pocket, the irony not lost on her. With her flyswatter she pursued and killed flies for the better part of half an hour, all the while talking to him, accusing him of never being a believer. It was the most important thing in my life, she said. My faith. And how could the man who used my own bed not cherish that.

I cherished it, he would have lied.

You cherished cherishing those girls, she told him.

He said nothing. He had a towel over his face. She plucked a string of her own hair from his sleeve.

In times, she said, when God's burden weighs us down, in His mercy He gives us leave. Such was the leave He allowed Lot's daughters who plied their father with drink and went in and laid with him to preserve their line. And Lot without guilt. Fat, blind, drunk, happy. His shamed daughters going into his cave. The eldest first. Mrs. Tate popped a fly out of the air. Men are so simple, she said. Get them drunk, satisfy them, and they sleep. It's the women who lie awake.

From outside she heard a gunshot. She went to the window and lowered her veil and peered into the night. The guard came trotting up and shrugged. Her gun had gone off again. Mrs. Tate let the drapes fall and raised her veil. She returned to her husband's side and took his hand and told him she was sorry about last Friday. How she'd been cold to him when it was his turn to go see that young Hester Hobbs. You appeared properly burdened by it, she said. Didn't even seem excited to go which is all I or any of us could ask for. Her so young, so pretty, and our need so necessary. And you not even eager to get out of the house. Pretending so well. And I was cold to you. Because I knew you wanted to go. You asked me to bring you a cup of water and I got the water and set it down so hard it spilled. Go, I said. Just go.

She looked at his shoulders and swatted a fly dead. And off you went. Walking slowly at first. I watched you out the window as your steps got faster and faster and you were almost running you wanted to get away from here so bad. Away from me.

She adjusted the cloth over his face and fluffed his handkerchief. Men are so simple, she said.

∞

On the Lord's Day, the Christian Deputies rested. Walton ordered his men to do very little about their camp other than pray and meditate or use their magnifying glasses to practice reading their tiny Bibles. He saluted the troops in their studious poses and retired to his tent and fastened the ties and attached his mosquito netting and removed his boots and polished them to spec and then reclined on his collapsible cot to pray. He fell instantly asleep and like a succubus from a fever dream the whore-child Evavangeline assembled herself from the air and *sans* pants climbed upon his chest like a degenerate muse and attached her steaming vulva to his neck. The dream was so real he had an emission and woke with a yelp, fumbling for a handheld pierglass so he might check his neck for "hickey" marks.

Mister Walton?

Deputy Ambrose. From outside.

Walton cleaned himself and donned his pants and hurried out, becoming entangled in the mosquito netting in the process and holding his boots. I thought I gave orders, he said.

Ambrose nodded toward the south. When Walton didn't seem to understand he pointed.

Stepping into his boots, left, then right, Walton followed his lieutenant's ebony finger over a series of fields and beheld a vista of distant, blue trees.

Lovely, Walton said. Indeed. What poultice to my chapped soul is Thy handiwork, Lord.

Not the scenery. Ambrose handed the leader a telescope. Look thew this.

He saw two deputies in full uniform and with all their equipment, creeping through the sugarcane toward the trees, leading their horses.

Deserters, he said.

Ambrose straightened his posture. You want me to git em?

Please.

There ye go, boss. It's about time. The Negro drew his rifle from its sheath and levered a cartridge into the chamber and half-cocked the hammer and took off his boots and left his hat spinning on his pommel and vanished into the cane. Walton located the deserters with the scope and tried to find Ambrose in among the "bamboo-like" plants. But his lieutenant's stealth did the deputy proud and Walton thought he'd give the Negro a commendation upon his return. Yes. A spot of incentive to soothe good "ole" Ambrose, grumpy as he'd been of late.

A gunshot startled Walton from his revery. He searched the field and landed his glass upon Deputy Ambrose bursting from the cane leaves. Behind his rifle, Ambrose approached one of the deserters who raised his hands in surrender and began to backpedal and beg. Excellent, Walton thought. He would order that deserter horsewhipped, by gum. That would put the fear of God into any future deserter, wouldn't it?

Now Deputy Ambrose had the barrel of his rifle in the second deserter's mouth. Quite effective. Measured savagery indeed a crucial ingredient of God's most contradictory design, Man.

Then Deputy Ambrose fired. The deserter's head burst open at its crown, the stump of its neck smoking. Ambrose shot again.

My Lord! Walton cried, nearly dropping his telescope, but its shivering globe next revealed Ambrose pursuing the second deserter, already shot once and attempting to crawl off in a piteous manner. The dark deputy approached the fellow from the rear in sideways dancy steps and put two bullets in the back of his head.

You ought to kill that crazy nigger, Loon said, peering through his own telescope. Fore he shoots the rest of us.

Negro, said Walton.

ᙢᙢ

On the Lord's Day Evavangeline rode the speckle-legged pony from the orphanage north. Ranging east, for a few hours, then back due north. Her gut pulling her clear as gravity. She was aware that the boy from the orphanage had broken his promise about looking after the other younguns and was following her on foot. A couple of times she heard him and once glimpsed his face peering from around the trunk of a tree like a coon. She would urge the pony to a run so they could ditch the boy, but each time, within an hour after slowing down, she perceived the horny little dickens still back there, tailing her.

She thought it was cute.

Presently she began to hear a dog barking far in front of her. It relieved her in a way she didn't know needed relieving—she'd been aware of something lately and that something was *Where were the dogs?* Normally they were everywhere, two or three following her, trying to rut on her leg. But it had been weeks since she'd seen a live dog. Back in Shreveport? Anxious now for this one, she wiggled her hips and the pony clopped to a run over the dry earth.

Closer she got she realized the dog was in an ill temper. She swung down off the pony for she'd sensed a man too somewhere about and so she left the pony feeding on crabgrass and stepped inside the trees off the path she'd been following and walked hidden that way toward what sounded like a dogfight.

Suddenly it was a fellow behind her, a gun barrel between her shoulders. A quick hand snatched her own firearms and pushed her along. She was impressed at the economy. Not many could get the drop on her.

Don't look back back back, he said.

She didn't and he prodded her along his barrel. She tried whistling, hoping the pony would hear and come help, but he kicked her in the seat of her pants. Hesh, he said. Next sound I'll bop ye in yer brain brain brainpan.

He'd faded a few steps back, too far behind to be jumped, and the cagey bastard had maneuvered them back to the path so there were fewer trees she could try to scale. For the time being, she gave up and tried to sense out his leaning, boy or girl, to see would that give her an angle.

They came presently to a decrepit woodshed wrapped in chains, the door banging and rattling from inside as the dog clawed and scratched and headbutted the wood.

Tell me ye name name, said the stranger behind her.

She told him.

That's a perty name perty name perty name perty name. You a whore?

Naw.

Are too. I can see the way ye walk. Wiggling wiggling wiggling like a little whore's ass, whore's ass.

The dog was growling and scratching the door. The gun barrel touched her spine, urging her forward. This here savage one is Lazarus the Redeemer the Redeemer the Redeemer, he said.

It's a damn mad-dog ain't it.

He's my good boy. Behind her, her captor sighed out a breath of air. But I didn't say ye could talk did I say did I say did I say did I say?

He hit her in the head with his rifle-stock and the woods exploded white before they faded to nothing.

Walton would have run all the way to the scene of violence had not Donny trotted up behind him and pushed his nose in the ticklish spot between the northerner's shoulders. Thus aback his steed, the head deputy closed the distance quickly and came upon Deputy Ambrose where he was kneeling at the corpses relieving them of their possessions.

What, yelled Walton, in the name of God are you doing?

The Negro paused in rolling one of the dead men's socks down over his calves and regarded Walton. This my stuff now, he said. I killed these ones and now I get they stuff.

Walton folded his arms to hide his trembling hands. Hardly, he said. Do you know what a "rig" like this costs, Deputy Ambrose? Do you know who pays that cost?

Ye momma.

Well. Yes, technically. But as her agent, I claim all these men's effects for the Christian Deputies, myself commander. Into the company store, so to speak.

Don't be so-to-speaking to me.

Poor grammar fails to augment your arguments, Walton said.

Now, continue to gather the equipment and we'll inventory it later, what do you say? I was thinking of giving you a commendation for your stealth.

You, Ambrose said, are the biggest fool I ever seen.

Pardon?

I said "fool." F-U-L. Big one. Big fool. He stretched out his arms, a sock in each hand.

Why, that's insubordination. Walton stabbed his pockets for a pencil, his cheeks stinging and his lungs light. I could have your badge!

My fucking badge? The Negro snatched it from his crimson shirt and threw it in the dust and stamped on it. Fuck my fucking badge, he said. He stamped it again. You know what I'm gone do? *I'm* gone teach a lesson now. He mimicked Walton in a prissy fashion, writing at his chalkboard. I call it <u>"How to Rob Two Dead Deserting Fuckers of All They Fucking Possessions and Then Cut Off They Tallywhackers and Stick Um in They Mouth Cause That How the Indians Do It So If Anybody Come Along They Gone Think It Was the Savages Done It."</u>

I see, Walton said.

He watched Ambrose pull one man's pants down over his hips and, a precise motion of his beltknife, slice off his member and place it without ceremony in its owner's mouth. He did the same to the second dead deputy. Then Walton watched the Negro *not* speak respectful words over the bodies and, arms full of "booty," languidly pursue his horse across the field and charm it calm and gather its reins.

Frozen at the site, Walton clutched his hat and quoted a few apt verses of Scripture to usher the dead men wherever their journey next took them. The leader then prodded Donny with gentle heels and followed his distant second-in-command whose silhouette now rode back toward the last two deputies, Loon and Onan, and soon the four of them rode together at a fair clip without speaking a word. Deputy Ambrose whistling and practicing with his sword, lopping off the tops of small trees.

The man had walloped the whore-lady in the back of her head, William R. McKissick Junior witnessed it from the bushes. He watched the walloper squat with his rifle and regard her a while, the whole time that dang dog trying to eat the door off. The man rose and William R. McKissick Junior saw that he was tall and wore overalls tucked into his boots and had no shirt on underneath the straps. There was a red kerchief around his neck and every patch of his skin the boy could see was covered with freckles. He'd never seen such a speckled man before, but this one was going through Evavangeline's pockets and touching her in all the secret places that William R. McKissick Junior wished he were touching. He'd best kill that man. He held the Mississippi Gambler by its blade tip and closed his eye and judged the distance and flung the knife.

It flew behind the man as he stepped over the prone girl and slashed into the brush. The freckled man, busy with his prisoner, set his rifle against the shed and took a forked stick and went to the door where the dog was still making its racket.

Shet up! he bellowed. Ye got-damn cannon mouth cannon mouth cannon mouth. He kicked the door which quieted the dog.

Then it was back, more savage still.

Creeping through the foliage, William R. McKissick Junior saw the man use the stick to unlatch a small trapdoor in the center of the larger door. He saw him throw down his stick and fling sweat from his fingers. When he lifted the girl her eyes were fluttering. The man tussled Evavangeline forward in his arms as if they were dancing, her feet off the ground, intending to job her arm in where the mad-dog was. Without a thought he was running from behind the shed out into the dappled light, falling on his hands once and getting back up. The speckled man had stuck Evavangeline's forearm in the hole but when he saw William R. McKissick Junior he dropped her and scrambled for the rifle and she fell, withdrawing her arm. William R. McKissick Junior grabbed the rifle but couldn't make it shoot before the man was on him. The man raised him up in the air by his collar and looked him in the face a moment then underhanded him into the shed wall where the boy slid to the ground and moved his elbow a second before the mad-dog's snout left frothy drool peeling down the wood. He cocked the rifle and aimed down the barrel where the boy lay scowling.

Then an idea seemed to dawn upon the man's long face. He resembled a horse, his lips bore a perpetual pucker of protruding yellow teeth which made him seem to be smiling. Scabs of beard dotted here and there among the freckles. He came forward leering behind the gun and grabbed the boy's foot.

I'm gone sell ye, ain't I, he said. Get a get a get a get a real good price.

He backed toward the whore dragging the boy and didn't see that she'd opened her eyes. The forked stick was within her grasp and her fingers closed around it. The speckled man was bent over, looping a rope over that boy from the orphanage. Her sodden brain couldn't call up his name but she pushed off the ground and held the stick in both hands and swung hard and whacked him a good one across the base of his skull and using the momentum of her first swing swung again as he turned to face her and this time she hit him hard across his mouth and burst his lips and nose. Then fell herself.

The boy helped her to her feet, staring at her breasts, their nipples targets in her thin sweaty shirt.

Thank ye, she said, holding her head in her hands.

He pulled the bloody hairs off the stick and offered it to her for a crutch.

Thank ye. He conked me a good one.

The boy kicked dirt on the downed man. I'd call ye even now. Is he dead?

As if in answer, the speckled man stirred. The two youngsters looked at him and then at each other and then at the shed door which had never ceased its rattle. It took them both to drag him to the door and push him up against its side and prop him there as he muttered and jerked and tried to wake up. They pushed his arm in the hole and fled as he hung, hooked by his own armpit, and the dog had its way. From the safety of the woods Evavangeline and the boy watched him come to his senses. He snatched out his arm which had been gnawed to a bloody stob. He glared at the woods, seeking them, then tore his handkerchief off his neck and did a rough onehanded job of bandaging his elbow.

Evavangeline knelt and squinted so she could see in the boy's blue eyes. Her vision was blurry, there seemed to be two of him. She blinked and tried to focus. What did ye say yer name is agin?

William R. McKissick Junior.

Well, Junior. Where's them younguns you promised to look after?

He pointed behind her.

There they were, three boys and the same number of girls. They were filthy and gaunt and hollow-eyed and holding hands. She might of gotten angry except it was then she noticed the dog-bite on her elbow.

9

THE EYE

MEANWHILE, MCKISSICK THE BAILIFF AND GATES THE BLACKSMITH had spent a few hours sleeping on the hard earth, the latter tossing and afraid, and after a morning of hard riding, he squirmed atop the pack mule, waiting for McKissick to return from moving his bowels. He could hardly keep from humming, close as he was to getting the eye.

It ought to of happened first thing today, according to what the bailiff had said was his gut's regular schedule.

Ever morning, he'd said.

You lucky, Gates thought. I done a bucketful earlier and I could fill up another one right now.

Perhaps the wound *had* irregulated his system, as McKissick claimed, which now worried Gates that Smonk's eyeball might of already popped out of the injury unbeknownst to them. Shit. Such a nag would eat at him like possums on a dead cow till he saw the eye. Until he knew it was safe, until he could roll it in his fingers and smell its smell. Insisting on privacy, McKissick had ridden his horse into a stand of mimosa trees a dern half-hour ago. Dang. Gates craned his neck. For all the blacksmith knew, his partner had shat the eye and played with it a spell and gone off to kill Smonk alone. Gates breeched his rifle. Still empty. He uncocked it and sighed. Everything was against him.

ᗧᐁᗤ

Meanwhile, naked as an Indian but for his borrowed shoes, McKissick plucked Smonk's eye from the rope of coal-black shit he'd deposited across a rotten log. He wiped the ball clean on his shoe-toe and admired it from several angles. How the light hit it. He had no intention of giving it back. He meant to keep it. Smonk had bullied his way into McKissick's life which had become the kind of situation where once E.O. was there he would never leave until somebody killed him.

He'd met Smonk several years before, when E.O. still had two eyes, one green, one blue, in the lost train of days when Smonk looked like a damn savage, red hair streaming down his back, those arms that were like battering rams and hairy as a bear's. He could crush a brick in his hand, which frequently won him drinks in saloons. His other bet was that he had a cock that hung below his knee. There were always takers against this boast, and Smonk would pull down his britches and show them the rooster on a noose tattooed on his shin. Laughter would be general, and the nature usually good, but on a couple of occasions McKissick had seen men get testy and challenge Smonk. Some fellows took his short, squat stature as weakness. Like one time this lanky dentist—said

he bare-knuckled his way through dental school—outright refused to pay. He was drunk on Smonk's shine. Threw a jarful in
Smonk's face and said the real cock in the room was Smonk his
self. Smonk grabbed the dentist's head in one hand and popped it
like a coconut. Then E.O. called for the man's brother who shuffled forward out of the crowd. You gone pay me? Smonk asked. I
am, said he. McKissick had covered Smonk in that altercation, and
had the brother said anything other than, "It's okay, Mister Smonk,
he always was a cheap skate," McKissick would of shot him in his
knee. Or higher up, depending on how much whiskey he'd had.

McKissick and Smonk had met in Utah in the sheep town of
Hornwall Bend, where Smonk was hiding out and McKissick was
in jail waiting to hang. While E.O. had been laying with some
man's wife, her husband and his friends had arrived home unex-
pectedly. Ike, the nigger Smonk traveled with, crowned the husband with a shotgun but another fellow got the drop on Ike and
they arrested him and pronounced him guilty without a trial and
had him scheduled to hang in the near future. Smonk got away
Scot free and mounted sugar bags on a horse he'd stolen from a
town fifty miles away. He fired a pistol and scared the horse off, it
running in the direction home, the weight bouncing on its back exactly Smonk's. From beneath the whorehouse, he watched most of
the town's men ride off in a posse, leaving an inexperienced deputy
to guard the prisoners.

Thus McKissick, jailed for murder (banker, strangled), sat in
the cell beside Ike and yelled it wasn't fair for a white man to be
caged up with a coon. Get this watermelon out of here. Ike never
said anything. Just sat with his arms folded and eyes closed.

Hey, McKissick called.

At midnight there came a scuffle from the front office where the deputy was sleeping. Ike sat up from his bunk and began lacing his shoes.

What the hell, McKissick wanted to know.

Then, lit by the lantern he held, in walked the strangest fellow you'd ever see. He looked like an orangutan McKissick had seen at a zoo once. Smonk told Ike there were no keys to be had, the sheriff had taken them. Under his arm he had a big shield of iron that he handed through the bars to Ike. Ike propped the plate up against his bunk and got behind it. Smonk—he hadn't acknowledged the other prisoner—was lighting a stick of dynamite.

Panic flickered over McKissick's face as Smonk stood the stick against the east wall and walked out of the room.

Ike said, Come on.

McKissick dove behind the iron shield as the TNT exploded and when he looked out the town newly revealed gleamed with rain.

To follow were years of robberies, blackmail schemes, McKissick and Smonk meeting in a city and making their money and fading in different directions and communicating via secret code in newspaper advertisements. (McKissick never again saw Ike during their transactions. For all he knew, in those years and in these, the nigger was gone.) Their partnership would dissolve every year or two because McKissick was the guilty sort, and each time an innocent was murdered in crossfire or blown to bits in the wrong place at the wrong time, he would give up his guns and go straight. He'd disappear.

Smonk always found him.

One time he found him and McKissick had got married. Lived

in a brick house in Carter Wyoming, happy the first time in his life. She was a reformed whore who would still use her whore tricks on him and did each night . . . until the dawn McKissick walked out naked on his porch to piss and saw Smonk sleeping there, a bottle for a pillow. Soon as his wife saw Smonk it started. It always did. Smonk got all the girls, they couldn't resist him. It was something of the animal about him, was McKissick's notion, a wild element men had left behind with the advent of such peacekeeping creations as the six-shooter or Gatling gun.

McKissick helped Smonk extort several thousand dollars from a mayor who was a secret octoroon in a nearby town. Later, after he caught Smonk in his, McKissick's, bedroom, with his, McKissick's, wife, McKissick took the girl and fled. They both pretended the baby was McKissick's, and hell, maybe he was. They lived in Oklahoma in poverty and the boy grew up skinny and by the time Smonk found them again McKissick was lean himself, short of fuse, unable to find work, happy to extort or threaten or burn or kill.

It's a tobaccy farmer, Smonk had said, pushing gold coins across the table, the boy hiding beneath. E.O. had lost his eye by now, lost his looks. He'd gotten fatter. Hairier. Brown spots on his skin. Chancre sores. But he was short none of the appeal he had for women. In these lean years McKissick's wife had stopped performing her wifely duties with McKissick, but here she was flirting with Smonk, and here was Smonk paying gold coin after gold coin to McKissick so he'd go outside and tend the one-eye's horse while he visited with the woman. McKissick kicked the dog across the yard on his way to the barn.

McKissick murdered the tobacco farmer and when he came

back his wife was gone, took off after Smonk. So with the boy in tow McKissick had chased them. He found his wife in a town in east Texas, whoring, but she refused to take him back and he shot her dead and with the boy behind him on his horse he rode off after Smonk. They'd chased E.O. all over the world it felt like, for years, winding up at last in the wilderness between the rivers. He'd installed himself as bailiff in the nearest town (Old Texas) and clipped his chin whiskers and cut his hair. He'd donned the overalls and bicycle cap of a town bumpkin and waited in disguise.

Now, naked, he thumped the eye in the air and caught it and popped it in his mouth. Its taste growing on him.

He turned to go and there stood E.O. Leaning against a tree. He had his cane in one hand and a pistol in the other. Somehow he looked even worse than he had the day before, coughing, dragging one leg as he came forward, blood oozing into his beard. McKissick stepped back, closing his hands. For the first time since he'd known the one-eye, Smonk looked *killable*. Like murdering him would do him a favor. McKissick was backing up, aware he was naked, his loin cloth draped over a branch near where he'd defecated.

That's yer stob? Smonk pointed his cane. No wonder that whore of yern used to fret so on mine.

McKissick's rifle lay across the log.

Smonk stepped closer. He wore an eyepatch but had it flipped up so you could see in the hole. The bailiff remembered Smonk telling the story of how, after he lost the eye, its attachments had rotted in his head and for dern near a year he'd had to stuff garlic in the hole to make it bearable and keep the gnats and flies away.

I recollect ye now, fellow, Smonk said. Here we are ain't we. A reunion in the woods.

McKissick kept backing up and Smonk paced him step for step. He was like a grizzly about to stand.

I want my rifle yonder, Smonk repeated. And I want my fucking eye.

McKissick edged to his right, toward Smonk's blind side, but the one-eye angled his head and wagged his finger at such a squarehead move.

McKissick, Smonk said, ye got nerve, boy. I'll give ye that. To come after me when you know what I'll do to ye.

It was cause of my boy.

Ye boy.

William Junior. Willie. He was at the trial when ye butchered the town. When I come to he was gone and I knew you must of took him.

Smonk's good eye narrowed. I remember that little sneak, he said. Ike caught him, all right. Done stole my mule. Knucklehead's got sand.

Where is he?

Hell if I know.

McKissick had been backing toward the log and when he was close enough he dove over it and, airborne, kicked the stock so the over & under flipped and he landed on his back behind the log and caught the gun. He'd swallowed the eye again, this time on purpose. He raised up to fire but Smonk was gone, except for his voice, which boomed in the high treetops and dropped acorns and seemed to shake the sand.

GIVE ME BACK MY FUCKING EYE!

❧

"Give me back my fucking eye"? the blacksmith repeated down to his mule. He gazed into the dark trees. Did you hear that?

The animal didn't answer.

The woods were soundless and still, a picture of woods with him sitting in the middle of it.

Well, shit my britches, he said, looking upward where dapples of blue highlit the leaves. He was poking the mule's ribs with his heels. Why don't we get the hell out of here.

He goaded the mule to a run in the direction of the tenant farm. If devilry were going on, if Smonk was out in the woods killing McKissick and saying such a string of words a Christian ought never hear, Gates could sneak back and see the whore for a quick suck and a spot of licker to sustain him on the long ride to come. He could charge it to the judge.

Yah! he said, kicking the mule harder.

❧

McKissick peered over the log.

He's done for, the bailiff thought. Or I'd be dead already.

He stood up. He scanned the spaces between the trees. He saw a sparrow. He saw a chipmunk. A butterfly blinking past.

The sniper's shot he half-expected never came.

So Smonk was gone. His eye, however, was working its way down the bailiff's gullet.

He strapped his loin cloth on and cinched its knot. If E.O. had indeed retreated, it showed weakness. Here was their chance. McKissick turned, he was running toward his horse. He'd circle

back, get Gates, and the two of them would track Smonk and kill
him once and for all.

⌘

Gates rolled off the mule at the farmhouse and reined it to the rail.
He mounted the stairs, brandishing the empty Winchester like
Daddy used to, when he hit Momma. He looked around, then
knocked on the wall with the rifle-stock. He knocked again, then
again, and finally creaked open the door. A slab of light fell into the
room and the dark corners tensed. He stepped in from the sun and
waited.

The mule brayed behind him.

Dry up, said the blacksmith. He lit a lamp and found a jar of
yellow liquid on a shelf and sipped it but spat it back out. Piss, he
said. I drunk piss! In a rage, he overturned chairs and kicked up the
rug and stomped through floorboards and tore apart the stove. Not
even a shot's worth. That lying tenant farmer. Hell. By now Gates
was so ready for a taste he'd of swallowed the jar of piss if it had
been a drunk had pissed it. He walked onto the porch and glared
down the hillside, nothing except more woods and sugarcane.
Mule 'd got loose. Out in the field pulling up grass. Shit.

At the insistence of his bowels, he left the porch and picked his
way through the weeds alongside the cabin. He saw the tenant
farmer spread out on the ground, his throat cut. His face covered
with ants. Serves ye right, Gates said, stepping over the body. He
searched the man's pockets and reclaimed the nail he'd given him
earlier but found nothing else. Dusting ants from his hands, he
walked a few yards farther, into a stand of oaks.

The whore stood up from a crouch and grinned. She was unhooking her slip from one shoulder and then the other. It fell from the skeleton and skin she was and she glowed white in a burst of sunlight where the forest roof hadn't yet stitched out the sky. His bowels forgotten, Gates rushed toward her fumbling with his britches and she met him with her teeth bared and they fell coupling. She was a zestful lover who growled and scratched and bit, just the way he liked, and when he flipped her to her stomach and held her arms behind her back she groaned and took his wad which was all he wanted from any lady, whore or otherwise.

Half an hour later, making good time on the horse, McKissick with his balls bouncing on the saddle and his thighs blistered and his burns coated with sand rode harder yet and seemed to lift from the horse's back. They skidded to a stop before the farmhouse, the mule chewing grass.

McKissick ran up the steps and through the open door, rifle at ready. The naked woman, tied to a chair, raised her head and bared her teeth and hissed, *Did ye come back for more?* She writhed against her ropes and flung her strings of hair about and, still bound, began to scoot toward him chair and all. *I got some sugar for ye*, she said and licked her tongue over her front teeth. *Come here let me give ye a kiss.*

He stepped back, onto the porch. I reckon I'll pass, he said.

She spat at him and snapped her teeth, foam clinging to the corners of her mouth and her fingers clawing the seat of her chair. She writhed in her ropes and craned out her neck and in her fervor to bite him upset herself and crashed to the floor.

McKissick wiped sweat out of his eyes with the back of his hand and cocked the over & under.

Now she was scootching toward him over the floorboards. He could see scabbed-over bite marks on her buttocks and legs and titties. A wide circumference of mouth, huge radius of teeth.

Smonk do extract a price, McKissick said. He raised the rifle and fired and the concussion rang in the room. She lay still with a trace of smoke rising from the hole in her forehead. Behind him the mule brayed and a dark cloud of crows blackened the sky. McKissick steadied himself against the wall. Dern. He bet she'd been a good ole girl in spite of it all and suddenly he missed his wife.

Meanwhile, Gates had crept up behind him, and before the bailiff could turn, his own partner had whacked him across the back of the head with a rifle butt. McKissick stumbled forward with blood hot like sunlight on his neck and fell across the whore.

10

THE MISSISSIPPI GAMBLER

THOUGH SHE HATED TO, EVAVANGELINE HAD FORSAKEN THE PONY with the star on its forehead since to reclaim it meant chancing upon the speckled man with the tore-up arm and the rifle. She wished the pony well, hoped it got out of the madman's way.

Her head throbbed from being conked and from time to time her vision blurred, but she kept walking, trying to ignore the dog-tooth marks on her elbow, leading Junior and the children away from the path and north through the tangled woods as fast as she could make their legs go, ducking briars and battling through a vicious crossfire of thistle and thorny weeds and sticker bushes, her skin redlined with cuts and clothes snagged to threads. Snake tails melted into the brush before her and twice whitetail deer rose on springs out of the bramble and bounded away as if the bushes were air. She shivered.

Presently they happened upon some luck, a dry creekbed curving through the bottom of a gully, and they began to follow it, the going easier through the sand and pebbles. She stopped in the lowest, shadiest place she could find and dug into the bottom for water but found only more sand. Walking a few yards behind her, the children held hands in a line, quiet and obedient, with Junior bringing up the rear, slicing at green snakes with his Mississippi Gambler.

Late in the afternoon there was light up the hillside on the left and they ascended the incline using vines and at the top the eight of them peered out at a field of sugarcane with another field after it and field upon field as far as any of their eyes could see. Evavangeline was about to push through out of the woods when Junior tugged her sleeve.

Miss Whore? he said. You don't want to go this a way. That goes where I jest come from. Old Texas. It's a bad place.

She looked back at the children, standing half-asleep, their clothes torn to rags, thorn welts laced over their skin.

It's a town ain't it? It's got people in it ain't it? Ain't it?

The boy didn't respond.

She repeated: Ain't they people there?

The boy shrugged.

Ain't they no children to play with?

He shook his head. I never seen nare one. Ner dog neither. We lived there for a while. Fore that we was traveling around. We went all over the wilderness till we fount Old Texas slap dab in the middle of nowheres. They was real happy to see us all the men was and ladies specially and they said what job did Daddy always want and he said he always fancied being a bailiff. Well what do ye know, they said, they happened to be bad in need of a bailiff.

William R. McKissick Junior wanted to tell Evavangeline more. How the ladies of Old Texas had watched him on the sly. They were all the time bringing covered dishes to the shack outside town where he lived with his father, trying to make Daddy send him to school and church, but Daddy said no. Schools and churches was for girls and sissies he'd said. Said a man had to make his own way and wasn't nothing a book could say a gun wouldn't say better. Said that's why he liked being a bailiff. You got to collect people's guns. What about the Scripture, the ladies of Old Texas had asked his daddy. It could sure tell ye plenty couldn't it? the ladies said. Was it words scratched on paper? Daddy asked them. Most certainly, said the ladies. Not interested, said Daddy. Thank ye for the turnip greens but we'll pass on the sermonizing. Herding them out. Yet when William R. McKissick Junior rode to town with Daddy and shot marbles in a circle drawn in dirt or played mumbly peg with Daddy's three-bladed pocketknife while he was doing whatever business he had to do, the boy had always perceived the ladies' eyes on him from behind their drapes.

He shuddered.

Well, Evavangeline said, I'm the oldest and I say we bound for Old Texas. She burst out into the field, the cane a pleasure to tromp through the way the sugarcane stalks broke apart, the train of children following her, even Junior, skulking along at the end of the line. They crossed several fields without talking until she paused to hold open two strands of a barbed wire fence for the children to squeeze through.

As Junior passed, she took his arm. Even if it ain't no children, it's got men and ladies, ain't it?

Not no men, he said. Not no more. He dipped through the fence and held it for her, trying to see down her shirt as she ducked.

She let the children get a little ahead and walked alongside the boy.

A town that ain't got children ner men neither?

I told ye. I don't know where the children went, I never seen none the whole time we was there, but Mister E. O. Smonk killed the men. Ever last one. I told ye. I seen him myself a day or two ago.

The boy drew out his Mississippi Gambler. He give me this knife.

Can I see it?

Nome. I don't let nobody hold my knife.

I'll trade ye, she said.

He looked slyly up. What ye got?

I got two size small titties and one genuine cooter with the hair shaved in a stripe. If ye give me that knife I'll let you see em all.

Thow in a pecker tug.

When they walked on a moment later she was slipping the knife down the back of her pants and he was smiling. Far ahead they saw a cluster of buzzards hanging in the air. More were coming from the south behind them, attending some event of death the way stars attended the night. Soon she spotted the faintest smudge of smoke on the horizon.

She looked back at the children, dazed and filthy. Why don't yall set down a bit. It's some shade over yonder.

They walked to where her finger pointed, a sapling pine grown out of the field, its needles brown but not yet dried to falling, and sat around it.

She looked toward the town. Then down at Junior. How in the hell can one fellow kill ever man in a town?

The boy shrugged. Mister E. O. Smonk ain't no normal fellow. He's of the devil.

Well. Even if they ain't no children, and even if the men's all dead, ain't it a bunch of ladies there?

He didn't answer.

Ain't it?

Yeah.

Then they could feed these younguns and doctor em and see to they needs and yers too, and I could be along my way. I can't lose no more time on account of a bunch of damn younguns.

Why? Where ye going?

She stopped. For the first time it occurred to her: She didn't know, she'd never thought of it. Well first, she said, I'm gone to get shed of the rest of yall and the closest place to do it in is Old Texas.

I ain't going up in there.

Fine. You can stay in the damn sugarpatch then.

I will.

Hell Mary, she said. She stood looking at him. Okay, wait here with the younguns, then. I'll go in and check it out. If I don't come back by dark, you get these here younguns to some other town. Do not, I repeat, do not, come up in there.

Yessum. Will ye do me one more time fore ye go?

She looked down. No. But I'll do ye twice when I see ye next.

He watched her go. Hell Mary, he whispered, believing that to be the whore's name. Hell Mary.

❧

Evavangeline had been smelling smoke for half an hour when she caught her foot on a set of rusted locomotive tracks that stretched as far as she could see east in one direction and west in the other. She doubted a train had rattled by in years, though. Nearby, an overflowing well-pipe gurgled water into a clay trough, its bottom coated with slick green moss. At her appearance several buzzards had flown from the rim of the trough, this likely the only water for miles. Lesser birds had congregated in the limbs of trees, waiting a turn that might never come. In the woods back from the road she saw the twin eyes of a wildcat and knew it had been watching her a long time. It wanted to eat her. Drink her blood.

There were flat stones arranged at the well for sitting and working and she imagined ladies washing clothes here. She dunked her head and shoulders in the trough and nearly lost her breath it was so cold. She straightened up and shook like a dog, keeping her eye on the wildcat. She drank handful after handful of the water— strong taste of sulfur—until she vomited it back up. She drank more in careful sips and looked around. The strip of shade she'd found to stand in was benefit a dead tree with medicine bottles and jars on the branches. She adjusted the knife in her waistband and walked up the hill into Old Texas.

The town was twelve or thirteen buildings facing one another across the road and houses scattered back among oak trees and dead gardens. Fences. Outbuildings. At the bottom the road turned a sharp right and there was a building still smoldering from a fire. Its chimney so tall it must of had stairs and a story up top. Across the street was what looked like a mercantile.

Women in black dresses and veils and holding rifles came onto their porches to watch as she walked along the street. She looked behind her and they were following her.

To ditch them she ducked right and went up the steps and through the screen door of what looked to be a nice house, hoping to find a lonesome gentleman who'd take her to his room. Maybe a bottle. There was a fellow reclining on a sideboard and she meant to sweep her hand up his leg to his crotch and see what he had. When she approached him, though, he was dead. Hence all the flies. His brown face had collapsed like a fallen cake.

Hell Mary, she said.

Beside him was a settee and a pitcher of water, a tall standing clock and a chaise lounge. There was a newspaper on a table. Out of nowhere her monthlies let go and ran down her legs into her boots. She began wadding the paper into a ball and stuffing it into her pants.

You can go on use my newspaper there to stop your flow, a woman said. I used to do it myself on occasion. Usually read it first, though.

Evavangeline spun. It was a bent little woman in black. White hair glowing under a black veil which obscured her features.

I'm sorry, the girl said. It come on me quick.

Do you get cramps?

Nome. Jest get a good ole hearty flood, then it's done.

My mother used to say, Aunt Flo's come to visit.

Evavangeline wished she'd had a momma to say wise things. Or a daddy one.

Well, it's a nickel, the woman said.

What is?

That newspaper.

Shit I ain't got no nickel. Can I take it out in trade? Maybe get a meal, too? I ain't eat in a number of days. Who's that?

That was my husband, the lady said of the dead man. He was

killed yesterday early in the three o'clock hour by a murdering devil and his gang of swine.

The woman indicated that Evavangeline follow her and they
passed from the foyer into a parlor bathed in amber light through
the drapes and sat together on the cushy fainting sofa.

What the hell's going on here? asked the girl.

Through the window, she saw women gathered in the street. A
dozen maybe.

The lady crossed her legs and made a steeple of her fingers on
her knees and cleared her throat.

My name is Mrs. Tate. I'll answer all your questions, if you'll
answer mine. Now. One. What's your name?

Evavangeline.

Is that your given name?

Well. Somebody give it to me.

Who did?

How long does this last?

Not much longer. What's your Christian name?

My what?

Your last name.

I ain't got nare.

The woman frowned. How old are you?

Perty old.

Where are your mother and father?

Dead I reckon. I never knew em.

The women outside had congregated on the porch. One separated and came inside.

Miss Evavangeline, Mrs. Tate said, this is Mrs. Hobbs. Mrs.

Hobbs, I'm just interviewing Miss Evavangeline here. For our position. You ladies can go on back to your dead.

Mrs. Hobbs nodded and left the room and reported to the others who disbanded and disappeared.

Well, said Mrs. Tate. We've been needing someone like you in our town.

Somebody like me what?

To draw men in. If we can clean you up, get you some decent clothes.

Evavangeline looked down at herself. Her hands on her thighs. She had blood under her fingernails, no idea whose.

Why can't ye draw men in ye self?

We're most of us too old. We have six women of childbearing years. Three were killed yesterday, along with all our men. We need husbands now. We need men to guard us. To do man's work, grow the sugarcane. Someone as young as you . . .

Well, I can sure as hell whore, the girl said. I need to git some money together, you see, cause I got a bunch of younguns—

Children? The woman had seized Evavangeline's forearm. I'm sorry. She unclenched and leaned back and poured herself a glass of water and drank it in one swallow under her veil. Her voice when it came was managed. Did you say you were guardian of children?

I was, Evavangeline said, if ye'd let me finish my damn story. Like I was saying. I got them children, rescued em from a dyke and her raper of a husband—nearest I can tell, her and that raper was stealing em to sell. So there I was trying to get em home when they jest up and lit out on me. I ought to of looked for em but I been in a hurry.

They were in the orphanage west of town? Where are the children now?

That's enough questions. Now it's my turn. Who the hell is E. O. Smonk?

The lady looked out the window behind her, as if he might be eavesdropping. He's . . . a curious creature.

Do what?

Some citizens claim he's of the devil but I say there's no of about it, he is the devil. He bought a big sugarcane farm out east of here a year ago. We were all glad at first, so few men about, but then he started in on us. One by one we ran afoul of his peculiar temper and we've all suffered injustice upon injustice at his hands. By his hands. She stood. But I don't want to talk about him any more. Did you say you were hungry?

Yeah. For some biscuits and gravy. Some meat if ye got it. I can eat a lot, too. As much as ye can make. Also, I like to take my food out and eat it away from ever body. If ye don't mind.

Well, why don't ye go on up the stairs to that second door while I go get it ready. You can get all cleaned up. Change your clothes. Just make sure you don't go in the first door.

Only the advent of her monthlies in conjunction with her hunger sent her upstairs. Mrs. Tate had gone toward the kitchen and Evavangeline paused at the first door. She checked behind her for the old woman and then turned the knob. It was dark when she entered, smell of piss. Someone wheezing. She nearly slipped on the floor crossing to open the heavy drapes. When she flung them back, light flooded the room.

A shriveled white man-thing roped to a filthy mattress convulsed when the sun hit it. Unnnnng, it said.

She slid the window up and stuck out her head and took in a breath of air and saw below her a pile of dead dogs at the edge of the cane. A woman in black pouring kerosene on the pile looked at her. Evavangeline stepped back and adjusted the drapes to regulate the light. She went to the thing on the bed and frowned at it. Its face chalky and cracked. It didn't have teeth and kept pulling back its lips to show rotten yellow gumwork. The eyes opaque in a way she'd seen before. She bent and looked closely into them. When she reached to touch its cheek it tried to bite her.

Shit, she said, and hurried out.

The room next door was the frilliest she'd ever seen. She could have walked into Hell's furnace and been less surprised. Frilly curtains with frilly lace and frilly pillows on the bed and a frilly quilt. A fringed rug underfoot that you damn near sank in, it was so soft. There was a dark slab of furniture against one wall with a pair of fancy doors she creaked opened.

Hell Mary. She'd never seen so many frilly dresses and of such colors that smelled so perty. It was like breathing a cloud. Violet and pink and bright yellow and roses sewn from lovely cloth. Blouses and skirts with stitching so fine you'd be able to see the skin underneath. Her plan, which she was still forming, would involve getting food and medicine and sneaking off to the children. Not bringing them back here, hell no. Maybe it was a town full of witches. She'd heard of those from Alice Hanover. She'd keep her guard up. Look at this perty dress here. Shorter, show a little calf-leg. She unhung it from its peg and slipped the dead crow hunter's boots off and stuck the knife in the wall and shucked the pants she'd stolen from Shreveport and that floppy gray shirt with the knife slits and stood naked before the mirror stand.

A knock came from the hall and she went and opened the door, uncaring of her nakedness.

Oh, Mrs. Tate said, holding a glass. I came to see if you were thirsty, and if you wanted a bath while I got dinner ready.

The gal took the glass and drank it.

The bath's this way, said the lady. Still naked, Evavangeline followed her down the candlelit hall past a line of closed doors into a room with pulled drapes and a tin washtub centered on a rug. There was a partition for changing and a toilet table with colored puff-bottles and powders and brushes and combs in neat rows. Evavangeline chewed her nails and watched the woman move boiling pots of water from the fireplace and pour them in and soon found herself steaming in sweet bubbles with Mrs. Tate behind her scrubbing her shoulders with a long brush and trickling hot oils on her neck and rubbing soap into her scalp.

You need to let your hair grow out more, she said.

Ummm, said the gal. She felt like going to sleep but the scar from Ned was starting to itch like hell. She tried to rise but Mrs. Tate's hands held her down. *Shhh*, the old woman said.

Meanwhile, the Christian Deputies were cantering their horses northward, a beatific Ambrose at point, Walton in the rear slouching in his saddle, when the distance revealed an uncovered farm wagon headed in their direction. As they drew nearer one another, the deputies noted that the pair of mules pulling the wagon wore straw sombreros, slits cut for their ears, the entire clattering operation driven by an elderly, thin Negro, his dark skin darker still from years of endless sun. He wore a Danbury hat—the exact style hung on Walton's hatrack in his apartments in Philadelphia, the ousted leader realized. Fur-lined brim. Lizard skin band made from genuine South American iguanas.

Ambrose raised his fist and the troop slowed and endured its own dustcloud as the wagon-driver clicked his teeth to halt his mules. Walton was aware that if something didn't happen, he would be the first white man in the history of these United States to lose his command to a Negro. He imagined drawing his pistol and shooting Ambrose in the back of the head and telling his mother about it.

Behind Ambrose, the remaining two deputies, Loon and Onan, walked their horses down the sloping land to within a few yards of where the elderly Negro had stopped his wagon. The two roads converged here into one, and the parties were going in the same direction. Walls of dense foliage would not permit both to pass at once, so one party would have to back up and let the other go. Whorls carved by countless wagon wheels—deep ruts, savage grooves cemented on the face of the land—indicated this juncture's history in rainier times, submerged in water and likely impassable. Walton unclipped the rawhide safety thong from his sidearm and spurred Donny and sat alongside his fellow deputies.

Back up, uncle, Ambrose ordered the wagon-driver. Let us thew.

The colored man wore canvas hunting pants and a denim shirt faded almost white with silver snaps on the breast pockets. A red scarf tied at his neck. He held the reins loose in one hand and a short whip lash in the other.

I ain't gone tell ye agin, Ambrose said. He drew his pistol and tapped it on his thigh. Abscond, ye rickety old nigger.

Ambrose, Walton said.

Yet the fellow sat perfectly still. One of the mules began to urinate, then the other followed suit.

That's bad luck for somebody, Onan pointed out. Two mules pissing same time facing east.

For uncle here it is, Ambrose said. He pointed his pistol at the stranger. I'm gone count to five, he said. One. Two. Three. Four. Fi—

Wait! It was Walton. He threw his leg over Donny's saddle and dismounted. His hand in the air signaling "Attention," he hurried over the ruts past Ambrose's horse to the wagon and laid a casual hand on the brake and lowered his goggles to show how earnest his eyes were.

Sir, he addressed the seated Negro, who didn't look down at him. We Christian Deputies will certainly employ diplomacy when possible. But we are in a remarkable hurry here.

No response.

Sir! Walton repeated, knocking on the side of the wagon as if it were a door. Please, he said. Let us pass. This need not grow into a "scuffle." There are several of us. You are a Negro, alone and unarmed. Quite elderly as well. We are most of us young, white and armed. We are trained, well-equipped professional lawmen on a mission to better this land for each us all, irregardless of the pigmentation of our skin. And, I hasten to add, we have already encountered two casualties today, witnessed by mine own eyes, two men murdered by yon fellow Negro. I worry in fact that he desires blood again. So I beseech you, sir: Let us pass.

The wagon-driver had been looking languidly at Deputy Am-

brose who was still aiming his pistol. Now the stranger fixed on
Walton those eyes with their enormous pupils.

Naw sir, the man said. It's yall. Need to get out my way cause
I'm in a hurry too. And what I got to deliver ain't gone wait and
ain't gone want to eat yallses dirt all the way to town.

I beg your pardon? Walton showed the sky his palms— What
in heaven's name was going on here? Had every Negro in Alabama
chosen today to assert his independence? Now, look here, the
Philadelphian said, his voice rising in pitch. I'm normally very
conscious of the lower races—

Hang on, Cap'n. It was Walton the driver addressed. What
kind a commander ride all his men to a low spot of trees without
sending one or two of em in thew the woods scout a ambush?

Walton glanced at the trees, their dusty twitching limbs and
leaves, dawning with danger. Each acorn the squat sight on some
hooligan's "scattergun," as if Death had stepped onto the road. He
swallowed. Why, sir, do you ask?

For a long moment no answer came. Then the Negro said, Ye
buck yonder's demonstration of counting's done inspired me. Pick
one ye men.

Walton peered past the mules to where his troop, such as it was,
sat their horses. Why, sir? he repeated.

Don't sir me. If ye don't pick one, the man said, I'm gone
choose for my own self. He raised his chin to better see the
deputies, who were eyeing the trees for ambushers.

I must insist, Walton pressed. Why?

Cause whichever one ye pick, Ambrose called, that feller
gone die.

Walton could not move. That's not true, is it? How? he asked. A demonstration of voodoo?

Voodoo? The colored man's eyes shrank and his hat flexed back on his head and the wagon began to shake, as if it were laughing. He nodded to Walton. That's right, boss, he said. Show is. Voodoo fixing blink its eye. Or a feller out in the woods, one. When I count up to five you can see.

The Christian Deputy leader threw Ambrose a panicked look.

One, counted the man.

Not Loon, Walton thought. Not Onan. Both were studying the trees, trying to spot the sniper.

Two.

Perhaps offer myself? thought Walton. As a gesture?

Three.

Ambrose! Of course! Here would be his chance.

Four.

Let him shoot Ambrose.

Walton glanced at Ambrose and the Negro saw, in Walton's eyes, that he was about to be "sold down the river."

Fi—

Wait! Ambrose swept his gloved hand toward the west. Go on, ye old snake-doctor. Fuck off with ye.

At which point, not even a display of gratitude, the uppity Negro cracked his whip lash and the farm wagon clacked forward, Walton leaping to the ground to avoid being crushed and the horses scrambling as the wagon banged over the whorls in the pass and then up the opposite hill where weeds grew in the road, dusty white grasshoppers fizzing in the air like fireworks set off by gnomes. When the wagon was gone the pass in the road seemed enormous.

Ambrose sheathed his pistol. Hey, Captain Fool?

Walton found it hard to stand as his knees had jellied. Give me a moment, he said. Please.

When ye ballsack descend back down out ye asshole, I want ye to write a entry in ye diary yonder says we jest got backed down by one old nigger and two old mules. The second-in-command took off his gloves and threw them in the dirt. Shit, he said and turned his horse and trotted away, in the opposite direction the farm wagon had gone.

Walton watched him, then turned to the wagon as it squeaked away. Before he had time to think better, he'd taken off, on foot, in pursuit of the old man. Walton was not one to "pull rank" because of his skin color, but this was uncalled-for behavior from a "darky" old enough to remember how conditions had been before Walton's northern associates had liberated the slaves. For emphasis, he drew his revolver, which he had no intention of using, and was closing on the wagon, about to grab its tail-gate, when suddenly the driver whoaed his mules and the wagon stopped and the Christian Deputy founder nearly walked into its rear end. He raised his pistol— perhaps a warning shot in the air?—the same instant the tarp in the wagon-bed rolled like a swell of water and a fat bearded man elbowed himself up from the hay on the floor.

Who interrupted my nap? he demanded.

Shrugging the tarp aside, he clomped the over & under barrels of a long black rifle on the wagon's back rail, so close to Walton the northerner could smell gun oil.

Toss ye iron in here, he said. Keep ye hands where I can see em.

Walton complied, blanching at the horrific fellow's goiter and grizzled brown skin and its pockmarks, gashes, scars, and moles. He wore dark lenses with an eyepatch under one and a bush of wild red hair in a braid hanging over his heart and a sprawling beard that made his head larger. His teeth were red and the rattle of his breath like a dog's low growl. Perhaps here was a "moonshiner," Walton thought. Which might account for his pensiveness.

What the hell you supposed to be in them outfits? the odd fellow said. A fucking Mountie? Canader's a few miles north ways, ain't it, I? He laughed and coughed.

I'd prefer less graphic language, Walton said, gazing into the rifle barrels. He raised his hands, showing no threat. I, sir, am Captain Phail Walton and those men behind me are my Christian Deputies.

Christian? The man coughed and sprayed Walton's face with blood. Deputies?

The leader moved to reach for a handkerchief in order to blot the blood from his face when the stranger bopped him on the head with the rifle barrels, dislodging his hat. I told ye don't move, sissy.

Ouch, Walton said, suddenly dizzy.

The fellow had began to chuckle and the wagon creaked with his mirth. Ye looks like a bunch of goggle-eye dandy boys, he said. In them faintsy getups.

We don't appreciate that kind of insinuation, Walton said.

Shit, said the one-eyed man. The driver whipped his mules and the operation clattered off, the eerie man in the back laughing or coughing, it was hard to tell which.

Walton began walking backward toward the others, wondering

what ilk of black magic he'd stumbled upon. Was the peculiar man in the receding wagon's bed some "haint" of the backwoods? What monsters still roamed these southern wildernesses? Why, here might be Darwin's "Missing Link" or a specimen of the fabled "Big Foot" of western climes. Walton put his hands on his hips and watched.

The wagon was nearly out of sight.

Meanwhile, loyal Donny wandered up on his own and nibbled Walton's ear as the old man's laughter or coughing hackled over the fields. Walton closed his eyes and summoned what wherewithal he had left and pulled the clammy sack of his body into the saddle without opening his eyes. He let Donny walk himself toward the others and thought about Ambrose. How he'd found the Negro face-down, beaten nearly to death, in a Memphis alley. Rats tearing at his pants leg. Walton recalled frightening off the large rodents and helping the wheezing wretch to his feet, procuring him a bowl of turtle soup and rice and giving his testimony while eating with him and several other hungry denizens of the underclass, the Philadelphian thrilled by his own display of openminded philanthropy.

And now here rode that same philanthropist with quite a different mind, shivering on his horse, backed down, again, ready in fact to give his own man up. He remembered Ambrose "watching his back" on the riverboat and deflecting the murderous intent to Red Man. Later siding with Walton about the burials. How he'd said "bunker" with such faithfulness.

Perhaps it was time, wasn't it, for Walton to face the fact: Ambrose was right. He, Walton, was indeed an F-U-L, *fool*. Wasn't he out here in the wilderness only because he'd backed out of a duel at a Halloween costume party at an Admiral's summer home in Boston? With Mother on his arm, he'd gone as a "gunslinger," red shirt and khaki pants with their extra pockets full of "loot," the polished riding boots, ascot and hat. For fun he'd worn a real gun, unloaded of course. After a misunderstanding, a meaty, red-faced Italian "thug" pulled Walton's leather gloves from his gunbelt and slapped him across the cheek several times despite Walton proclaiming his innocence in the matter of the Italian's wife. Yet the Italian, dressed as a giant rabbit, shoved Walton into the seaman's rosebushes. He then kicked him in the crotch and spat upon him and threw drinks in his face. He hit Walton in the back of the head with his, Walton's, own pistol.

Walton's cheeks burned at the memory. Hadn't he, bleeding from rose thorns, knelt and begged his beefy opponent not to murder him? The man flipping off his rabbit hood now, blood speckled on his faux fur. Hadn't the Italian agreed to let him go only if Walton removed his pants, crimson shirt and underwear and crawled naked from the party? The mob of them (including a "loose" woman) following in their buggy—not part of the agreement—costumed in masks and gaudy outfits and top hats, swinging lanterns and spewing him with bottles of champagne. Banging cans and firing pistols at the stars. Later, the first strains of morning light had caught him sneaking through a back alley; a Boston police captain on his way to the station-house nabbed him as he tried to sneak into Mother's hotel. Wrapped in a dirty shirt, Walton was thrown in jail. His head shoved in the chamber pot by the degenerates in his cell. Lice in his hair. Instances of painful sodomy. Mother, her carriage-driver holding her arm, her handkerchief over her mouth and nose, fetched him out of the jailhouse. She'd brought him a scarlet hood and would only suffer his company if he wore it. His darling betrothed Miss Annie's younger brother had returned Walton's grandmother's diamond ring along with a letter he'd only read once but could recite from memory: *Dear Phail, please tell me which Parties you plan on attending in the Future so I will not. Never speak to me again. You should spell yr. Name with a "f." I wish you were dead. Or I was. Somebody. I hate you. —Sincerely, A.*

Hadn't Walton traveled "coach" on the railways south to this wasteland of dry sugarcane and human detritus in the very costume of his shame and with the sole intention of getting himself murdered? Would that not show them all? *Did you hear? Phail's dead! Killed in battle in a southern wilderness. He was no coward after all. We were so wrong about him. They're going to publish his logbook.* A perfect plan: South then dead. Yet somehow he'd discovered a niche for himself. His leadership had given these shiftless men shift. He added focus to their lives. He was their salvation. And might they not be his?

He gazed across the fields of brown to where faithful Loon and Onan waited, glancing at the trees around them. Thus far Walton had squandered chance upon chance for the glory of death in battle, "kill or be killed," to even his score on God's night sky of a chalkboard. Red Man should have been Walton's kill, not Ambrose's. Hadn't that rightly been Walton's mutiny to quell? And those deserters ought to have died impaled by Walton's sword, not killed by Ambrose's Winchester. And only moments ago, this wretched man-thing with his enormous rifle and rebellious Negro! They were obviously criminals. Yet was the man-thing dead? Was the Negro?

Was Walton? Had he fought like a man or surrendered his sidearm without a thought? The Christian Deputy leader straightened in his saddle. Strength had returned full force to his knees and he rose in the stirrups and clasped his pommel and nodded as he rode up alongside his men.

Deputy Loon, he said. Deputy Onan. He smiled grimly. Let's go get that son-of-a-bitch.

Neither man moved.

I see, their leader said. He lowered his gaze. So I've lost my authority completely. Not that I blame you—

Naw, Onan said from the side of his mouth. It ain't that. He and Loon were casting their eyes fearfully at the trees. We jest don't want that nigger's friend in the woods to shoot us.

෨෨

Ned's face in her dreams but gone when she opened her eyes. She lay in warm hay, it moved with her breath. She was glad there wasn't any shit in the stall now but there had been some here before. Her face was away from them but she knew that of the three women behind her two were having her time of the month and one was past prime. She tried to sit up but her hands were bound behind her. She rolled over.

They wore black dresses and veils. She didn't know who the two in back were but the one in front was Mrs. Tate, she could tell from her smell of her dead husband. She blinked and blew hay from her face and rolled over. They'd put her in a barn stall made secure with bars like a jail cell. Hay for sleeping. Slop jar in the corner. Nothing else.

Mrs. Tate held the Mississippi Gambler in her hand. What did you plan to do with this? Cut my throat?

Yall poisoned me, she said.

The ladies said nothing.

Mrs. Tate, Evavangeline said. Did I answer ye questions wrong and this is what I get?

I'm sorry, said the little woman. She handed the knife away. But you can't say names here. We don't have names here. You've been bitten by a struck dog. I saw the marks on your arm while you bathed. These other ladies have witnessed them as well. So we have no choice but to confine you. For your own safety. See if the ray bees have got you.

No, she said. She wriggled up against the wall and fell forward, her ankles bound as well. I ain't got none, I swar. That dog was my own pet dog. It never had no ray bees.

If you don't exhibit any symptoms, we'll set you free and you can be a citizen of our town. And if you do have them, we'll shoot you quickly and burn your remains.

But I got to go, Evavangeline said.

Why? Because of those children? If you tell us where they are, Mrs. Tate said, we'll bring you some milk.

I had enough of yallses milk.

Well. If you change your mind, tell the guard here and she'll let me know.

Mrs. Tate and another lady walked out of the barn. The guard moved a wooden bucket near the door and spread a dish towel over it and sat holding a pistol. She flung the knife which stuck in the wall. For near an hour Evavangeline tried to talk to her, but she may as well have been asking a salt block for a nickel for all the good it did.

Jest give me my knife, she begged.

The lady ignored her.

Eventually she gave up and fell asleep and dreamt again of Ned, this time wringing a pullet's neck with his hands and tossing it to her to pluck and secret the feathers away in a bag for a surprise pillow she was stuffing. Settling against the kitchen wall and breaking wind and letting her pull off his boots and then dragging down his britches. She woke with hay stuck to her face and beyond the bars her guard knitting a boy's sweater.

Ned had made whiskey money by whoring her out to passing men, signs along the road saying "Yung Gurl One Dolar" and with arrows directing customers to their house. Once a town lady big in her church stole a bunch of the signs and Ned tracked her to her house and killed her dogs and a peacock and threw them on the roof and said if she ever messed with his signs again he'd come back and burn her place to hell with her in it and all the younguns. She and her children had replaced the signs immediately, and after that everybody left them alone and a man or two a week was their average. More at Christmastime.

Once he was showing her how to make stew with the coons she'd brought in. Their hides were nailed to the logs outside to dry, hung over holes in the walls to stop the wind. It was not so cold that she needed to be bundled up, the fireplace glowing in one room and the stove in the other, and she moved around the dark smoky kitchen in a short dress made from a flour sack. He was at the woodstove dropping carrots and taters and onions into a bubbling pot that painted the air the color of a pretty picture. She walked barefoot on the dirt floor, then began to dance, humming, Ned's large fingers dropping in celery and parsnip and she grazes the slope of his shoulders with her little biddy tits and he spins in his chair and grabs her onehanded by her ribcage and pulls her face into his beard.

Another time she got mad at him for bedding a coon-ass whore and tried to poison him with gun powder but he smelled it in the grits and put her out and said never come back and she'd lived outside in the yard for near a month with him never once looking at her as she shrank and shriveled from lack of food not willing to catch a coon ner wildcat ner skunk jest waiting for him to forgive her fore she died. He'd come out to feed the chickens and step over her where she was asleep in the dirt. If he was riding his mule he'd ride it right over her. If the mule hadn't liked her so much it would of stepped on her a hundred times. But then Ned forgive her when the thaw come and he was out of money and more men was showing up needing they corks pulled. He took her back and burned her clothes and fed her and doctored her wounds and wormed her and cured her of the head lice and scrubbed her red in a tub and dried her on his shirt and then held her nekkid up in front of him lying down his arm purring.

He said, Evavangeline.

It was the only time she ever heard him say her name. Till then she hadn't known she had one other than Gurl. Every morning after that when she opened her eyes she repeated it to herself, so she wouldn't forget it. She remembered every hit, kiss, bite. She remembered the time he fed her watermelon heart. She would of drawn his face in the dirt with a stick but earth and wood couldn't do him justice. She could of smelled him in wind blown past a dead skunk if only there were wind of him to blow. He told her he must of got the ray bees from one of them coons though he never saw no sign of em. He said he hadn't told her yet cause he didn't want to scare her. Wanted to be sure she didn't have em too. But now it was time for him to do what he had to, he said, before he got all cross-eyed. He said he could feel his eyes crossing right now.

They were sitting beside one another by a fire in the yard. He'd been burning furniture out of the cabin all morning and not saying why. She leaned in to look at his eyes. There was something wrong with them, they were yellow and jumpy, toadfrogs drowning in shots of milk.

I can't drank water, he told her, slobbering. Can't stand the sight of it. He twitched. My thoat's all swoll. Come I's to hit ye last night? It's cause ye offered me a sup of water. Member?

Yessir.

It's the ray bees, he said. I run around all night shivering with em. I wanted to come in there with ye. I ain't never seen no ray bee but I heard of em. I feel ever minute like there's less of me and more of them. I feel like biting ye right now. He snapped his teeth at her.

She jumped back.

It ain't that I want to, he said. But it's part of me does. He snapped his teeth again and she slid a knife out of her shoe.

He looked hard at her and bared his teeth. I can't see ye as clear as I used to could, neither. And I got no idea what my name is.

Ned—

Ye look like food, he said. I would eat you starting with ye face. I would start with ye eyes.

Ned—

He clicked his teeth.

Ned! She put her hands over her ears.

Gurl, he said. I was jest fooling with ye, he said. Come give ole Ned a love.

His beard twisted into a grin that frightened her but she hurled herself into his arms nevertheless and hugged his neck with her arms and his belly with her legs. She burrowed her face deep into his collar and ground her cooter against him. He was nibbling her shoulder, hard, groaning, sucking, it would leave a good hickey.

A second later he was eating into her neck and a cold shock went through her. She squirmed from his grasp and dragged her knife through his back and twisted the blade and catapulted herself away. He fell with his legs quivering and blood painting the sand and the knife buried halfway up its handle. She tumbled over the dirt and slid into the foliage and lay panting on her belly and bleeding from her neck and watching through her fingers as he lolled and howled and flailed his arms, jibbering like a shot animal, tearing his shirt off and rolling and growling and clawing at his chest. She was still watching when rain began to fall and she was watching still as thunder crashed overhead and the horizon flickered in the distance like the backdrop of creation and he shook in a fit and his tongue flagged out black and thick and his beard was foaming.

She watched with her mouth wide open and cried until she gagged. She gagged until she vomited. He heard her and began to claw himself toward her in the dirt. He was drooling. His lips cracked and bleeding. She vomited more until there was nothing left to vomit and all she could do was retch herself inside out and cry and see him crawling at her till he couldn't crawl any more and then see him flapping his arms at her and baring his teeth, no pupil to be seen in the milky holes his eyes were.

In the morning he still wasn't dead. She was cried plumb out and shivering, her face salt-raw and scaling. His belly jerking up and down. The flies had found him, all the flies there were, it seemed. She waited as he grew black with them until he'd twitch and they'd all lift and for a moment hover above him like a cloud before descending back. She watched. DIE! she would scream. She hated him. Why wouldn't he just DIE? She wished she could go inside the shack and get his shotgun and shoot him in the head but she couldn't move. She was rooted to this spot. She watched the slow tack of the world as the shadow of the roof inched toward her over the yard and then past her and she lay bathed in its cooler air and remembered a thousand things, all bad. She pissed where she lay and didn't bat the flies. She slept at last deep in the night and was not surprised come dawn when his belly somehow still moved. She watched for hours hating the sun.

Now, in her cell in Old Texas, she wriggles to the backmost corner and grinds into the hay. Tries not to think of how at dusk, that day so long ago, Ned's upper thighs wobbled and spread a little and a red cone emerged from a hole in his pants. She watched, not breathing. It was a fat possum, covered in blood. It wiggled its way out, then Ned's stomach wiggled more and another fat, bloody possum rolled out and she understood that they had been inside him eating his guts. Suddenly a swirl of buzzards landed like an event of weather and the black hellish flesheaters stood swiveling their necks and hissing and looking at her with eyes soulless as bullet holes.

※

Let's ride, men, Walton repeated.

He'll shoot us, Loon answered, watching the trees.

Good heavens! I told you, there's no gunman in the woods, Walton insisted. I'm afraid we've been "bluffed." We've been shown leniency as well, I should imagine. That feral-looking "cuss" might have shot us all.

Bluffed? Onan said. By that old nigger in his wagon?

Negro. Yes. And didn't, just moments ago, Ambrose take his leave as well? Was he shot? No.

The deputies looked at one another.

Who? Loon asked.

Walton stared at one then the other. Ambrose? Our former second-in-command?

That stumpy nigger, ye mean?

Negro, please.

Hell, I didn't know he ranked me, Onan told Loon. I'd of been done killed him if I'd knew that.

Yeah, added Loon. We ain't got to kill nobody.

Could we continue this discussion, Walton said, in transit? He swept back his hand to indicate the road.

What about that feller in the woods?

Walton clenched his fists. For the last time, there is no "feller" in the woods! It's absurd to think that pointing would occasion murder. Look. He jabbed a finger at Onan, who yelled and covered his face with his hands.

Nothing happened.

See?

Onan lowered his hands. Then a shot cracked and the deputy flew backward out of his saddle.

Meanwhile, the children from the orphanage lay flat on their bellies with their hands over their ears, as William R. McKissick Junior had told them to, before he left. No matter what they heard, he'd said. He'd said witch ladies were about. If they saw a witch lady to run as far as they could and when they were far enough he told them to lay on the ground flat as a flapjack and quiet as a dead mouse. The children had seen two witch ladies dressed in black earlier and run a mile away and been lying in the sugarcane for the hours since. They'd never once spoken and barely moved and slept in fits, one little girl starting awake when her hand slipped from her ear and she half-heard a distant voice calling, *Baby? Honey?* It was a lady's voice. *Darling? Sweet pea? Doll? Angel?* then repeating the cycle but ending this time with *Dolly,* which was what this girl's mother had pet-named her. Dolly clambered up, still half-asleep. With straw in her hair and her nightdress torn and soiled she toddled off toward the lady beginning her list again. *Baby? Honey? Darling? Sweet pea?*

11

THE TOWN

THE BAILIFF, MCKISSICK, RAISED HIS ELBOW TO WARD OFF THE blacksmith's next blow and heard his wrist snap. He called out his own name and said that they had Smonk on the run, he was theirs for the taking, but Gates seemed intent on murder. He raised the stock again and brought it down and McKissick's world darkened at its edges and the room began to peel away and he was sinking in a warm, pleasant sea.

Gates stood panting. The rifle slick with blood. His face red with it. He staggered back against the log walls, his hands shaking. He couldn't get his breath, he thought he might vomit. McKissick lay still in his own blood. Dead? Gates watched a gorgeous blue knot unwhorl from the bailiff's temple as if his brains were about to rupture. Alive yet, or how might a knot rise? The blacksmith clenched his fists to still his hands and stepped past the dead whore and searched among the wreckage of the cabin until he found a huge butcher knife stuck in a wall and fell across his former partner. McKissick was naked and wearing his, Gates's, shoes. He touched the blade to the bailiff's chest where he imagined the heart to be and raised his other hand, palm flat. He closed his eyes.

He opened them.

McKissick had him by the balls. Gates forgot the knife and tried to twist away but the bailiff only squeezed harder. Somehow McKissick had gained the knife and swiped Gates across the chest and the gush of blood was such that the bailiff nearly choked on it before he could scrabble away and watch the man twitch and gurgle.

He tried to pull himself up and overturned a table. He couldn't focus his eyes. He sat against the wall, trying to catch his breath. The room seemed bright. Then it seemed very bright.

⚮

Meanwhile, from the hill at the edge of the east woods, Ike gazed at the irregular houses and buildings and oak trees of Old Texas. He'd done this slow circuit dozens of times before, the town globed in his spyglass as he scanned the angles and doors of each building and outbuilding. A ladder that wasn't there yesterday. The alterations of firewood piles and how long it took a splotch of birdshit to fade from a windowsill. There were ten widows in the town, ages he'd calculated from forty to eighty-five, and half a dozen young women and girls. He knew who lived where. Who'd had which husband.

Ike squatted and studied the ruin of the hotel. Looked like nothing saved, a total loss. He smiled grimly—Smonk always had been thorough—and focused the telescope when he saw a widow go in the livery barn's side door and, a moment later, the girl he'd seen go in three hours ago come out.

Shift change. What were they guarding?

Near dusk, from beside a tall oak in the southeast, he spied a wildcat crawling on its belly toward the well. It raised to its hind legs to drink but at the sight of the water it convulsed and ran down into the town snapping its teeth. A widow hurried out and shot it with a snake charmer four-ten. She returned a moment later carrying a pitchfork with which she speared the cat and lugged it out of his sight. Ike moved for a better vantage and found himself watching the smoldering pile of dead animals they always kept burning. The widow tending it, in her early forties, used her stick to help the other dislodge the wildcat from her tines. When the first left, Ike watched the second douse the new arrival in kerosene and strike a match and drop it on the animal which burst into flame. The dog and cat faces in his spyglass frozen in waxen agony.

Later, as night fell, he saw a lone boy crouching in from the west, ducking through the cane. Good stealth on him. Centered in Ike's spyglass, the boy became William R. McKissick Junior, the mule thief. Ike pursed his lips. How come he hadn't took off like a boy with sense would of? What in the hell would keep a body *here*?

He swung his attention back to the livery barn and wondered what or who they were watching in shifts. Could be something simple as a stock animal in labor, of course, but nothing about Old Texas and its citizenry seemed simple.

He was about to creep back around to his camp when something made him freeze. He flattened himself against the ground as two old ladies and the six dazed-looking children they led passed within fifty feet of him.

Come on sugar, the ladies were saying. Come on, sweetie.

When they were gone Ike lowered his eyes. Still at it, he thought. All these years.

∽◦⌇◦∾

On the other side of the town, as he lay waiting to sneak in and find the whore, William R. McKissick Junior saw the children, too. Captured.

Dern, he thought. Now Hell Mary would be mad. He might not get his handjobs. Double-dern. He wished he hadn't traded her the Mississippi Gambler knife. If he had it to do over, he wouldn't trade.

Yes he would. He wished he had it to do over so he could see her titties and cooter again. That stripe of hair between her legs. Her hand on his devil's tool as his own was now.

He got a nut and relaxed.

Naw. He oughtn't to of traded his only knife. Especially one give to him by Mister E. O. Smonk. William R. McKissick Junior thought if he saw Mister E. O. Smonk again he would cut his thoat with that knife. He thought that if Mister E. O. Smonk hadn't come and made Momma squeal so hard maybe she wouldn't of kept running off. Killing a man like Mister E. O. Smonk wouldn't be easy, though. The boy knew this. Such a man had survived dozens of attempts on his life. Man who'd shot his way out of fights up and down the map, yesterday killing a whole town's worth of men including his, William R. McKissick Junior's, daddy. A fellow like that wouldn't go quiet.

But William R. McKissick Junior had picked up a thing or two about murder in all the long years of his life. Number One: Whenever you're fixing to kill somebody using a knife, get behind them. His daddy had taught him that. Five years ago in the country of Texas America Mister E. O. Smonk had sent Daddy after that sheriff over in Throckmorton County. The sheriff had written a letter, against Smonk, to the newspaper, accusing Smonk of all manner of activities up to and including murder, by his own hand and by order. William R. McKissick Junior's daddy had to take the boy along on the trip to assassinate the sheriff because his momma had run off again.

His daddy said it would be a good plan, though, that nobody would ever suspect a man would carry his own son with him to kill a sheriff. And if he—William R. McKissick Junior's daddy—got killed before he finished the job, the boy was to get home by himself. Daddy said if he couldn't find the way he didn't deserve to get there. The boy remembered how him and his daddy took the train together and Daddy kept slipping nips from his flask. Then they loitered in the sheriff's town for an afternoon. Jest getting the lay, his daddy said. They used fake names (the boy was Cole Younger James) and sat for an hour on the porch of a general mercantile, drinking Co-Colas and watching the jail down the way. They had oyster crackers and tobacco. Hard candy. His daddy bought him another Co-Cola and the boy drank it in one gulp and belched so hard his eyes watered and the old men who were lined up on the bench laughed. They bought him another Co-Cola and they were all burping and laughing and the old men started giving him pennies and ruffing his hair and up till his first handjob it'd been the best time of his life, that hour.

Then his daddy saw the sheriff had got back in town and they excused their selves and went behind a building. Him, his daddy said. That's the man we're gone assassinate.

Assassinate.

That night they'd waited in the dark alley beside the jail. A stray dog tagged along with them—this back when dogs were everywhere. Get away, the boy's daddy kept saying, but the dog just wagged its tail and panted.

The sheriff walked by, right on schedule. He heard the dog panting and raised his kerosene lantern and looked in the alley.

The town clock bells starting bonging.

Is it something going on back in here? the sheriff called. Is that you, Roscoe?

Hello, his daddy yelled to the sheriff. We back here. I think we got us a mad-dog, he called. It's acting all crazy. But I'm a stranger to this town and don't want to shoot a dog that may belong to a citizen of this very nice town. I'd like to meet the sheriff of this very nice town and congratulate him on such a pleasant place. I'll certainly direct some business this way. If that's what the good citizens want.

A mad-dog, say? Toting the lantern, the sheriff had bumbled back to his own death in the dark where the boy's daddy hid behind a pole. As soon as the sheriff walked past him, his daddy appeared behind him in the yellow lanternlight and clamped his arm around the sheriff's throat and drove his knife so far through his back that the tip came out in the sheriff's belly and split the shirt. The lantern fell and burst. A fire started. The sheriff staggered to his knees, jerking Daddy off his feet behind him, and the boy watched as the two men struggled on the ground in the firelight. William R. McKissick Junior had begun to vomit, then, from all the Co-Cola. Ain't you shamed, his daddy said once he stood up. He flung blood off his fingers. See if I brang you one more got-dern time.

That had been in Butler Alabama. But this was Old Texas Alabama. His daddy was dead. Killed by Mister E. O. Smonk. Same man that stole his momma. Now, William R. McKissick Junior, hidden on the edge of the town, holding his devil's tool in his left hand, laid his head on the ground asleep, an ash of grass rattling under his nose.

∞

Meantime, having doubled back and hidden in the trees near the three-way crossing, it was a snickering Ambrose who'd shot Onan off his horse. He would've shot Walton next, in the head, and then Loon, in the gut maybe, but his Winchester jammed. He'd spent the next two hours trying to fix it but gave up in the end and decided it would be good enough fun to let the fools sit there terrified, pointer-fingers buried in their pockets.

Leaving his rifle stuck in the ground, Ambrose unraveled the ascot which he'd always hated and stuffed it in his back pocket like a handkerchief. He fumbled through his pants pockets and ditched the clanking paraphernalia he'd argued against toting. A sextant? A goddamn jew's harp? He boinged it into the shrubs and turned his hat backward which was how his father had worn hats. He rolled his sleeves up and unbuttoned his top buttons so his chest showed, its tiny black springs of hair, and retraced his steps to where his mount waited, eating poison ivy. Fool animal, he said and climbed on and donned his boots and egged the horse to a trot over the parched land, leaving Walton and Loon still on their horses, in the sun, waiting for doom. Ambrose began to whistle.

❦

Meanwhile night with its endless lines had etched the county black, and from the west two figures conjoined in shadow negotiated the rails of the fence at the edge of the field and hobbled together across the dust toward the dark back windows of Old Texas. There were no dogs to bark the alarm, and though the ladies had posted armed guards at the well and next to the blacksmith's place, with still another guard walking the street, they'd left exposed the rears of the stores. In broad-brimmed sombreros, Smonk and Ike disappeared between buildings and a few moments later the Negro returned and crossed back toward the cane.

At the Tate house, Smonk used a pair of nippers to pick the lock. He leaned against the doorjamb in the parlor. He held his walking cane in his right hand and a gourd in the other. The old lady Mrs. Tate snored, slumped in a rocking chair next to her husband dead on the sideboard. Odor of rot swirling in Smonk's nostrils. Something else too. His stomach growled. She'd lain her head beside the dead man in the nest her arms made, shoulders rising with each breath she haled and falling when she let it go. Smonk wiped his lips with the back of his hand and came clicking in his bones toward her and bent at the waist and nosed himself to within an inch of her mouth. She was tiny as a child but her face was a thousand years old. Hair so thin it looked like dandelion puffs. Her veil lay on the floor next to her foot, fallen there or thrown he didn't know.

Ike had returned in his soundless way with a pair of scatter-guns, barrels sawn down the way Smonk liked them. He had Smonk's lucky detonator and several coils of wire. His pockets full of TNT. He set it all down and indicated upstairs with his chin and Smonk watched him start to tote things up.

Without a look over his shoulder, the one-eye left Mrs. Tate to her slumber and ascended the stairs toting the detonator, resting halfway to the top and again on the landing. There was a door by his ear and he inclined his head and listened. He set the detonator box down and twisted the knob and the thing on the bed leaned its head toward him and snapped its gums. Smonk was about to go in when Ike came to the door behind him, the satchel cradled in his arms.

Eugene, he said. You ought not go in there.

Naw, Smonk said. He stepped in the room and closed the door on the old colored man and clicked its lock and crossed the floor. Moonlight enough he could see the ruined body, the contorted face. The eyes that he covered with his hand as he sank his knife in the invalid's chest.

Meanwhile, the field in which the two remaining Christian Deputies displayed stooped posture upon their horses had seemed its brightest as the sun died over the treetops; dusk had lingered, then, but at last night had commenced its slow overland bleed, shadowing the trees and shrouding the deputies in its cloak. Loon remained convicted that pointing meant instant death, though the proof had vanished as Onan's horse had tottered off several hours earlier, dragging the dead masturbator with it and leaving a swipe the width of his shoulders on the parched ground.

Now? Walton said. May we go?

Loon glanced around. It *is* perty dark.

Indeed. Surely yon "sniper," if he even exists, cannot see us now, the leader said.

Yeah, Loon said out of the side of his mouth, but he might be a dang Smonk or something.

A skunk? Are they nocturnal? I suppose they are.

No, a *Smonk*. Loon barely moved his lips.

Is this a local "tall tale"? Walton wanted his logbook, to make a cultural entry, but was afraid to retrieve it from his thigh-pocket. His goggles hung loosely around his neck.

Well, Loon confided, some niggers thinks he's the booger-man, I reckon. Say he goes about killing innocent white folk by tearing they dang thoats out. The ones that lives catches the ray bees and dies going mad.

Wait. Could this "Smonk" be akin to the hirsute gentleman we encountered earlier?

Do what?

The hairy gentleman in the back of the wagon? Was he a "Smonk"?

Might of been, hell. If that warn't the booger-man the booger-man missed a good chance.

Walton gazed into the night, toward their attacker's last known coordinates, as Loon told more gory Smonk anecdotes, and as the leader listened, he became increasingly nervous. Smonk burning down churches, eating children, laying with animals, peeing on young girls, biting people's noses off.

Loon was saying, It was one time, he caught a fellow in the woods—

Enough! Walton said. I'm going.

Go on, Loon said out of the side of his mouth. I ain't going nowhere. And don't ye pint at me, neither, ye dang shit-kicker, and do me like ye done that other fellow.

You mean Deputy Onan? Don't you know anybody's names?

Yeah I know they names.

What's mine?

Yer what?

Name, Loon. What? Is? My? Name?

Hang on. Who the hell's "Loon"?

Why, you are.

Since when?

Since quite early in the adventure.

Dang a bunch of loons. My name is Oswald Heidebrecht.

Whatever. I'm still going.

Jest don't kill me like ye did that other knucklehead. Omar, was it?

I told you. *Onan.* And that was coincidence.

Oh? Loon held up his fist and slowly unfurled his "pointer" finger in Walton's direction.

Fine, fine, the leader said, tugging his ascot. You've made your point.

They stared at one another, surprised at the pun.

Loon began to giggle.

Walton, despite his best efforts, joined him.

Their laughter rang out, an alien noise in this diorama of drought.

Stop, Walton said. *Shhhhh.* If he thinks we're laughing at him, he may open fire again.

The mood sombered, and soon the sky had pushed a red moon out of the eastern trees.

I'm going, Walton said.

Watch ye ass, said Loon.

Watch "ye" own, the leader responded. He tapped Donny's flanks with his heels and the horse sprang into a trot, eager to quit this part of the state's geography. Walton held his breath and bounced along in the dark with his eyes closed, trusting Donny's finely shod hooves. Here he was, alone in the South—truly alone—for the first time, fully expecting to be shot at any moment, prickles of fear hiving his skin and "butterflies" flittering in his abdomen.

Yet he was strangely happy.

❧

In the Tate house, Ike climbed the stairs to Smonk's room and dribbled piss in the slop jar and stood over Eugene watching as the one-eye labored for air and tossed and flinched in pain. Each breath one closer to his merciful last. Ike folded his arms. What a specimen Eugene had been long ago, down in Mexico. Out in the west past the Rocky Mountains. Ike remembered showing him the Grand Canyon. The Mississippi River. How to hold a largemouth bass by its jaw. He remembered Eugene's fight with a boy a couple of years older than he was. Ike and Smonk had been fishing in a deep-woods Texas pond that wore moss like a beard when a white boy of seventeen or so had crashed out of the bushes. He had several dead squirrels hanging on his belt and brandished his paltry twenty-gauge shotgun to rob them. Smonk had looked at Ike with eyes that were nearly white. *No,* Ike had said but Smonk was already on the boy who never fired a shot, and when Ike snatched E.O. off—careful of those teeth—he saw the bites on the screaming boy's neck. Instead of letting the boy suffer the horror of the ray bees, Ike dragged him into the pond and held him under. With Smonk skipping rocks across the water, Ike waited and watched and turned away only when bubbles stopped blooping in the moss. Then Ike had gathered their things, wondering (not for the first time) how Eugene could watch death's red flower bloom and throw another rock, eat another apple, go back to sleep.

Now the colored man took up his shotgun from the corner. Jest sleep on, he thought and closed the door behind him and turned the key in its lock and descended the stairs, stepping around boards that might creak, not looking at the dead man in the parlor or his widow drooling on the sideboard.

He went out into the alley and down the back of the doctor's and let himself in through a window. In the office he struck a match and read the labels of the brown medicine bottles and selected this one and that. He moved through the house and peered into the main room where the doctor lay dead, his widow standing at the window staring out. She sensed him and turned. He caught her before she could scream and clamped a cloth rag over her mouth, her husband's own chloroform fainting her instantly.

Outside he crept building to building wiring dynamite. He'd just finished and stood to stretch his back when he spied another lady in black walking along the livery barn wall with a bucket. She set it down and reached back in her hair and shadowed her face with a veil. Then she and her pail slipped in the livery door and a moment later the same door opened and another lady came out covering a yawn. She threw back her veil to the air.

Ike crept along the livery's shadowed east wall. The barn had spaces between boards and it was through such a space that he saw the girl in the cell. Lanternlight yellowing the hay. The lady he'd seen go in was guarding her. The bucket was her stool.

He twisted his head to better see.

It was her.

O God here she was. He'd never seen her before, but he knew it was her. He turned his shoulders to the wall and leaned against it, sinking to his backside where he sat for a long minute. He looked up at the sky. He didn't believe it. What you gone do next? he asked the stars. What ain't you gone do?

He hurried back through the alley to the house and inside, past Mrs. Tate in her restless sleep, up the stairs into the room. Eugene hadn't stirred. His belly rose and fell and the air seemed fouler from his dying. Ike set the medicine bottles along the table and selected one and another and mixed them and poured them into Eugene's whiskey gourd. He sat in a chair in the corner thinking. Then stood and squeaked opened the chifforobe and gazed at the colors. A moment later, his arms full of clothes, Ike left the room.

ॐ

When the key clicked in the lock Smonk opened his eyes. He rocked back and forth on the bed, gathering momentum, then rolled onto the floor. Ike was gone. He stood sucking air into the bloody scraps of his lungs. He reached for his glasses and gourd and unstoppered it and drank deeply.

Little morphine kick, he said, raising the licker. Brother Isaac, I thank ye.

He drank again and hung the gourd around his neck and took

one of the bottles and stripped the sheet from the bed. He hefted his lucky detonator and grabbed the coil of wire. Downstairs Ike was gone, and Mrs. Tate had barely moved, just the hitch of her shoulders as she snored. She wore black, which made her tinier.

He set his wares down quietly and undid the gourd and drank again. He found the snake of wire Ike had left and twisted it to the wire he'd brought and hitched it up to the detonator. He disappeared down the hall and returned holding a broom and, behind the old woman, flapped out the bedsheet and within a moment had employed a trick he'd learned from Kansas City teamsters where you fasten your victim to his chair with a sheet, tightening the sheet by a broom handle affixed to the back. With nothing showing but her neck and head, he twisted the handle and stood behind her where she couldn't see him and held her until she stopped convulsing.

I got some questions for ye, he said, blowing hot sulfur breath in her ear.

He thumbstruck a match and lit a candle on the sideboard by Justice Tate's head.

The old lady wriggled in her cocoon and he tightened it a turn. She was trying to shake her head but his hand had her face. Behind her, he looked down her length, points of her feet at the bottom.

You won't get away, he said. Especially if I have to strangulate ye. But if ye swar to be a good ole girl, I'll let ye loose at the mouth. All right?

Rage in her roiling eyes and the electric rod of her body, but he held her as long as she could flex and presently she went limp and he loosened the broom.

Okay. There. He lifted his palm from her mouth and moved

around into the candlelight. Red bars the shape of his fingers and thumb on her cheeks.

Who—her voice a jar of wet sand opened—Who are you?

He leaned his head closer and removed the hat and glasses, his good eye twinkling in the candlelight.

When she saw who it was her body spasmed anew.

What's the matter? he asked, muffling her screams. Ain't ye glad to see me?

❧

Christian Deputy Loon, meanwhile, heard a horse fast approaching and, careful not to point, tried to flag down its rider who seemed to be naked, burnt to a crisp, caked in dusty blood and carrying a giant rifle. But the stranger passed in the moonlight, racing toward Old Texas. Deputy Loon sighed. He took off his right boot and scratched between his toes. He put the boot back on. He sat for what seemed an hour of time and eventually lay forward on his horse's neck and entwined his fingers in its mane and closed his eyes and slept and dreamed of a town burning and a horde of women fleeing the flames and overtaking him on the horse, dragging him down, tearing him into pieces. Boy was he glad it was only a dream.

12

THE WAKE

EVAVANGELINE SAT UP. SUDDENLY THIS TALL NIGGER SHE'D NEVER seen before had appeared in the livery room and clamped a cloth to the guard's nose before she could rise from her stool and sound the cowbell. He let her drop to the hay and peered through the bars. He brought up a long finger for silence and knelt and looked her so hard in the eye it made her fidget in her bonds. He rubbed his chin, like a gambler wondering what his discard should be, then lifted the key off its nail and unlocked the cage and cut her loose and handed her a bundle of clothing and underthings. Up close she could see his coiled white hair beneath his hat brim. The gray goatee. The lines of his face that would tell stories if a person could read such maps.

He nodded at the clothes and turned to give her privacy. She stretched and flexed and stripped from the shift they'd dressed her in and stood naked in the hay and held things up to discern them arm or leg then wormed her feet down the stockings and dress and fitted her fists down the sleeves. When she was finished he crooked his finger for her to follow. On her way out she unstuck the Mississippi Gambler from the wall and concealed it in her dress.

Outside, the widow-guards began to shoot at them but hit nowhere near Evavangeline as she followed the mysterious stranger over a rail fence into the crisp sugarcane leaves and after a time into the woods. The dress impeded her walking so she lagged back and used the knife to cut off the bottom half. Under it the stockings came near to her thigh. The skirt material was pretty and, still following the old nigger, she fashioned a headdress from the cloth. It was too hot to wear, so she left it collapsed over a stump like a bride weeping in the woods. Because the top half of the dress was cumbersome yet, she ripped off the sleeves at the shoulders and rolled them down her arms and left them strung along twigs of knuckled black oak like tunnels of spiderweb. When it was still hard to breathe she unfastened the top buttons of the blouse and then the bottom ones, noticing how the wires in the corset made her tits bigger. She pushed through a brake bush and into the nigger-man's campsite where he sat smoking a pipe. Arms folded, wrapped in his coat despite the heat. He had a small fire with a pail of something bubbling over it, held aloft by a spit and sticks. But if he was surprised by her appearance it never showed on his face.

❧

I miss the sound of a dog at night, Mrs. Tate said, bound by the bedsheet to her chair. He'd hung a shawl over her shoulders to conceal her confinement and they'd sat for half an hour without a word spoken between them. Once in a while Smonk would elicit a squeak of air from her by tightening the broom handle.

From outside came the sound of gunshots, no surprise as the guard-women were prone to accidental discharges even when they weren't terrified. Still, Smonk signaled for silence as voices clanged in the street and footsteps clumped over the porch. A breathless guard-widow burst in the parlor and reported that a nigger had stole the girl they'd captured. What should they do?

Unseen behind the door, Smonk touched the tip of his sword with his tongue.

Let them go, Mrs. Tate said. We'll find them tomorrow.

The widow looked doubtful but nodded and took this order outside.

Meanwhile a flock, or a swarm—or whatever their group designation was—of *bats* had inexplicably attacked Walton and Donny, occasioning the understandably panicked horse to throw its rider. Walton's boot was entangled in the stirrup which battered him along behind the horse as it fled, shrieking madly. When he'd come loose at last, the flying rodents pursued their equine target and left the human one stunned in the dust. The same had occurred with the late Onan, dragged as he'd been by his departing mount. The stirrups, in opposition to what that sales clerk had said, were obviously inferior.

Yet somehow unscathed he rose, searching his arms for pinprick bites, worried about the dread "hydrophobia," sorry that his rifle had been scabbarded on his saddle and sorrier still that he'd surrendered his pistol to the horrific man in the wagon. Also, his sword was missing, as were most of the pieces of equipment from his extra pockets, victim to his being floundered over the terrain. He felt a passing anger at the tailor who'd assured him the pocket flaps were guaranteed "tip-top," and wondered what the rotund Italian craftsman would think knowing the terrain over which his pants walked tonight.

A quick inventory revealed that Walton had retained only his medicinal flask, magnifying glass, fishing kit and whistle, which he brought to his lips but decided against blowing. Perhaps stealth might prove a better tactic out here in such sprawling wilderness. Even his goggles were gone. His compass as well, so he had no idea which direction he should go. Perhaps he ought to remain here, near the site of his fall, hoping to retrieve pieces of the valuable equipment on the morrow.

Wait! The North Star. Nature's omnipresent Saint of the Lost. He gazed into the heavens and spotted that beacon of hope glimmering and counted it a small personal success. He wished he had his logbook. He rubbed his backside and thought of the bats and shuddered. Perhaps he'd best make haste. The full moon gave ample light for him to traipse through the "cane," beyond which he could discern a copse of trees. He made this his target and began to run, hoping the shelter would remove the danger of another bat-attack.

In the copse, he soon lost himself in total darkness and became entangled in a crosshatch of spiderweb, ivy, vine, weed and briar, quite a morass. Walton shoved at the morass but it shoved back and he thought he felt spiders in his hair. In a panic, he began to flail his arms and bat his way through, an immediate mistake as a low horizontal limb at throat's height laid him flat and knocked out his breath.

When he opened his eyes, he thought he heard voices. He rolled onto his belly, his neck sore and skin burning from its various cuts and abrasions, but his head felt clear, in fact very clear, and he knew the thing to do was steal closer to the voices without giving himself away. Remaining prone, he passed beneath the thickest of the thicket and presently the underbrush thinned to a civil level and he crept forward tree to tree, moonlight beaming through in columns.

Soon he'd spotted a campfire and, after discerning the wind's direction by licking his finger and pointing in the air, he prepared to come in "downwind." He'd have removed his hat had he had it. Instead, he separated each metal item from the other to avoid clinking and began to scuttle forward, noiselessly, soon raising his eyes over a fallen log to fix them upon the precocious Negro wagon-driver from before and, seeing her from the rear, what looked to be a bride with her clothing rent.

Walton's heart began to pound; he forced himself to breathe deeply.

Here. Here was his chance. He raised his eyes to the trapezoids of twinkling sky the forest roof allowed him and experienced the sensation of having arrived at his destination after a long journey. He bore no doubt that he was a fool. A coward. A—there was no other word—fop. Yet what other fop was here, what other coward, what other fool? Who else to help this woman? To save her from the uppity Negro who even now seemed to be thumping her a coin. Attempting to buy this decent woman for a "thrill."

Well, Phail Walton wouldn't have it. He'd reached for his pistol but it was gone. As were his sword and rifle. His knife. Here he was on a mission of reconnaissance, armed with a fishing kit, whistle, flask and magnifying glass. Think, Phail, think! What would Mother do?

She'd take a drink. He removed the flask and unscrewed its lid and endured the burning scratch of alcohol down his throat. He endured another. What was he to do, Mother?

But it wasn't his mother who seemed to lend wisdom: It was his own inner voice. Just calm down, Phail, it said. Take another drink and listen to the people talk. What are they saying?

&&&

They gazed at one another over the fire, the old nigger-man so openly, with such appraisal, it made Evavangeline fidget.

What's ye name? she asked him, finally.

Ecsenator Isaac. Call me Ike. What's yern?

She didn't say.

He puffed his pipe and blew a smoke ring so perfect she nearly chased off after it.

Where ye from? he asked.

That's what ever body wants to know.

Not ever body. Jest me.

I'm heading north.

You rather ride a horse or pony?

Not no horse.

He nodded. Why ain't ye wearing that hat ye made from ye dress bottom back yonder in the woods?

She watched him.

No matter how many fellows ye lay with, he said, ye don't never get knocked up. Do ye.

She shot him a snake's gaze. You a damn fortune-teller?

Naw, miss. It's jest . . . it's jest something I need to tell ye. Something important. It's gone sound crazy.

Be a dollar, she said.

He considered her, pipe raised halfway. A dollar for what?

Me to listen.

He brought the cob to his lips and the leaves in the bowl simmered and a line of smoke rose from the corner of his mouth and traced up his cheek and curled around the brim of his hat.

She looked at him and looked away and looked again. A dollar, she repeated. I don't care yer a nigger. She lowered to her haunches across the fire from him and hooked her arms around her knees.

Well now, he said. Since you don't care I'm a nigger. He extended his legs, longer than they'd seemed, his shoes store-bought and new, which she'd never seen on a nigger's feet. He removed a leather purse from his pocket and unclasped it and over the fire flipped her a heavy silver coin which she caught and bit and raised to him as if in toast and then popped into her mouth and swallowed for safekeeping. It got lodged halfway down and she plucked at her throat and hacked.

Can I get a taste of yer— She pointed to the whiskey gourd by his log and he tossed it across the flames and she caught it and unstoppered it and smelled it then sipped politely.

Go on finish it.

She grinned and turned it up and he caught it back empty when she was done.

Thank ye, she said. Shit. She pounded her chest. Whoo. That's some bust-head licker for a nigger to have.

Nigger's got a lot more than that.

He got anything to eat?

He smiled like a tired uncle and dug a handful of jerked beef from his pocket and tossed it over.

Chew it good, he said. Else it'll repeat on ye.

I hope it do. I ain't had no grub in I couldn't say when.

Can ye listen while ye chew?

She nodded.

Then let me get my dollar's worth.

☙❧

Meanwhile, William R. McKissick Junior was slipping through the alleys of Old Texas and peeking in its windows. His plan: rescue the whore and get his handjob. She hadn't come back like she said she would, which meant the widow-witches must've nabbed her. He hoped, as he searched, that he might see a nekkid lady. But so far he'd seen little more than ladies sleeping in chairs by dead men on tables or sideboards. In one of the houses he saw the six children he was supposed to have been watching. Asleep on pallets on the floor. They looked cleaned up, at least. He hoped the widows had given them something to eat and wouldn't have minded a cob of corn himself.

He went along the back of the house and stood breathing in the shadows. Something pulled at his britches-leg and gave him a hard bite. Rat. He kicked it against a wall and it fell and got up and lurched at him again, hissing, its ears back. There was a pitchfork against the nearest wall and the boy seized it and skewered the rat and left it to wiggle itself to death and went on, scratching at the bite.

⤫

I remember last October, Mrs. Tate said. When you first came to our town. I knew what you were.

What was I?

She stared at her dead husband but spoke nothing.

Smonk chuckled and stubbed out his cigar in Elmer Tate's hair and collected a dip of snuff between his fingers. I remember too, he said. That day ye mean.

A year before.

With Ike watching from the east hills, Smonk had ridden into town on a blind mule named Fargo, now deceased, past the well and up the hill and off the mule into the store. The man behind the counter had paled at Smonk's countenance and demeanor and his impatient claws clacking the countertop. He'd pointed him down the street to the town clerk who could help him with the parcel of land and the deserted sugarcane plantation he wanted to purchase. On his way, already limping with the gout, he'd stopped in the street before this very house. He'd stood staring for so long that Tate finally came out onto the porch with a rifle, making tiny, careful steps. Casting wary eyes. Said, Could I help ye, stranger? Naw, Smonk had answered, looking past Tate to the woman's face through the window-glass.

I wondered why ye didn't invite me in for a gourd of licker, he said now. Dusty as these Octobers can get.

She said nothing.

He offered a pinch of snuff and she shook her head. Go on have a dip.

It's vulgar, she said. A man's nasty habit.

You want to tell me ye don't take a dip ever twilight I'm gone call ye a liar. I can smell it thew ye skin. Besides, we been watching ye, my partner and me. Out there in the sugarcane watching ye town a whole goddamn year. So don't believe that it's a thing about all you old heifers I don't know or ain't seen. Yer pansy menfolk went down easier 'n a goddamn orphan-house full a blind babies. We know who ye bailiff is, too. My former employee. Followed me here. Did he tell ye that? Born killer, that one. Did ye know what was walking among ye?

She said nothing.

We know ye killed the judge, too, though I can't blame ye there. We know ye burn ever animal ye can catch. Know the ones of ye that still suffers her monthlies is suffering em now. And we know, he said, about yer church.

She glared for a moment, but then her wrinkles relaxed in her forehead and her bottom lip furled down. She lowered her head. I think I've changed my mind, she said.

There ye go. He came and with two of his sharp yellow nails deposited the pinch of snuff-powder against her gums.

You want ye teeth in?

They were in a jar of water on the table. He fished them out and held her jaw—Don't bite now, he said, grinning—and fitted them in and she contorted her face until they worked into place.

Smonk returned to his chair behind the old woman and they sat

quietly. He drank and replaced the gourd on the detonator. You got
a bowl for spitting?

No, I do not.

He leaned and spat on her rug.

Animal, she said.

Smonk cranked the broom handle and she peeped. Animal, he
said. Is that what I am.

I reckon evil happen ever now and again, Ike said to Evavangeline.
Here and there in the world. Can't keep it at bay. Start this way or
that way. People dabbling where they ought not. Witches and they
conjures. Tarot cards, crystal balls. Doctors with they potions and
scalpels. Men in congress with dogs and eating live monkey brains
and the like. All of em, meddling up in God business. Reaching too
far back in the drawer. Evil happen. Here, there. Started in Old
Texas a long time ago, after the War commenced, when the North
started they work and ever white man and boy in town and them
farmers beyond, ever one who could get on a horse and go got on
one and went. Volunteered like fools to die fighting the Yankees.

Evavangeline chewed jerky and listened as Ike's story began.
He told how when the War started only a few men and boys—too
old, young or sickly—had remained in Old Texas with the ladies
and farms. But one was a tall preacher named Snowden Wright.
He'd been born with one arm—where the other should have been,
up at his shoulder, was a nub with six tiny fingernails. As desperate
as the army was for soldiery, they still sent him back home (all four
times) he tried to sign up.

Once he'd resolved to stay, however, he took charge of the town, swearing to help all the wives while their men were gone fighting. He did their farmwork and preached Sunday sermons and counseled the ladies at their daily lives. He solved their disputes. Advised them. Whipped their unmindful boys and girls and comforted the wives in their darkest hours.

Then one morning, as he collected eggs in his henhouse, a possum dropped from the rafters onto his neck and bit him. He suspected the animal had the ray bees as daylight appearances were unusual for its kind, as was the savagery this specimen displayed. He caught it and put it in a cage and watched it refuse water and bat itself against the wire and slobber and try to bite him.

A thoughtful, self-educated man, the Reverend Wright had squatted before the cage for hours, clutching his Bible and staring as the creature snapped at him and ground its face through the wire mesh with no thought to pain or self-preservation, as if all the world's rapture lay in the union of tooth and flesh. Day, night, Wright watched the creature thrash itself to death, the preacher thinking, *What will I learn O God upon my journey.*

He burned the possum when it finally succumbed, and on waking several mornings later with sweats and shivers, ill at the sight of water, he had the ladies of his church lock him in a makeshift cell he'd built in the livery barn and assign a guard. Day and night he fought the disease, alternately praying and cursing God, ripping his clothes off, tearing his skin with his own fingernails. Bruises flowered on his chest and shoulders from his battering the bars. He endured fits where he couldn't remember his own name but also relished spells of clarity, his eyes pooling at the beauty of sunlight patterned on wood and a chain's oiled grace. In these calm moments he knew the position of every insect in the barn and could tell one sparrow's voice from another and see in the dark.

He called for his daughter, a girl abnormally tiny and sixteen years of age. She had good handwriting and as he lectured and preached she copied down what she heard. How his condition had revealed truth he otherwise wouldn't have known. The ray bees, he said, were the living key to God and God had told Snowden Wright that He, God, was making him, Wright, a prophet, that they should alter their church to the ways of his telling.

Write! he would shriek at his daughter when she fell asleep at the school desk they'd set outside the cage. He spoke rapidly, babbling at times, contradicting himself at others, his eyes opaquing as he squatted in the hay, naked as Adam in the bliss before the serpent, saying his strange, brilliant things.

And when Wright called to her from his cell, his daughter put down her tablet and pencils and slipped out of the school desk, straightened her skirts.

Get the key off the wall, her daddy said.

Because he was her father, she obeyed, she let herself into his cell where he rose naked from the hay. Because he was her father, she submitted to his will. Then he called for her younger sister, and for the other daughters of the town, and they were brought to his cell and he had his way with them.

In two days, when he started trying to bite the girls, they became afraid to go in, and he died within a week after being bitten, snapping his teeth to the last and incoherent in his babbling, his daughter still trying to write it all down. When they were sure he'd passed away, the girl disappeared upstairs in the large house where the family lived. She missed her father's funeral, so consumed was she to compare the views he'd dictated and create her definitive version. The document she presented to her sister and the other ladies of the church two days later was what came to be known as the Scripture.

What did it say, Evavangeline asked.

Ike paused. It laid out they new beliefs. And they mission. The ladies was to keep em a mad-dog, ye see. They call it a struck dog, I call it a mad-dog. Keep it in a cage, and that Scripture say the ladies supposed to infect ever boy child with the ray bees. The little boys they had already, six or seven of em too young to go die in the War, was the first to be *blessed*—that's they word—*blessed* by that mad-dog. They call him Lazarus the Redeemer. Them first boys to get bit, well, they all died of the ray bees. Ever one. But it was more little boys on the way, cause most of them girls who'd laid with Snowden Wright was now in a family way, including both his daughters.

All them girls, Ike went on, they knowed what was in store for they babies when they come. The girls had seen the ladies of the church let the mad-dog bite they brothers and they'd seen the boys in they cages. Going mad. Trying to bite they mothers when they come visit em. Ulrica and her little sister Elrica and all the other girls knocked up by Snowden Wright knew they'd have to let that mad-dog bite they boys when they was old enough. They mothers would make em.

Why? asked Evavangeline.

Cause they believed that when that chosen child got born, all they faith would be rewarded. All them other boys the ray bees had killed would rise up from the dead like Judgement Day.

∞

Stop! hissed Mrs. Tate, hearing the same tale from Smonk. How do you know these impossible lies?

Who was that turnip, Smonk asked, up the steps yonder?

Her eyes followed his finger. My Chester, she said. My boy. She blinked at him. You killed him.

I did. Chester's bit his last.

For a long moment Mrs. Tate stared at him through the candlelight. A tear wending down the wrinkles in her face.

Those were impossible days, she said. You won't understand. You weren't there. We ladies and children cut off from the rest of the county while the North destroyed us a boy, a man, at a time. We were all alone out here, fourteen ladies and twenty children. No letters, no news. Four long years. One one-armed preacher and one damned possum.

Tell me about ye daddy, Smonk said.

Mrs. Tate sighed her foul breath into the air. Daddy, she said. Well. He was fair enough to look at, I guess. Except for his absent arm. I used to be afraid of the little nubbins up on his shoulder. He could wiggle them. Used to make the boys giggle and scare us girls upstairs.

Her face changed.

But he had lovely black hair, Daddy did. He wore it long. Wore his beard long too. Gray at the edges. His back muscles were so pretty and shiny when he'd cut wood in that onehanded way of his with his shirt off.

The old woman inhaled and closed her eyes. He was a good speaker, too, she said. Of sermons, I mean. Every Sunday, a new one. He'd read from the Song of Songs. We ladies and girls fanning ourselves and squirming in our pews. She lowered her voice. If he got you off alone he could sweet-talk you, too, make you feel special, and so, by the time the War ended, we were all in love with him—even my sister Elrica and me, his own daughters. Our mother had died ten years before. Daddy would visit this lady or that each night and lend council. That's what he called it. But it was good council because he was in constant demand. Fix this fence. It's a fox after our chickens! My Jimmy's got the measles and high fevers. Come sit the night with him, come comfort my soul.

Smonk tilted his gourd. He offered it to Mrs. Tate but she ignored him.

When that possum bit Daddy we were all terrified. In danger of losing our only man. But he calmed us down. Daddy. He told us what would happen. Said it was God's plan. God was watching us, couldn't we feel His eye? And we could, somehow, Daddy, we could. You felt bathed in His light. It felt as if He had noticed us. God. As if His eye had fixed on Old Texas.

Smonk belched.

❧

Ike told how Ulrica, always a child who'd lived in fantasies, who'd played with sprites and danced with fairies, believed in the Scripture she'd written, and as her belly swelled with her daddy's child she prayed for the strength to trust the Lord as Abraham had on that unthinkable walk up the mountain when he was about to sacrifice his only son. But Ulrica's sister Elrica, who was fourteen, didn't believe the Scripture. The younger sister hated her daddy for doing what he'd done to her and hated herself for letting him do it.

But her love for the baby inside her got bigger as he did. She would not let the church ladies have him, she decided, she would not let them feed her child to a mad-dog. She left the house one midnight and walked out to the place called Niggertown and had the baby there but died having it, he was so big and she so tiny. Before she died, though, she made the midwife promise never to let Old Texas get her son. She told what horrors transpired in that fallen town. Even as her baby suckled its first and last from its mother.

What you want the baby called? the midwife asked.

But Elrica Wright was already dead.

Now that midwife, Ike said, she had always been barren. And always wanted a youngun. And now here was a baby. Like a gift from God. Saved from death. Her and her husband decided they'd take that child and move to the next county and get a house and raise him. He had dark enough skin, and cutting cane the way they did for a living, well, they knew he'd grow darker still from the sun. Soon he'd pass for colored and they would have they child.

All this time Evavangeline had been watching the old man's face. The orange pulse from his pipe gleaming twins of itself across his cheekbones. His eyes such bowls of black it seemed as if he could see past tonight and into her life before.

What happened? she asked.

Wasn't to be, he said. Those eyes of his looking down. Wasn't long fore the midwife figured out she had the ray bees. Cause he'd bit her. That baby had. Teeth already in. When the shivers come on her some days later her husband snuck to town. He seen with his own two eyes what was going on. Seen a boy mad in a cage and the ladies praying round him. Which was how his wife was fixing to die, too, he knew. Mad. Drooling like a dog. But she was a good, good woman. Name Inetta. And she knew what them ladies didn't know. Knew the redeemed boy they was looking for was already here, born with ray bees.

What happened to the midwife?

Her husband. He shot her in the head when she starting getting mean. He shot her in the head and burned her in a fire along with they house, and he knew he ought to thow in that squalling baby too. Baby born out of a sinful union and carrying the ray bees that killed his wife. Be better for ever body he was to jest go on thow it in the fire. Jest thow it on in. But he didn't. He couldn't. It warn't that baby's fault things were how things were. He didn't evil his self into the world. He was jest a baby. And then that poor heartbroke man smelled the baby's head and got drunk on it. He didn't thow him in. That night he left, rode a mule and led a goat on a rope and fed the baby on goatmilk from a bottle and raised him up his own self and loved him even though he was a evil little—

Wait, said Evavangeline. It was you.

Meanwhile, William R. McKissick Junior crept toward the south end of town, approaching the single-room church building which also served as the schoolhouse, and crept up the wide plank steps and stood on the porch looking in the window. The ladies had tried to get him inside this place before. Saying he needed God and learning. That was two things could never be took from ye, they told him. God and learning. William R. McKissick Junior didn't give a good dern for neither God ner learning. Heck. If air one of them ladies had jest flashed him a titty he would of gone.

Behind him somebody was coming so he jumped off the porch and ran east alongside the building and paused in the shadow of a cord of stacked firewood, looking behind him, waiting, listening. The rat-bite on his leg stinging. He crept to the church window and took the sill in his fingers and scrabbled up the clapboards and peered in. In the pews in the shadows he saw them. Dozens of them, very still. Praying maybe. Or maybe being punished. Grown folk did that sometimes if you misbehaved. Back in Oklahoma William R. McKissick Junior had gone to school for two days while his daddy stalked and killed a ranch hand. That teacher-lady had made him stay late and bang chalk erasers both days because he'd beat up several other boys. He learned to crawl under the school during play time and peep through the cracks in the floorboards and see up her dress. Then his daddy said it was time to move on and they'd moved on.

William R. McKissick Junior looked through the glass, smeared with his own breath, and imagined his head among theirs, bowing, praying, learning to write and read and add numbers. He pushed the top of the window but it was locked. He dropped to the ground and crept alongside the building. Back door locked too. The other windows. Then—heck—it was somebody coming. He slipped under the church and rolled through spiderwebs to the dark center and watched the guard-widow's black skirt-tails trundling the dust.

❧

Smonk could feel the morphine working. To test himself he hovered his heavy, flat hand over the detonator handle.

How do you know these lies? Mrs. Tate asked.

Smonk moved his hand. Tell ye what else I know, too, he said. War 'd been done almost a year when four, five of ye men begun to trickle home. Didn't they? Fellows with they eyes empty and they beliefs all sacked. They was skeletons, warn't they? Had arms off, legs gone.

How do you know this?

They wanted to know where the younguns was, didn't they. And how come all the unmarried daughters was knocked up?

She lowered her chin. Yes, she said. Some came back. Yes, they wanted answers. We told them what happened in a simple version. Told them about Daddy's vision and even as we told it, it began to sound false. But the simple men believed it. If they hadn't been so eaten up by the War they might have done something else. Might have called it all madness. Might have said that Daddy 'd gone crazy with the ray bees and made us all crazy, too. How had we listened to him? How many little boys had we given to our struck dog?

But them men, they didn't say none of that, did they?

No. Because of what they'd seen in that War. That Goddamned War. Because of what they'd done there. One man— boy!—who I'd known from girlhood and once had held hands with—in this very parlor—he returned home with that selfsame hand blown off. The other women sent him to visit me and he saw in my eyes I had a secret. He took hold of my hand with the hand he had left and twisted until I told him that Elrica had gone to the darkies to have her baby.

So the men collected they guns and rode out to Niggertown, Smonk said, and the niggers said the girl never had been there and said the midwife died of natural causes.

I suppose.

But when they dug the midwife up out the ground, it was a bullet hole in her head and it warn't nothing natural about that, was it.

I suppose not.

They found another fresh grave, too, didn't they?

I suppose they did. Without a marker I suppose. And when they dug it up they found Elrica wrapped in bloody sheets. But no baby. The Old Texas men tortured the darkies and burned their houses and barns until they found out that the midwife's husband had stolen the child and run off.

Out west.

We didn't know where. But before our men entered pursuit, they came here first. All covered in blood. They had Elrica in a wagon. My baby sister. Under a sheet. Said it was my job to clean her up. Put her best dress on. Bury her like white people. The worms had already been at her but I didn't care. Here was my 'Rica returned to me, and men with arms and legs off were already departing on their horses to find our stolen child.

She was weeping.

Them fellows never found the nigger, did they. Or the youngun.

We don't know, she sobbed. They never came back.

Wait, Smonk said. If them fellers never come back, then who the hell was all those sons-of-bitches got killed yesterday?

Mrs. Tate's breath hitched. Strays, she said. Men who showed up over the years. Drummers, some. Some thrown off riverboats. Others lost in the woods. Running from the law. We needed them to work the fields. We took them as our husbands and as the husbands of our daughters. We let them have any job they wanted to make them stay. We let them have their way with us when they wanted, with our daughters, hoping for boy children so we might find our promised child.

What if a fellow didn't want his youngun bit by a mad-dog?

Any man who objected was given to Lazarus the Redeemer.

Boards creaking, Smonk moved around front so she could see him. He lowered his good eye to within a foot of her face and she turned away. Loose strands of her white hair stirring in gusts of his breath.

Please, she said. Go ahead and kill me.

Shhhhh. He raised his swordblade to her cheek and turned her to face him. When she wouldn't open her eyes, he prized them apart with his fingernails.

Don't ye recognize ye sister's son? he said.

Meanwhile, a riveted Walton watched the old Negro and the unidentified white woman—age hard to judge from her back. He'd heard almost everything the colored man had said, a tale worthy of that delightful E. A. Poe, indeed, a tale he'd not have believed except he heard it with his own ears. And as earlier today he himself had witnessed the churlish villain "Smonk" in the flesh, Walton felt no need to doubt the veracity of the Negro's narration.

Now the young woman in her fetching dress tottered and the "darky" reached over the fire to steady her. When she turned away and Walton saw her face, he clapped his hand over his lips. It was her!

Evavangeline!

He stopped breathing.

He'd found her!

This ain't from no licker, she was yelling to the old colored man. She raised her shaking hands and snatched her arm away from him and her face seemed like it might cry. I got em ain't I? The ray bees?

Rabies? Walton thought.

They got me, the girl cried, ain't they?

Naw, miss. You gone be fine, the colored man said. He coughed. Jest don't bite nobody ye don't want dead.

A kind of "Typhoid Mary"? Walton wondered.

My head's hurting, the girl said.

I speck it is.

Why you telling me this shit?

Cause you got to go back up in there. Back up in Old Texas.

The girl sat down. To a bunch of old witches that done put me in jail once? Sorry to disappoint ye, Mister Ike, but I'm gone pass. I got a itch to get going north and nothing's gone sway it.

Miss, he said. Old Texas *is* north. You gone pass right thew it. That itch ye got ain't nothing more than burning ray bees in the air. It's piles of dogs and coons and possums burning all around. You done smelled it and followed it here.

I ain't smelled nothing.

And while ye there, Ike said, in Old Texas, ye might think about collecting that passel of younguns, including that McKissick boy. Help em find they way home.

Walton thought, *Children. In peril!*

How come you don't go git em? Evavangeline asked.

The old man looked into the fire. I'm done for, he said. He opened his coat and Walton saw that his shirt was bloody.

The girl was silent. Then she said, When 'd ye catch one?

His eyes shut. For the first time he seemed pained. When I was rescuing you, miss.

She came across the fire and sat down next to him and put her hand on his arm and listened as he talked quietly, so low Walton couldn't hear. The girl didn't move for several minutes after he'd had his say. Then she got to her feet and walked away from the Negro, away from Walton, to the edge of the trees.

It's one more thing, he said, looking directly at Walton where he eavesdropped from hiding.

She paused. You gone be all right?

Yeah, he said. Jest don't go in that church. Whatever ye do.

Meanwhile, William R. McKissick Junior used his head to bump at a board overhead. Then another. When he found a loose one he lay on his back and kicked it free and stuck his head through the floor. Instantly he snatched it back, the smell awful. Holding his breath, he tried it again and slipped his entire body through and up into the room. It was dark but he could see shoes and the ends of benches and an aisle down the middle.

Hey, he said. He rose into the church.

No answer. The pews, from where he stood, seemed full of boys his age.

Hey! he called, stepping away from the hole. Ye bunch a town sissies.

Behind him was a table. Still eyeing the shadowy audience, he swept his hand over the dust until he felt a box of matches. He turned, his breath held. The box rattled in his fingers. He snapped the first stick in half and dropped the second. The third flared,

showing a pair of candles on the table. He lit them and held both
candles out before him and faced to the room like a celebrant, and,
remembering to breathe, stepped into the aisle. Flickering down
the front pews and hazy in the rows behind were the faces of boys.
Dozens of boys. All wearing neckties, dark church suits. Some of
their heads were cocked to the side and some tilted forward, showing widow's peaks and cowlicks. Some tilted back. Many of their
eyes were closed, others half-mast. They looked sleepy. Their
mouths were open. William R. McKissick Junior bent closer to
the front row. Some of the boys seemed to be tied with twine to
keep them upright. Their cheeks were drawn and gray.

Hey, sissies, he whispered. I can whirp ye all.

As if in answer, a cockroach flickered across the face closest to
him and William R. McKissick Junior banged back into the table,
its leg chirping on the floor. He clambered underneath dropping
the candles and scrabbled out the other side overturning the pulpit
and began to claw the floor for the hole he'd used to get in. He
couldn't find it, couldn't find it, couldn't find it. Hell Mary! he
yelled. Behind him, in the light from the burning rug, the heads
were moving.

13

THE FIRE

MEANWHILE, SOUTH END OF TOWN, MCKISSICK SLOWED HIS HORSE and leapt off despite his aching side and broken wrist. He splashed water from the trough onto his face and covered his privates with his hand as a guard-lady approached down the hill with a shotgun trained on him. He moved behind the trough to hide his pecker and balls and recognized the attractive daughter of Hobbs the undertaker. He bet Smonk had bedded her. She frowned at him, the blood, his burnt skin.

Bailiff McKissick? Is that you?

Yeah. You can go on put that gun down.

She pointed it away from him and craned her neck to see his crotch. You all right? Who done that to ye head? It's all swoll. She circled and he circled opposite her, keeping the trough between them.

Can I borry ye wrap yonder?

She looked doubtful a moment then unsnagged it from her shoulders and tossed it over the water. He caught it and fastened it around his waist.

She watched him. Did ye find Smonk?

I did.

And done with him?

Yeah. Have ye seen Willie?

Naw, but Mrs. Tate might did. They fount a bunch a younguns. Praise Jesus ye killed him. You want to come back to our barn?

Not jest yet, he said. Stay here. If ye hear shooting, get behind the trough yonder and murder whoever comes running.

She let him pass, inspecting his buttocks, and he put Smonk's over & under under his arm and crutched up the hill with his broken wrist held by his heart. He hobbled along the backs of buildings to the Tate house where he tried the rear door handle. It was unlocked so he entered and stood within the hall in the dark. He clicked the rifle's safety off and the sound was enormous in the room. He squeaked open the parlor door, inserting the barrels, and saw Mrs. Tate sitting by her dead husband.

Bailiff McKissick? She strained to see. Is that you?

He stepped into the room.

Yes ma'am, he said. I'll give ye Smonk's eye if ye know where my boy is—!

A giant hand had fallen upon his head. McKissick felt himself turned like an auger. Hot breath blasted his face, flecks of blood in his eyes. The rifle slipped from his grip and Smonk's other hand caught it before it landed.

Thank ye for bringing this Winchester back, fellow, he said. I was always partial to it. Now where's my fucking eye?

First tell me where my boy is.

Smonk pushed McKissick's head away like a tent evangelical and the bailiff backpedaled toward the detonator and fell beside it and knocked it askant with his broken arm.

Get up, killer. Smonk checked the 45-70's loads and snapped the gun shut and lurched over to McKissick, the room seeming to tilt with his weight. Give me my eye.

The bailiff had no strength left and no feeling in his broken wrist. His side was bleeding, his head felt like an anvil. He noticed the detonator and spidered his good hand up to the corner of the casing and seized the bottom of the plunger the way a man grips an ax.

Back, he panted, or I'll blow it.

Including ye boy, Smonk said. He's down yonder other end of town with a bunch of younguns these old whores stold. Auntie here and her coven of witches is fixing to turn they mad-dog on em.

McKissick's grip failed and his hand melted from the handle. Willie? He's here?

Smonk had advanced. He edged the detonator away with his foot and touched the fallen man's throat with the tip of his sword and traced it down his gullet, slowly, a long welt in its wake and then a faint line of blood.

My . . . Willie? McKissick gasped.

Smonk straddled the bailiff and sat so hard upon the man's chest that blood spewed out of his mouth and burst like a fist from his wound, a penny like magic in Smonk's fingernails.

Here's ye tip, bailiff, he said. I thank ye for my rifle's safe return.

I would, McKissick gasped. Wouldn't take no penny from you—

I insist, Smonk growled, and with a slight lift of his eyebrows he ground the coin into McKissick's left eye socket with his thumb. Under him the man's shoulders shuddered and his legs kicked and floundered. Mrs. Tate screamed until Smonk reached his free hand up and cranked the broom handle and she blacked out. Meanwhile the one-eye had snaked his long trigger finger around the side of the bailiff's head and dug it into his earhole. He wormed it deep in the canal past a spongy substance until his finger touched his thumb.

Two hummingbirds, McKissick's mouth said without sound. Father and son.

And he expired.

Smonk groped to his feet using a rail of wainscotting and lifted the man once an assassin, once a bailiff into the air by his head and held him there limply like a large catfish and raked his sword down McKissick's front. Among what sloshed across the rug was one rolling eye.

☙

Evavangeline trotted to the edge of the woods and kicked off her shoes and scrabbled up an oak and wove to the tree's topmost where the capping branchwork was thin as her own interlaced fingers. She swayed among the leaves as if she weighed nothing at all, the dark squares and rectangles of Old Texas in the distance like blocks laid out by a child and painted otherworldly by the moon's red glare. This town Ike had called cursed by God for what it did. Where the people reached. What they pulled out.

Eugene is pure evil turned into God's right hand, Ike had whispered in her ear, *and it done swept thew Old Texas. It took the men, that right hand. Took em all. And it's time for the other hand to land.*

She'd said, *He's my daddy, ain't he?*

Ike hadn't answered except to say, *You don't need to see him. No matter what.*

Now in the sky the girl's hair blew. It was up to her. Kill the women. Rescue the children. Don't see Smonk. Well hell Mary, she told the air.

❧

Back at the campfire, Walton stepped out of the bramble behind where the old Negro had lain down. The Philadelphian had a cudgel of wood for his weapon and was half-drunk from his flask. As he closed in on the prone man, he raised the log high.

You gone hit me with that, the Negro said, make it a good shot. Jest one, if ye will.

Walton's club froze. He circled the fire lowering his arm until he could see the man's face. There was blood on the ground and an empty pail.

The lost Mountie, said the Negro.

Yes. It is I, Phail Walton. We met earlier. I'm afraid I'm somewhat tipsy.

Forget earlier, the man said. It seemed to hurt him to speak. You been spying on me bout a hour, so you know you got to go help that girl. Help her git them younguns out that town fore Smonk blow ever thing up or them ladies feeds em to they mad-dog.

Sir, Walton said. Excuse me. I have a few question, if you don't—

But the man's eyes had closed.

Sir? *Sir?*

Walton waited in the immensity of trees. Around them the

night. When he looked up he saw how far-scattered were the stars which were but an infinitesimal amount of God's power and reach. The unscrolling dust cast by His hand.

He knelt at the Negro's side and folded the man's hands over his chest and placed the Danbury hat over his face. He relieved him of his scattergun and a skinning knife. Had he his logbook he'd have written a receipt. Then he was glad he didn't have it. He closed his eyes. Lord, he prayed silently, I do not know this man from your own Adam made from dirt, but I cannot name a thing I've witnessed of him that causes me to question his integrity. In fact, one thing I can truthfully say of him is this: "He hath bested a fool." Travel with me, O Lord, on this journey to save Thy children. I ask it of You in Your Own Name. Amen.

❧

Meanwhile, Evavangeline descended the tree like something poured down its trunk and landed in a crouch. She left her shoes on the ground and ran through the woods and fields to the outskirts of Old Texas. She watched the row of houses in back of the stores, the dark windows. She scampered unnoticed by the moon over the dry grass toward the first house and entered through the back door, easy as it was to pick with a nail.

Inside she sank to all fours and skittered over the floorboards and crept along the wall in the front room. Here was the town's dead lawyer displayed on his own desk and his widow asleep in her chair, head thrown back. Evavangeline circled her on the floor and twined through the chair legs and buried her head in the lady's skirts. She chose the left calf and warmed the skin with her breath then kissed it open-mouthed, nuzzled the soft meat, slowly latching on. Above her the widow stirred but Evavangeline chewed so gently the crone only sighed and slumbered deeper into a dream of the trip south early in her life when her family slept beneath the wagon and a coral snake crawled into Uncle Lloyd's bedroll and bit him several times. Uncle Lloyd never woke because such a snake chews, doesn't strike, its poison in.

At the town clerk's house she found his widow strewn across her bed, the husband unattended in the next room, his humors puddling on the floor. Evavangeline lay on the bed alongside the woman's thigh and peeled down her stocking and kissed her behind the knee and tongued the mole that grew there and rubbed her teeth against the skin as the woman shifted and groaned and the girl nibbled and tasted blood and closed her eyes. Her skin buzzing and hot. In one house the stolen children were sleeping on the floor and their guard sleeping in a rocking chair. Evavangeline bit the guard on her side and, as she crawled through a window, one little girl raised her head but saw only drapes flapping.

Evavangeline found the liveryman's widow awake, gazing at the empty jail cell, and used a hoe to knock her flat and bit her under the right tit which had plopped out of her dress when she fell. She found the doctor's widow tied to her chair but asleep and without wondering at this oddity gnawed the ray bees into her calf which was shaved and soft.

She dropped from a rafter behind the guard at the blacksmith's and boxed her ears and slugged her across the face and left a reddening imprint of her teeth on the left cheek of the woman's ass and at the opposite end of town shattered a bottle from the bottle tree over the guard's head and bit her on the neck. She bit Mrs. Hobbs, the undertaker's widow, on her nipple and the woman convulsed but never woke. On through the town, house to house, widow to widow, calf to armpit to lower back to thigh, the women dreaming of moist sugarcane you bite and suck. Of their nursing babies of long ago, the pricks of pleasure from their first teeth. Of Snowden Wright in his heyday as he swung his ax in that one-handed way of his, visiting each lady as he did in the dark hours and ministering to their needs as their husbands would have had they not been off killing and dying.

Lastly she walked along the street with dust curling over her feet. Evavangeline Smonk. In her left hand the Mississippi Gambler and in the right a four-ten snake charmer unclenched from a sleeping widow's hand. She had one shell. She ran her tongue across her teeth. In the moonlight she could smell him. A thick odor, woodsmoke with old meat cooking over it. She wanted to bite something. She took the porch stairs in one step and crossed the planks and the door swung in.

She heard voices. A man's, a woman's. She floated through the dark, drunk on his scent, repeating what Ike said.

You don't need to see him. No matter what.

She opened the parlor door and there he sat. In his red enormity. Eugene Oregon Smonk.

Upon her entrance he'd simultaneously raised the over & under barrels of his 45-70 and snuffed the candle. But it didn't matter, she could see in the dark. Could see a detonator and its wire coiling out of the room. See tiny Mrs. Tate contained in a sheet, only her neck and head showing. The points of her feet. Her dead husband on the table with a cloth over his face and another dead fellow half-naked on the floor, his guts soaking the rug.

Evavangeline closed the door. Smonk lowered his rifle and sat it across his knees and took a long hard pull off his gourd, watching her. Where'd ye come from? he growled.

She shrugged. She liked his blue glasses.

What town, girl? The air sulfury with his breath.

I don't know. I been in Shreveport.

Shreveport, he said. I been there. He showed his teeth.

Mobile, she said. I been there once.

Yeah.

She liked his voice. San Antonio.

Yeah, he said. I spent a year there one week. He flapped a hand at her. Put that gun down, youngun, so we can enjoy our reunion here without fear of getting shot. You wouldn't murder ye daddy, would ye?

She kept the four-ten aimed true at his heart. I ain't decided yet.

Ain't decided yet. He grinned at her. What about ye momma?

I never knew her. Is my name Smonk?

No. It was Mrs. Tate who answered. Smonk is a darky word, she said, not to be spoken within these walls.

Shut yer yap, Smonk said. He pulled on his beard.

Snow! Mrs. Tate hissed. Light a candle so I can see my great-niece.

He twisted the broom handle and air squeaked out. Call me that one more time and I'll crank so tight yule bleed from ever hole.

No, the girl said. Don't kill her. Not till I figured this all out. Jest go on light a damn candle. *Daddy*.

He struck a match up his leg and touched the flame to one of the candles on the table by the late Justice Tate. For a moment Mrs. Tate squinted at Evavangeline, trying to puzzle her out of the dark. Then her wrinkles narrowed.

You!

Yeah, said the girl. It's me, escaped. Now say ye damn piece.

Mrs. Tate haled in a breath of air and exhaled it and did this several times as her color paled to its normal white.

Why don't ye come over here, Smonk said to the girl. Set on my lap.

Listen at her first. Evavangeline pointed the knife at Mrs. Tate, but Smonk wouldn't take his eye from the girl.

This is hard to tell. The old lady frowned, as if she needed to belch. But my time, she said, with Daddy, it bestowed Chester unto me. Chester. He was the only boy to survive after Lazarus the Redeemer blessed him. But even though Chess didn't die, he still wasn't— She writhed within her sheet, as if she needed her hands to talk. He still wasn't right. In his head.

What about before ye let that dog at him? Smonk asked.

She didn't answer.

What about him? the girl asked, pointing the knife at Smonk.

Mrs. Tate sagged in her sheet. My sister Elrica, she said. My sister Elrica's time with Daddy resulted in him.

E. O. Smonk, he said, patting his thigh for her to come sit. At yer service.

That Ike, the girl said, her arm growing heavy with the snake charmer's weight, he said we evil.

Evil! Smonk spat on the floor. Horseshit. If we so evil how come Ike never killed us? I seen him kill plenty of evil folks but he never killed me. Did he kill you? He tossed the gourd to the gal.

She caught it in her elbow crook and uncorked it with her teeth and turned it up.

Stop drinking, both of you, Mrs. Tate said. Don't yall see? If I bore Chester from Daddy's seed, and Elrica bore you, Snow, from Daddy, then it's obvious that it's something within our family. I don't know who this girl is but she must be some relation of ours, a second or third cousin, there are Wrights all over Texas. The ray bees have chosen the Tates. Chester wasn't right in the head but the ray bees didn't kill him, either. Somehow he lived. That must mean we—we Tates—are carriers of them, of the ray bees. Our family alone. Don't you see, the two of you? Don't you?

I see a perty little gal, Smonk said, grinning at Evavangeline. That's what I see.

I don't see shit, the girl said.

Mrs. Tate leaned forward. You must seed this child, Snowden, right now, or our name will die. Our *kind* will.

Oh I plan to, Smonk said, but I done told ye about calling me that. He laid his hand on her tiny shoulder and shoved himself upright, upsetting her so that she squawked and tipped and crashed to the floor, still affixed to her chair.

Smonk stood on uncertain legs, opened his arms. Come here, gal, he said. Give ye ole daddy a *hug*.

Evavangeline took a step forward. The knife dropped to the floor and stuck upright. The gun slithered out of her hand and fell to the rug. It's evil, she said. But when she looked at Smonk a strange thing happened. Somehow he didn't seem evil and he wasn't ugly and misshapen and old and bloody. He was her daddy. He was only her daddy and she thought he was beautiful. Her guts felt like they'd shifted in his direction and she could feel the ray bees all through herself. They were buzzing in her teeth. Her hair stood on end, her skin tingling. Her nipples hot knobs. The gourd fell from her grip and her hands when she raised them to her mouth were shaking.

❧

Meanwhile, the town seemed peaceful, somnolent, not a "smidgen" of evil in the October moon's crimson light. But while it might appear lovely, Walton had learned that in such desolate southern climes things were "seldom as they seemed," a world of plague and temptation, madmen and monsters. He broke open the shotgun and a shell's brass butt rose from its port. Should've further searched the old Negro for additional ammunition. He thumbed it back in and closed the gun quietly as folding a handkerchief and ducked between the rails of the fence and hurried past a pungent pile of burnt animals and rested in the shadow of a cane wagon.

He crept through a long alley and faced the main street, peering out to look it south and north. No sign of movement, the street bright in the moonlight. The windows dark.

Except—he craned his neck—for one. The large residence at the end of the street. In a front room the window pulsed with candlelight. Perhaps a citizen with insomnia. Unthinkable as it was to drop by without an invitation, Walton shouldered the shotgun and marched down the street.

He nearly tripped over an elderly woman flat on her back, clad in a veil and a long, black funereal dress. He knelt and eased his hand behind her neck and raised her head gently and folded back the veil.

Ma'am, he whispered. Are you ill?

She stirred. Her eyes fluttered. Help us, she said.

Smonk, meantime, loomed over Evavangeline and she wanted nothing more than to throw herself into his outspread arms and be hugged to death. She heard Ike's voice—*Don't, don't, don't*—and took a step back. Her foot touched something and she picked up the snake charmer.

Get her, Snow, Mrs. Tate hissed. Seed her!

Smonk swiped for the girl but she ducked. Daddy, she said, wait—

Come own, he said.

Evavangeline was backing across the room and didn't see Mrs. Tate shift her legs.

Daddy—

Dragging his foot, he came at her, the rug bunching at his ankles, the disemboweled bailiff flopped aside, Smonk's enormous fists balling and unballing and the air aswirl with sulfur.

Do like ye daddy tells ye, he rasped.

We got to go git them younguns, Evavangeline said. She tripped on Mrs. Tate's legs and fell. Before she could get up Smonk's face contorted with teeth and he kicked the old lady out of his way and stood panting over the girl.

Take off ye clothes.

She raised the snake charmer. Get back, I'll shoot ye.

Shoot ye daddy?

If you don't get back I will.

Shit. Smonk feigned away as if giving up but quick as a rattler grabbed for the gun. She fired into his trunk then he had the snake charmer tossing it away. She tried to dodge him but he caught her

by her midriff and raised her into the air with his left hand and
backed up, tangled in the rug. He shoved the dead justice from the
sideboard and threw her across the tablecloth there.

From the floor, straining to watch, Mrs. Tate began to speak in
tongues. *Hela-bo-sheila-bo—*

Smonk pinned the girl and tore her dressfront away as she
kicked and scratched and bit and thumbed out his glass eye which
landed on the sideboard and rolled onto the floor and down a
groove in the rug and past Mrs. Tate's face squinched in babbling
prayer. Holding the girl, Smonk opened a brown bottle from his
pocket and spilled liquid over her face and she ceased to battle and
he fell across her, panting.

Do it, Snowden, Mrs. Tate hissed. *Do it now.*

✣

So much for peace!

Walton had carried the elderly woman to a porch and laid her
down. He'd returned for her shotgun and his own, intending to in-
vestigate the large house down the way, when, almost simultaneously, a gun discharged in that very house and now here came a
child running toward him from the other end of town. Walton
raised his hand for attention and the boy slid to a stop before him.

Hello, young man, the Christian Deputy leader said. Are you a
resident here?

It's a bunch a resurrecting folks up yonder, the boy gasped. In
the church.

Walton squatted before the boy and took his shoulders in his
hands. Resurrecting folks?

The church ladies killed em, the boy panted, and Mister E. O. Smonk killed the men. We got to find Hell Mary. Cause them dead younguns down yonder's done come back to life.

Hail Mary? Are you a little Catholic?

Let go, sissy! The boy jerked his arm free and ran up the street. Walton stood. Sissy?

Behind him screams and banging doors. They were spilling onto the street, he saw, women in black, each armed. The one on the porch had sat up reaching for her gun.

More than a little "spooked," Walton broke into a run. He followed the boy to the large residence and hurried up the porch steps and stood peering in the open front door.

Excuse me? he called. He rapped on the doorjamb. Anyone home?

He heard raised voices. Through the foyer door he saw movement. He crossed the threshold and came forward behind his shotgun and what he beheld when he entered the parlor struck him like a boot to the nose.

The large "booger-man" known as Smonk was peeling a stocking off of Evavangeline's leg, the girl comely and prone and seemingly unconscious on a table. Also prone, but on the floor, bound by bedding, was an elderly woman, black juice dribbling down her chin; a snuff-dipper, like Walton's own mother. This lady was speaking rapidly in a foreign tongue, perhaps German. Beside her—Walton blanched—the mauled and near-naked body of an eviscerated man, a cornucopia of entrails in the rug's hills and channels. And finally, completing the mix, here came the little Catholic boy from outside, flinging himself against Smonk's back.

Killed my daddy, he was yelling. Killed my daddy!

Everyone, Walton called, stop! Cease or I'll fire!

No one seemed to notice his entreaty over the boy's yelling and the prone woman's babbling and Smonk's own loud exhortations of breath, so Walton hurried forward. His intention was to grab the young boy but instead his foot slipped in blood from the disemboweled gentleman and Walton's ballet skills aided him once again and he spun in the air, his right leg outspread, and landed on the opposite foot. The elderly woman began to scream—in English—at the boy on Smonk's shoulder.

Let him be, Willie, she cried. Let him be! He'll save us all!

Smonk, who had Evavangeline nearly out of her clothing, shrugged the boy off like a peacoat and sailed him across the room where he bounced from a wall and landed on all fours. Smonk tilted back his gourd and drank while he pulled down the girl's last stocking.

Stop, Walton yelled, or I'll fire!

No one stopped; instead, the boy clambered up holding a knife and raced across the floor and up Smonk's back and grabbed him by the hair.

Killed my daddy!

Smonk rolled the bludgeon of his head and bucked but the boy clung on, his fist embedded in that matted red hair. There was a sound like something uncorked and yellow bile spewed as Smonk's goiter burst and then, while Walton watched, fascinated, a great wash of blood sprayed the girl where she lay on the sideboard. Walton understood that the boy had cut the one-eye's jugular and was currently riding out Smonk's death throes, the big "cyclops" jerking and swinging his arms like poles, shattering a lamp and raking pictures off the walls. He staggered past a detonator as the boy rode his neck. He tripped over the woman screaming on the floor and tottered over them all, the boy leaping free as Smonk's life bled down his chest like water over a fall.

Snow! croaked the old woman from the floor. There's still time.

But Smonk was done for. When he crashed to his knees the window-panes rattled. He fell forward and grappled for the handle of his detonator but his reach failed and his glasses slid over the floor and his hand thudded on the wood and the fingers unfurled from the fist they'd made and his palm lay open like a bear trap. Lying on his stomach, he flashed his eye once around the room and said, I knew I should of— And then his body sagged out its last hale of air and Eugene Oregon Smonk closed his eye forever.

Meanwhile, William R. McKissick Junior bent over the prone Evavangeline and was wiping blood from her eyes and saying, Get up, wake up. Mister E. O. Smonk killed my daddy but I killed Mister E. O. Smonk. Get up.

Walton backed to the wall, letting it support him, and was therefore out of sight when the town women, young and old, began streaming into the house. They saw Smonk and saw the girl Evavangeline and the boy William R. McKissick Junior. They saw Mrs. Tate screaming and writhing on the floor like a carp and when the Hobbs daughter saw the gutted bailiff she began to scream.

Hush, said her mother and the girl jammed her fist in her mouth.

Quiet her, too, Mrs. Hobbs said of Mrs. Tate, and two women hurried forth and knelt beside the flouncing widow and tried to keep her still. And get him, Mrs. Hobbs said of William R. McKissick Junior, still brandishing his slick Mississippi Gambler. A young woman obeyed, jabbing her rifle barrel at him until he dropped the knife. She took him by his shirt collar and shoved him into a corner where he froze, watching their guns play on him.

Smonk killed my daddy, he said. I killed Smonk. I ain't scared.

It's the McKissick boy, one said.

Let's take him to Lazarus!

Let's take all the children!

No! barked Mrs. Tate from the floor, but with the women closing on the boy, no one heard.

From concealment, Walton saw his chance. He raised the shotgun and fired into the air and the room stilled and every conscious person turned to him, dusted in powder from the ceiling.

Excuse me, he said to the ladies. He sneezed. I'm only dimly aware of what's going on here, but I'll be rescuing this child and the unconscious young woman now. If anybody tries to interfere, I'll be forced to action. (At which point he realized he'd fired his only barrel.) In other words, he said, drop your weapons, ladies.

He sneezed again.

They grumbled until he clicked back the shotgun's hammer in one final "bluff," and at last their guns began to clunk one, another, to the floor.

Thank you, Walton said, for your cooperation.

He glanced at Evavangeline, naked on the sideboard, and saw her fingers flutter. Her eyes opened.

Son, he said to the boy, please help the young woman to her feet.

From the floor, Mrs. Tate hissed, Who are you to interfere in our affairs?

Phail Walton, said he, founder and leader of the Christian Deputies.

Christian! croaked Mrs. Tate. Get him! she said to the bristling widows. Don't let them go!

The women muttered and milled.

Hurry, child, Walton said to the boy.

William R. McKissick Junior grabbed the over & under rifle in one hand and pulled Evavangeline to her feet where she steadied herself on the boy's shoulder like a drunk. They hobbled across the room but paused when they came to where Smonk and McKissick lay, very near one another. For a long moment Walton and his captives watched Evavangeline stare down at the face of Smonk.

She was crying. Pushing Junior away, she went to her dead daddy where he lay drenched in his own blood. She knelt over him and closed his good eye and ran her fingers into his pockets and found a wad of paper money and several heavy gold coins. She found three pistols and a pair of brass knuckles. A stick of dynamite. She picked up the glass eye from the floor and put it in her mouth.

William R. McKissick Junior had knelt, too. He rolled McKissick over and adjusted his father's loin cloth and yanked at the rug until he'd covered him and stood and looked, only his daddy's shoes showing.

Get those, Evavangeline said.

The boy reached down and pulled off the left shoe, the right, and when he did a small package wrapped in brown paper fell out. He took it.

Come on, Evavangeline said, her father's last things gathered to her chest.

The boy didn't even notice her titties. The Winchester in the crook of his arm, he held the package in one hand and the shoes in the other and followed Evavangeline's dirty shoulders into the hall. Walton, covering the widows, was aware of some of the younger ones' lecherous gazes, and once the girl and boy were outside, he thanked the ladies again and bowed and made his exit.

In the parlor, the women seized their guns and gathered around Mrs. Tate.

Release me, she said.

No, said Mrs. Hobbs. I think we done listened to you long enough.

Meanwhile, Mrs. Hobbs's daughter's neck was itching. Like she had a rash. When she felt the circle of cuts on her throat she began to scream—I been bit! I been bit!—and in a moment other women joined her in a discordant harmony as they discovered their own marks.

That was them, wasn't it? Mrs. Hobbs asked, displaying her ample right bosom with its ring of teethprints around the nipple. Mrs. Tate? Wasn't it? Them was the chosen ones!

Mrs. Tate turned her face to the wall. It's done, she said.

The church! someone yelled. If that was them—!

The children!

The women flung away their guns and shoved each other and stampeded outside, toward the waiting miracle. And indeed the buildings at that end of the street were glowing orange, as if the sun were coming up from the west, at midnight.

৩০

Walton had given Evavangeline his shirt to cover her naked flesh and she led him and the boy to where the children were kept. Walton posted William R. McKissick Junior at the window as he roused the sleeping youngsters, thin, listless angels with under-circled eyes. He examined their arms for dog-bites but found none. We're in time, he told Evavangeline but she didn't seem to hear, leaning as she was against the wall.

They coming, the boy said.

Walton crossed the room and peered out to the street where the women were collecting like a "lynch mob."

Little boy, Walton said. What's your name.

William R. McKissick Junior.

William, said the northerner. Can you do something for me? Can you lead these children and this young woman out the back, to safety? Cut through the sugarcane and don't stop. The wind's coming from the north so go that way. He pointed, and then, without waiting for an answer, Walton propelled the lad away.

Good-bye, he told them both, and said to Evavangeline: I regret that we weren't able to chat further; I'd love to have given you my testimony.

She looked at him. It's a dollar.

Walton had turned to the boy. Go.

William R. McKissick Junior nodded, which was the last thing Walton saw as he turned and let himself out through the front door, locking it behind him. Unarmed, he stepped out and faced the mob of women semi-circling the porch.

He raised his hands. Ladies, I'd like to give you all my testimony. He cleared his throat. Excuse me. Have any of you ever heard of the word "bunker"?

Get him, said Mrs. Hobbs, and the widows came forward. Walton closed his eyes, outspread his arms and blocked the door. He would not be moved. He awaited the impact of their weight, being shoved forcefully into the wood, the women swarming him and pushing him into the air and hoisting him aloft above them and then sucking him down to the floor. He waited, eyes shut tightly, trying to think of an appropriate Verse of Scripture with which to comfort himself. Perhaps lines from the Book of Judges, the scene wherein Samson slew one thousand Philistines with the jawbone of an ass. Walton could picture the statuesque Biblical hero atop a mound of fresh corpses with various jaw-shaped abrasions on their persons. Samson in mid-swing, the bone high in the air, half a dozen opponents frozen in the act of falling.

Yet . . . Walton opened his eyes. He was unharmed, alone. He looked down the street, where the church was on fire. Ah. Instead of mobbing him, the widows had noticed the burning church and were heading there now, collecting handfuls of dust to hurl at the flames. One stout woman mounted the porch and slammed her shoulder against the door, which fell in, engulfing her in fire which swarmed the eaves and roof and up the steeple, igniting the cross.

Below, women had flocked to the windows and were peering in, and perhaps it was the fire that seemed to quake the redeemed as they burned in their seats. Wailing, the widows clambered over the burning corpse of the stout woman on the porch. They flung themselves into the door and stumbled back out, dresses afire, circling the church as its flames licked the bottom of the sky, windows exploding, the steeple creaking, sinking into itself, toppling. It fell for a long time and splintered into a thousand fires and the trees alongside the building and the oaks lining Main Street ignited one after another like torches and dropped burning cobs and cones and limbs and leaves, the red moon blazing over all, heedless how the fire spat itself building to building along the street, Mrs. Tate in her house on her floor still bound as fire raged in from the porch through the open door. She found that she could roll herself in her sheet and rolled through the stew of the dead bailiff's guts bubbling with heat and rolled past Smonk's great dead face, his head the marble head of some ancient, unearthed idol. She rolled alongside the detonator as her swaddling began to burn and bent her knees and curled into a U and rocked herself upright enough to place her chin on the handle and closed her eyes and plunged it down.

Meanwhile, Walton had descended the steps and stood in the street watching the widows hurl themselves into the burning church. He might have tarried a spell longer had not the building he'd just quit *exploded*, of all things, and sent him flying. From somewhere a horse was running past and with no thought whatsoever Walton, in midair, twisted his body and landed on his feet alongside the horse and seized its halter and bounced once, twice, thrice in its rhythm and threw his leg over and stabbed his feet into the stirrups. He leaned alongside the horse's neck and retrieved the reins and soon had the steed whoaed and panting.

There, there, big fellow, he said, reaching to scruff between its ears.

He looked back. His plan was to return to Old Texas and see to the others, help Evavangeline find the children's homes; surely no nobler challenge could arise before a man of God. Perhaps he would ask for the young woman's hand as well.

But as he turned the horse he saw that the burning sugarcane had cast its fire east and west and now closed upon him like a pair of apocalyptic arms, affording him no chance but to heel his mount and flee south. Farewell, he called to the youngsters and the youngsters leading them. I'll try to find you—

He was interrupted by a falling tree and without command the horse began to run. Behind them, the stores and houses of Old Texas had exploded one by one from the Tate residence down the street, and when the church blew, the widows left alive were lifted in a basket of hot air and thrown into the darkness of the canefield like dice and left to sit up and gaze in wonder at the burning shreds of sky landing around them. They were deaf. They gaped at the hole where the church had been as sections of their own murdered boys fell soundlessly. The sugarcane began to burn. Mrs. Hobbs cackled and tore down her dressfront and with her fingers hooked into claws she fled the burning town, pulling out her own hair.

Moments later the other women followed Mrs. Hobbs, howling and ripping their clothing. Walton in the meantime reversed directions and nearly collided with the mob of shrieking women; they clawed and snapped at his legs, the khaki of his pants darkened with their saliva and his extra pockets shorn away, until the horse broke free and galloped south.

When Walton saw Loon in the same spot he'd left him he slowed his new mount and called, Come on, deputy, if you want to live.

Loon kept his hands out of sight. Naw. I reckon not.

Loon, Walton said, Oswald. There are times to trust another. This is one of those times. Please, I beg you. Put your faith in me.

Naw, Cap'n, I believe I'll stick to my position here.

The horde of screaming women burst into the field and Walton kicked his horse. Suit yourself.

He rode on.

A moment later the women spotted Loon and changed direction and raged toward him. When the deputy began to point his deadly fingers, no shots answered—not when the naked ladies grew close and closer, not when they pulled him sideways off the horse and fell upon him and began to bite him. Not even when he pointed to his own forehead.

Riding, with Loon's screams muted in the smoke behind him, Walton unpocketed his flask and drank until there was nothing more to drink and pitched the flask into the dark. Whether the cool tears tracking his cheeks and neck were the result of the alcohol, the copious smoke or his own stripped emotions, he was too tired to consider. What he did instead was close his eyes and cling to the horse, it seemed to be flying, and race the fire into the night.

Meanwhile Evavangeline, William R. McKissick Junior and the children had left the house moments before it exploded. They rattled through the sugarcane and headed north, into the wind, the fire cracking like rifles behind them. Soon they forded the shallow Tombigbee, William R. McKissick Junior carrying the littlest girl, and by the time anyone looked back they were in another county and it was beginning to rain. That night they rested in a barn and Evavangeline blew up the new balloon and she and the children batted it to one another until they fell asleep in the hay.

In the morning before the barn's owner stirred Evavangeline emptied the henhouse of its eggs and led the younguns away. Within two days they came upon the town of Suggsville, where the first little stolen boy lived. His weeping parents fed them ham and biscuits and cow's milk and Evavangeline and William R. McKissick

Junior would have been heroes in that town had they not collected the other children before first light the following day and left.

In the end it would take seven weeks to get all the children home, Evavangeline rewarding Junior with a handjob upon each child's safe return. Near Christmastime, after they'd seen the last little girl reunited with her parents, William R. McKissick Junior was himself adopted by a wealthy childless couple in a lumber town called Fulton. The house he would live in had indoor plumbing, and there was a big sweet gum tree to climb, right outside the window of his bedroom.

On Christmas morning before anyone else was awake Evavangeline left riding north on a spotted pony she called Little Bit, the season's first crumbles of snow glistening in the animal's mane and in her own eyelashes. She'd not produced a mile's worth of tracks when she turned to see the boy in his new sheepskin overcoat and galoshes. He was running to catch her, his breath trailing like a scarf.

Hey, she said.

Hey, he panted. His cheeks red apples. I needed me one last one. He held up a silver dollar.

The pony looked back over its shoulder. Well hell Mary, Evavangeline said. She rolled off and flapped her blanket out over the weeds and lay on her back and scooched down her britches with snow landing all around. We can do better 'n a damn handjob, she said. Come here, honey.

Three months later, she feels a thump in her middle. She stops on the sidewalk in Memphis under a striped awning beside a short nigger in the doorway sweeping. The nigger looks up.

In the coming weeks she finds work in an upscale house of harlotry for men who desire girls in a family way. She is treated well by this class of specialist, a cost of forty dollars a night, the house taking half, she the rest plus meals and licker. Her little baby likes shrimp and champagne. He kicks all the time, and hits and rolls, especially when she smokes opium or skunkweed. Sometimes he keeps pounding on her right side and she knows to go right. Or he'll get so hungry he runs in place. His sharp little toes. Right there in her tummy.

A goddamn miracle.

And now, after tonight's daddy has gotten his nut and rolled off snoring his beer and farting his steak, she watches clouds out the window and sucks E.O.'s eye in her jaw and cradles her melon of a belly. She has known death and love and danger and Alabama in her long tally of years, and she swears to God in the sky or the devil in the dirt—whoever bets the highest—that it's her honor to be knocked up with a tiny new Smonk, and if he takes her life when he fights out into the world of light and air, nothing will make her happier. And if little Ned wants to suck on her plump titties as she closes her eyes, then that too will pleasure her, yall. Infinitely. Which means forever.

ACKNOWLEDGMENTS

I want to thank Beth Ann Fennelly—my wife, best friend and first reader—for her loving work on the *Smonk* manuscript; for her advice, criticism, insight and wisdom; and, mainly, for never running screaming from the house. Thanks to my daughter, Claire, whose mishearing of "skunk" gave this book its name, and to my son, Thomas, for joining our family. To my generous, understanding parents, Gerald and Betty Franklin. To my colleagues and students at Ole Miss. To Nat Sobel, more uncle than agent, Judith Weber, and their amazing staff. To *Smonk*'s early readers: Chris Gay, William Gay, Michael Knight, Hardy Jackson, Jack Pendarvis and Steve Whitton. To Kathy Pories. To the Fairhope, Alabama, gang and especially Sonny Brewer and Joe Formichella. A raised Bud Light to my pals (there and gone) at City Grocery: John, Whitey, Joe, Chip, Enright and Norm. Thanks to Jim Dees, John T. Edge, Tom Howorth, Walter Neill, Ron Shapiro and Franklin Williams.

To Richard and Lisa Howorth, Lyn Roberts, and everyone at Square Books. To Earl Brown who took me back to 1876 and Steve Wallace who told me about Old Texas. Continued thanks to all the folks at William Morrow and HarperCollins, especially Tim Brazier, Kevin Callahan, Lisa Gallagher, Michael Morrison, Michael Morris, Sharyn Rosenblum and Claire Wachtel, my editor. And in memory of the writers Larry Brown and James Whitehead.

Portions of *Smonk* appeared in *Murdaland, 9th Letter, Climbing Mt. Cheaha: Emerging Alabama Writers* and *Verb: An Audioquarterly,* and I thank these editors.